Awakening
Teen Telepaths Book 1

James Gaskin

ISBN 978-1-933177-03-8

© 2022 James Gaskin
All Rights Reserved

Printed in the United States of America
Published by WAGbooks
www.WAGbooks.com

To Milo and Jonesy.
Let the new generation show us a better way.

Table of Contents

Acknowledgements

Writers work by themselves, fingers pounding on a keyboard or procrastinating, but some writers have a group of friends who understand the writing process. I'm lucky because I have a handful of writer friends beside and behind me, pushing me forward. Together we run the Dallas Mystery Writers group (DallasMysteryWriters.com), the North Texas chapter of the Mystery Writers of America (you can find them at the website MysteryWriters.org).

Please give a big hand to LaRee Bryant, Sandy Steen, and Janis Susan May Patterson, the smart ones in the leadership group. All three have been writing fiction professionally for decades, and helped start the Romance Writers of America. As sometimes happens, their romantic thoughts turned to murder.

And shine a special spotlight on Sandy, because she worked with me for months getting the tone, characters, locations, and vibe right for the Teen Telepaths world. Check out her "cozy werewolf" stories at SandySteenWrites.com to find fun books full of an interesting twist on a story you think you know.

There are more, of course, like Tex Thompson for a book doctor checkup. A special thanks to friends in the Dallas Mystery Writers and Dallas Filmmakers Alliance groups who always offer encouragement, like Aina Swartz and Steve Savage and Jennifer Bolden and Alan Elliot and Frank St. Claire and Shelley Kaehr.

Chapter 1: Sorry My Friend

I slid my laptop into my backpack, careful not to catch my tie in the zipper as I closed it with as much stealth as possible. Not quietly enough because Mr. Hamilton looked at me.

"Paul," said the government teacher who made impeachments and Civil Rights riots as thrilling as cold oatmeal.

The minute hand on the old wall clock clunked from 3:28 to 3:29. "Aww, the bell's almost ringing," I said.

"Tomorrow is Paul's eighteenth birthday, everyone." He glanced at the back of the note in case the announcement continued.

The Grigori teens, about a third of the class, clapped and stomped for me. Everyone else acted annoyed. They always complained about how big a deal Grigori families make about turning eighteen.

"Speech!" yelled Jaxon from the rear of the room right before the bell rang to end the school week. "Too late!" he added.

Everyone raced to the door like every Friday afternoon but the Grigori kids slapped me on the back or waved. Amina Gonzalez, with her long wavy hair and soft brown eyes and softer-looking lips, stepped in front of me.

"Sorry, didn't bring a dollar to pin to your shirt."

"Aren't I worth more than that?"

She smiled and patted my cheek tenderly. "Haven't convinced me yet."

"Well, I–"

"Be ready, because eighteen is a huge deal."

"What's the big deal about another day older?"

She turned, twirling her school plaid skirt, and waved over her shoulder as she left. After a few steps C.W., her jerk of a boyfriend, grabbed her arm, glared back at me, and walked her out of the room.

Two sophomores, Boy Taylor and Girl Taylor, or Taylor Squared as they liked to be called, stopped me on the outside stairs. Both blonde, her green eyes matched by his blue ones, they'd been glued together since they found each other in elementary school, and so adorable they should be on calendars. They only came up to my chest and reminded me of Labrador pups.

1

"We heard," said Boy Taylor.

"Boost me," Girl Taylor told him. He picked her up, and she kissed me on the cheek.

"Not a big deal," I said.

"Got major plans?" Boy Taylor asked.

"Course. Parties everywhere. Haven't decided which one tonight." They laughed and ran away with the grace of drunk puppies.

I continued down the steps, waved back to a few people, and walked to the Lincoln Town Car waiting to take me home.

The driver, who I think is our doorman's cousin, asked, "Another successful week of school, Master Paul?"

"Everybody's working for the weekend."

At home I had well over two hours before my parents finished work, so I settled into my gaming chair in front of the TV in my room. I pointed back and forth to my PlayStation and X-Box. "OK, which party tonight?"

* * * * *

"Relax, man, I got this," said Max Orlov, Number One running buddy since first grade, the next day at lunch. "Your cake day today." He put his credit card on top of the bill. This new waitress at Central Park West Diner, our favorite place, had the wrinkles and attitude of a long-time NYC deli server. She scooped the card up and disappeared.

"Not going to finish your burger?" He pointed at the few fries and two bites of bread on my plate.

"That's not burger," I said. "That's barren bread."

"What the hell is barren bread?"

"You know, no burger, no mustard, no pickle, not even lettuce. Barren. You better pay more attention in English class."

Our server came back but without Max's card and receipt. "Excuse me, sir, but may I please see some ID?"

"Why?" I asked. Max shook his head at me and showed his ID. She nodded and left.

"Relax, man, just Dining While Black, same as Driving While Black. If she knows the city, she'll be a lot nicer after checking the address."

She returned. "Thank you, Mr. Orlov, please come see us again soon."

"Can you tell Ruby we're ready for our extra bit?"

Ruby, the owner, came out a minute later carrying a cupcake with a lit candle and a piece of cherry pie. "Here you go, Paul, Happy Birthday." She patted my head like she's been doing since I was four years old. "This is what, eighteen?"

"Yes, ma'am. Thanks."

"Such a big boy, no, big young man, you've become."

She put the pie in front of Max. "I didn't order any pie, Ruby."

"Sorry for the new girl. And I can't let my favorite basketball player sit there and starve as Paul smears icing on his face."

Max smiled way big. "Favorite player? You mean Carmelo's number two now?"

"Until Mr. Anthony comes back in, number one you shall be. Enjoy, boys."

The carrot cake cupcake, my favorite, must be from Karla's Kupcakes, three blocks down. "Aren't you special for remembering my favorite flavor," I said with a grin.

"Uh, yeah, no problem."

"Lying weasel! Junie got this, didn't she?"

"Duh! Of course! What else are girlfriends good for?"

"It's been a while but I remember a lot more fun things to do with a girl than make her run errands."

"Thumbs up. Hurry and find somebody new or Junie's gonna fix you up with a friend so we can all hang again."

Running down the list of her close friends, several good options and one catastrophe popped up. "Why didn't Junie come to lunch with us? Afraid of me feeling bad being the third wheel again?"

"No, man, not at all," he said, nodding yes. "Hanging with one of those friends. Maybe bribing her to lower her standards and go out with you."

"I'll have you know the New York City Most Eligible Bachelor Committee called me yesterday. They threatened a restraining order if I keep sending them my pictures, but hey, they called."

Max laughed, choked a little, and grabbed his soda. "Jerk! You made me snort cherry pie up my nose!"

"Yeah, I'm about ready to help with her bribe fund myself."

"Since our parents are strict about us dating only Grigori girls, that gives us a small pond to fish in."

I licked the cream cheese icing off the bottom of my candle. "About tonight, I'm pissed you and Junie can't come."

"Relax, man. Not our kind of party. I couldn't invite you and Lucy to mine, remember? They say it's your party, but it's all about our parents and their friends."

"Direct hit. Caterers and the DJ and helpers everywhere today. Gonna be a serious crowd. Your parent's and Junie's are coming, so you guys decide where to hang?"

"Her place." He waggled his eyebrows. "Got a list of fun things to do with girls?"

"One thing to remember: the chill part is a lot more fun when you Netflix a romance. Play any *Fast and Furious* movie and she'll throw your butt out before the credits roll."

"You better donate a big wad to her bribe fund."

"Yeah, well, this shit'll be over soon. Birthday and party and all."

"The fun starts after you become an eighteener. You can do, ah, you know, more."

That got my attention. "More? Cool. Like what?"

"Sorry, man, thinking of something else. But you can vote, go to R-rated movies, yada, yada, yada."

"I can do those now except for the voting. But what do I know? I'm about the last of our class to turn eighteen."

"Don't worry," Max said, getting up. We left the diner, blowing kisses to Ruby on the way out. "Nobody dies because of the party. Let'em make a big fuss, be a smile robot for all the strangers, and enjoy what you can."

"Gonna be boring as hell."

We reached the corner where our paths diverged. "On average, it'll be a glorious night," said Max.

"Average of what?"

"You, sad and lonely at your party, and me chillin' with Junie."

"Was I this much of an asshole when I had a girlfriend and you didn't?"

"Way worse," he laughed. "Payback, baby." He waved goodbye, pulled his coat closed against the early spring wind, and headed home.

The wind pushed at my back as I walked down Central Park West Drive. Like he said, nobody dies, and I'll be fine. Bored, maybe, but the same next Saturday as this Saturday, only a week older.

Chapter 2: Bigger Life

"Stand up straight, Paul. Let me fix your bow tie."

"This tie is stupid, Mom. Won't stay straight."

"Don't blame the tie for your inexperience. But I have to tie your father's as well."

Mom stood tall in her Jimmy Choo hot pink party heels, but still looked up to my six foot two. "Almost there."

"Still wish my friends could come. Eighteen is a big deal."

She tugged my tie to the left, frowned, then tugged it to the right. "As I explained before, Jewish boys have their Bar Mitzvah at thirteen. Hispanic girls have their Quinceanera at fifteen."

"And their friends can come."

"This event carries far more significance than those. When a Grigori turns eighteen, they truly become an adult, and this party introduces you to the organization." Mom cocked her head to the right. One more tug of the tie and she smiled. "We can talk about a reception for your friends next week."

"Yeah, great."

Everything reflected in my full-length mirror was new for this party. Kitoni black dress shoes, Armani classic black tuxedo, and stupid bow tie.

"Glad you got a haircut yesterday. Nice to see your bright blue eyes without having to search through that messy black hair."

"C'mon, Mom, turning eighteen, not six."

"No matter your age, you look great." She peered into the mirror to straighten her white Vera Wang party dress. "Don't worry about being uneasy. It's natural and you're among friends."

How did she know I worried about being nervous and not just regular nervous? "No, my friends don't make me nervous. I'm among family and your friends, since mine can't come."

Mom finally adjusted her dress to her satisfaction and smiled. "We're better behind the scenes. You'll survive one night in the spotlight. Let's get your father and make your grand entrance."

Like he'd read her mind, Dad marched in like a general inspecting his troops. His tux, also a new Armani, fit perfect.

6

He's an inch shorter than me and has darker blue eyes and gray on the temples of his black hair. Two fun days: when I got taller than him and when he moped around after finding his first gray hair that same week. Good times.

"The crowd is ready. Let's roll." He sent a text and the music thumping in the great room nosedived to nothing.

Reaching to adjust my tie again got my hand slapped and a look from Mom. "Ready?" she asked.

Deep breath. "OK." The three of us left my bedroom. Me, followed by my parents, arm in arm.

When we reached the end of the hallway, my feet froze to the carpet. After a few seconds, Dad pushed me so hard it I had to take the next step or fall on my face.

Flashes from cameras and phones came from all directions. The DJ boomed out, "Ladies and gentlemen! Paul Atreides Barylan, presented by his parents Atticus and Caroline Barylan, has come of age!" Flashes slowed as people clapped and cheered. "The Grigori Research Association welcomes its newest member!" Cheers swelled.

* * * * *

Smashed between two sets of aunts and uncles, my radiant smile sagged more and more. So many damn pictures! But they flew from Los Angeles for the party, so I appreciated that. Left my cousins at home, which I didn't appreciate, but no kids means no kids. My parents made the reverse trip for my two cousins, Quinn, and Lance, for their eighteenth birthdays three and six months earlier. Sucks they weren't here. His California Cool helps me relax, and she gooses me when things get serious. Or just because she's bored and wants to see me jump.

When the photos eventually stopped, it was time to find a shrimp station. Nice to hide for a bit away from the crowd. Many of my friends' parents, like Max and Junie's, were here, along with relatives from California and Europe. Lots of business friends of my parents, too, most of them strangers to me.

But not their boss, Holden Goldstone, head of the fifth largest hedge fund in the world. But, as Dad always added, the second most profitable. Holden was also my godfather. "With a lower case 'g', not an uppercase one," he said, "Unless you owe me a favor." He's kidding, I think.

If Max and his girlfriend Junie were here, they'd grief me about being the only people of color except for their parents. Blame me like the guest list was my idea. While picking up a third shrimp, someone said my name. With a sigh, I returned the shrimp to the pile.

The Mayor of New York City, tall and topped with almost-white hair, pushed through the crowd. Why the hell was the Mayor at my party? We weren't all that political.

"Paul! The young man of the hour!" boomed His Honor, the Mayor. He grabbed, squeezed, and wrapped my hand with both of his.

"Mister Mayor, I-I'm surprised to see you here."

"My pleasure, my boy, my pleasure." People armed with cameras followed the Mayor and crowded around the two of us. "Your parents are grand friends of New York City. I look forward to your help in the future as well."

My damn easy-to-blush cheeks got warm while the Mayor gripped my hand. "Do you have your mind made up, son?" he asked. "Take the business, legal, or government path?" He released my hand and patted me on the shoulder.

"Not really sure, sir, not yet."

"No matter, young Mr. Barylan, no matter. I know you've been accepted to Harvard and Yale, but I'd like to pitch you on Columbia. Stay in the city, you know."

"What? I'm in at Harvard AND Yale?"

"You haven't heard? Your connections guarantee your application gets approved the first day. Official word soon."

The Mayor stepped closer and put his arm around me. He motioned the people crowding us to step back a little, and they obeyed.

"If you're worried about living with your parents, don't. Plenty of luxury apartments close to campus. Pick the one you want, and I'll get you in."

"Thank you, sir. But I didn't apply to Columbia."

"An oversight I can remedy." The Mayor waved his hand in the air and yelled, "Darwin, got a live one!"

Soon, a man stepped up and shook my hand. His white hair and goatee seemed familiar, but no name came to me.

The Mayor put his arms around both of us and pulled us tight to him. "Darwin, we need to keep Paul in the city and not let him escape to Cambridge or New Haven. Have a spot for him at Columbia?"

Darwin winked at me. "You bet, Mr. Mayor. We're disappointed he didn't apply already."

My eyebrows sometimes have a life of their own, and they jumped up. "You're in admissions?"

The Mayor laughed. "A little above admissions. He's the President of Columbia."

Darwin held out a business card. "When you're ready for a tour, I'll show you around myself."

The Mayor leaned even closer to me. "I know your mother pushes for Harvard, where she went. Your father blathers on about Yale. My suggestion is not to play favorites and go to Columbia."

Darwin agreed. "I'm biased, but I bet your parents will enjoy having you close to home."

An assistant tugged on the Mayor's arm. He released the two of us and shook my hand again.

"Paul, a pleasure to meet you."

"Thank you, sir. The pleasure was all mine."

As soon as the Mayor and Darwin walked away, my tight shoulders tried to relax. Before they could, my parents and Holden Goldstone grabbed me.

Holden always seemed more family than boss. Watching his classic features and full head of silver hair on TV always made me smirk. The man I called "Unka Hoeden" when young was on TV? Weird.

He wrapped his arms around me tight enough to keep me from thinking about breathing. When he let me go, he bent to put his face at my level. Now he only had to bend a couple of inches. When I was small he dropped to his knees to get face to face.

"Paul, Paul, Paul. What a glorious night!"

"Thanks, Holden. Glad you came. At least I have one friend here."

"Wouldn't miss it." He turned to a young woman so gorgeous and in such a beautiful evening gown she could walk the red carpet at the Oscars. A softball-sized box appeared in his hand.

"Great birthdays demand great presents!" He tilted the lid open and revealed the contents.

"Damn!"

"Go ahead, put it on."

A gold Rolex Submariner glittered in the light and its bright blue face glowed as if back-lit. Perfect fit on my left wrist.

Held up for a better view, the Rolex seemed to weigh three pounds. "I don't know what to say. Thanks. Barrels of thanks."

"Wear it in good health, my young friend. Wear it when you come to work for me after college. Your parents have been superb partners. If you follow them, it will thrill us all."

Mesmerized by my new Rolex, everything else faded away.

"OK," he said. "Give me one of your strange songs to fit the situation."

Didn't take me but a second. "Have to say 'Time Is' from It's a Beautiful Day, because the song title and group both name fit."

His laugh carried over the entire crowd. "Perfect," he said, turning to the young woman with him. "Don't you think such a command of obscure music shows real genius?"

"Sounds right to me, sir."

"Wait, do you work for me?"

She gave him a thousand-watt smile. "I do tonight."

He whipped around, bumped fists, and said, "Paul, it's been great, but we're leaving early."

An endless stream of adults shook my hand then said things that made no sense. A smile and a "thank you" on repeat mode like a friendly robot got me through the pain, like Max promised.

"We look forward to you coming into your own."

"Big changes coming, young man, big changes."

"An important week ahead of you, son. Good luck."

"I see a great deal of power in your future, young man."

"The Grigori are lucky to have you."

10

"Like Uncle Ben told Spider-Man, with great power comes great responsibility."

"Nothing is impossible with determination."

"You step into a new world soon. Embrace it."

After the receiving line finished, I had to find more food to hold off the shakes. Got lucky and found sliders made with Kobe beef that were damn tasty. Two disappeared in two bites each when a group of people moved closer. They parted, and Senator "Big Dave" Kingston stepped forward with his hand out.

"Paul, we haven't met. I'm Big Dave from Texas."

He could play the perfect modern Hollywood cowboy. Tanned but not too weathered, trim but still powerful, his calloused right hand gave me a Terminator grip. The Stetson was the cherry on top.

"I've heard about you, Senator. Thanks for coming."

"Wouldn't miss it." He pulled me away from the group and handed me a business card.

"My private cell number's on the back. You're going to have a strange couple of weeks."

Great, something else bizarre. "Strange, sir?" Maybe it was lucky my friends couldn't come. Max would give me shit for weeks about the crazy things people said tonight.

"If things get a little too out there, let me know. I'm ready to help however I can."

"Ah, thanks, Senator, but things are going great right now."

"Of course, grand party, but are people saying odd things to you?"

"I've heard a few, ah, interesting things."

"If you want to know the story behind those things, the Grigori story your parents won't tell you, call me anytime."

"You have stories? I'd like to—" The Senator turned and walked away. He and his group flew past my parents with a quick tip of his hat.

That was odd. Not rude like they ignored them, but more like he didn't know my parents.

That became my Number One Weird Thing of the party. Why would a United States Senator I'd never met, who didn't know my parents, come to my birthday party? The Mayor coming was crazy enough, but a Senator from Texas? Double crazy.

11

Chapter 3: A Fun Study Group

I sighed at my phone and typed a few words to answer a text. "Parents again?" asked Junie.

"Fourth time in fifteen minutes. This one from my dad is all caps. He even yells with his thumbs." I sat at Junie's dining table, along with her and Max and another classmate.

Junie Johnson played volleyball, not basketball like Max, and stood nose to nose with him in high heels. Not tall enough to be a killer striker, Junie's blazing quickness as a digger made her a standout.

"Something serious?" asked Kayla. She "dropped by" an hour after Madison was "in the area." Junie loved playing matchmaker, but no luck so far. Kayla's cute, but no spark on the mental side.

"Worried I'll be out late. Stupid."

"Out late doing homework on a Tuesday night? Must be up to no good." She touched my arm and flashed me a half-grin.

"That's me, trashing all five boroughs, and not even nine o'clock."

"Nine?" asked Junie. "Did you notice it's almost nine, Kayla?"

Kayla's eyebrows lowered into a frown. "Nine? Oh. Sorry, Paul, there's this a, ah, thing so I better get going." I walked her to the door, and she looked ready to kiss me goodnight, so I hugged her before she did.

Back at the table, Junie said, "Sorry. She overheard me invite Madison and begged me to let her come."

"That's a surprise. We've never hung out that I remember."

"Time for truth, Paul to Max. What's wrong with Kayla?"

I glanced at Junie. Max was my guy forever, and we told each other things we'd never tell regular girls and seldom a girlfriend.

She gave me the "come on" hand gesture. "Aren't I one of the guys yet?"

"Locker room showers would be a lot more fun," Max said, winking at Junie.

She winked back. "That'd be great! I could comparison shop!"

"Hey!"

"OK, Kayla's sweet, and there's no spark, not a big mental match," I said.

Junie and Max both nodded their heads. "Haven't talked to her much in a while, so I hoped she'd caught up," she said.

"No problem. Kinda fun tonight. Thanks." I closed my laptop.

"Oh no, you can't leave yet."

I flipped the laptop back open. "Who's going to drop by next?"

"Amina."

"Gonzalez?" That was a surprise. "I know she's still with C.W. because I checked with her friends."

"She's ready to pull that plug."

"Sounds good, but I don't wanna be a rebound guy."

"You're more like her escape hatch guy."

"Interesting. C.W.'s a dick-head half the time, and jerks don't deserve a girl that hot. Except for Max dating you." I hit Max with another drive-by insult.

"Hey! Again!" he said.

Junie patted his hand. "So now she deserves a better guy."

"What's wrong with you?" asked Max. "Rebounders release all their anger and frustration having super sex with a new guy. It's great when they—"

Junie glared at him while drumming her fingers on the table.

"Or so I've heard," he said, recovering. Before Junie started on him, the doorbell rang.

"The bell just saved your ass." Junie waggled her finger at Max, adding, "We'll talk later."

Amina's bright red lips curved in a smile big enough to balance her huge brown eyes, framed in wavy long dark hair. Long hair, straight, wavy, or curly, grabs my attention and hers fell in waves like the ocean. Her sense of humor was as sharp as her cheekbones and a brain even sharper. We sat, and I saw Max already moved our chairs closer together.

"Your birthday fun?" she asked.

"Fun and getting funner every minute."

"Aren't you being sweet." She curled some hair around her index finger.

"This year started, ah, rough, but things are getting better."

13

"I keep having that same thought. Heard a lot about what happened from, well, you know who, and understand why you've been slow to jump back in." She took a deep breath. "Ready yet?"

Lyrics from the Cherry Poppin' Daddies song, "No Mercy for Swine," from their *Zoot Suit Riot* CD played in my head: "The way to get over someone, just to get onto someone else." I blinked to turn off the music in my head and concentrated on Amina. I put my hand on hers and said, "I'm ready for the right person."

She smiled and licked her lips. We kept talking and got closer and closer until I held both her hands. Max and Junie became invisible because we looked only at each other.

Junie's phone vibrated. She looked, ditched the call, and turned it over. A few seconds later it buzzed again. "Sorry." She turned and whispered into the phone, "Gemma, people are here. Can't talk. Who left you? Sorry, but you shouldn't have gone hunting Saturday night... listen, I'll call you back, so stay put."

She hung up and put her phone back on the table. "Sorry for the interruption."

"What interruption?" Amina asked, and squeezed my hands.

"Didn't hear a thing," I said, and squeezed back.

When Amina had to leave, I walked her to the door. "We should do this again soon."

She pulled me down by my shirt and kissed my cheek. "Give me a few days. I'm worth waiting for, I promise."

My face smiled by itself. "Really? Haven't proved it to me yet."

She grinned, grabbed my face, pulled my head down, and gave me a kiss that made everything down to my toes tingle. I put my arms around her and pulled her close and hoped to keep that feeling for another hour or two, but it was over far too soon. "Good enough to buy me time so I can arrange some things?"

Fanning myself with my hand, I nodded, and she laughed. "I'll wait as long as you need," I said, as I opened the door and watched her walk to the elevator. Halfway down, she turned around and blew me a kiss.

Back with Junie and Max, the memory of her sweet lips on mine must've shown on my face.

"Spark?" asked Junie.

"Forest fire."

14

Max gave Junie a fist bump.

A few minutes later, I waited in the hall for Max and Junie to say goodnight, which took a while since she remembered his rebound sex comment. But he always charms away her bad moods, like he charms away everybody's bad moods. Memories of Amina's lips on mine kept me company while waiting for Max.

Chapter 4: Up from the Gutter

Outside Junie's building, the sidewalk looked brighter than normal for nighttime. I glance up and saw the fattest, roundest moon I ever remember beaming between the buildings.

"Damn, the moon's huge tonight," I said.

"Full moon? Shit, we gotta run." Max zoomed. After a half-block, I caught up with him.

"What's the hurry?"

"You can't say I told you, but the first full moon after you turn eighteen is a big jump. Your brain will, ah, transform."

"The moon changes my brain? That's stupid."

"Your parents didn't tell you anything? Damn. Hey, let's cut through this alley."

I turned the corner right behind him, and something warned me to stop. Max came back and grabbed my arm and dragged me into the darkness.

"*Come on, kids, come to me,*" I heard, but it sounded unnatural.

"Did you hear somebody?" I asked.

"Heard nothing except the clock ticking. C'mon." Max pulled me along faster and the shadows swallowed us. We passed a dumpster, and a man yelled, flew out from behind it, and slammed me into piles of restaurant garbage.

Max skidded to a stop and spun around to face a mugger pointing a silver revolver at him. He did the smart thing and put his hands in the air. I slipped on moldy lasagna noodles as I struggled to stand and collapsed again.

The mugger kept pointing the gun at Max as he walked over to me. He looked at me, targeted Max again, then grabbed my arm and pulled me upright. When I was standing, he gripped my arm as if he had a metal clamp for a hand and poked the gun barrel into my ribs. Dad says to stay calm in emergencies, but it's tough when you're covered in rotten food and a gun keeps scraping your ribs. My knees were shaky, and it was hard to breathe.

I stared at the asshole holding me so I could describe him for the police later. His clothes, black with darker stains, included a hoodie that put a shadow over half his face. Only his scruffy beard and filthy teeth were visible.

Max took a step closer, and his pistol gun moved from my ribs to point at his chest. I tried to pull my arm away, but while the attacker was shorter than me, he was way thicker and his hand squeezed my arm harder.

He waved the run at Max. "Put your wallet on the ground and step back." His voice was deep but nervous-sounding, as if he needed another fix fast.

All I heard was my heart thudding in my chest and the blood rushing through my ears. He turned to me, and said, "Nice watch. Hand it over." As awful as the disgusting food covering me smelled, his breath was worse. His teeth were so filthy they looked fuzzy.

I looked at the Rolex I'd gotten just three days earlier at my birthday party, so new it still sparkled in the sliver of moonlight that fought past the filth in the alley. Dad's advice played in my head, repeating what he always told me. "Stay calm, give them what they want, don't be a hero."

Unfortunately, the words that came out of my mouth were, "Go to hell!"

That surprised the mugger and me. His mouth set in a thin line, and he changed the revolver from Max to my temple.

"Da fuck you say? Gimme that watch!"

The hard circle of the barrel on my temple stopped my breathing. I imagined my tombstone reading, "Killed by a bully in an alley." I fucking hate bullies, but I opened my mouth to tell him he could steal my brand new Rolex. Again, what came out was, "Hell no."

He drew the hammer back and cocked the revolver. The metallic click slammed my ear like a thunderclap.

"Gonna take it one way or the other." He shoved the gun barrel harder against my head. My heart beats and blood rush in my ears stopped. The world became silent and I felt the cold barrel digging into my skin.

"Wait, let's talk about this," yelled Max.

The mugger didn't even look. "Don't need to talk 'cause I got the gun."

"You don't know who you're messing with. We're–"

17

"Two punk-ass rich kids in fancy school uniforms, that's who."

"We're connected to a group you don't want to piss off."

The mugger looked at him and shook his head. "Mafia don't recruit in private schools."

Max stepped forward.

"Don't do it, bro. Not worth it," I told him. I couldn't stand to see him hurt over a watch, no matter how new or how nice. "Look, here, I'm taking off my watch."

Max took another step, and the gun barrel left my temple and targeted him. Somehow, Max kicked a brick up from the ground and hit the mugger's hand holding the gun. Knocked upwards, his finger pulled the trigger and one shot boomed before the gun spun away into the blackness. Deafening echoes crashed through the alley. My heart thumped as the searchlight-bright flash of gunpowder in the dark seared my eyes and drilled through my optic nerves to my brain.

My body shook as my head exploded from the inside out. The pain grew more intense by the second, so I wrenched my arm free and pushed my hands against my splitting head.

The thug turned his filthy beard and filthier teeth towards me and drew back his fist. My head still throbbed as if someone kept pounding me with a hammer and I couldn't pull my hands away to protect myself, so I yelled, "GET AWAY FROM ME!"

Suddenly, he flew backwards and slid on his back through the alley faster than I could run, screaming the entire time. His body slid into a darker space twenty yards away and he disappeared from view, but I still heard him shriek. Those ended when a bunch of trashcans rattled, followed by a groan. The filthy alley hushed.

The pain in my head grew worse, my body jerked as if electrocuted, agony washed over me like an acid shower, and I lost my balance. I collapsed back into the pile of rotting garbage and passed out.

Surprised, I stood in a thick, soundless fog, alone. A shaped floated closer until I recognized a man with long stringy hair, Grigori Rasputin, and he was talking in Russian.

For some reason I understood him. "Today is your day. I am your father."

Madame Matej, in Romani clothing with a circular chakra tattooed on her forehead, floated out of the fog. "I am your mother."

I knew who they were because of lessons on our heritage given to children of Grigori families during special summer classes. In unison, they repeated, "Our strength is now your strength. Our strength is now your strength," over and over.

I tried to move, but my legs refused to obey. "The minds of men are as water," Rasputin added, then disappeared.

The next thing I remember, Max was shaking and slapping me. "Get up, man, get up! I gotta get you home! *Don't die, please don't die!*"

He kept shaking me. "OK, I'm OK. I'm not dead yet." He grabbed my school blazer and hauled me to my feet. I breathed normally again and my heart didn't bang against my chest, but my head still hurt as if someone split it with an ax. I touched my Rolex on my wrist.

"You heard me say please don't die?"

"Yeah."

"I didn't say it out loud, just thought it."

Horrible odors assaulted my nose. My clothes smelled worse than leftover lasagna baked in a dumpster in the scorching sun for a week. Rancid restaurant scraps from the food piles were all over me. I wiped moist sticky chunks and sauces off my school jacket and pants and dug a wad of gross schmutz out of my hair.

"My clothes stink so bad rats run away and you wanna talk crazy?"

"*Is this crazy talk?*"

"Stop talking weird!"

"Damn! Your Change happened right here in the alley!"

"What are you talking about?" I wobbled when I walked, so Max grabbed my arm.

"*Careful around that puddle.*"

"Who cares about a damn puddle when you almost get shot? Hey, you sounded weird again, like when you said please don't die."

"That wasn't my regular voice. You heard my Inside Voice, my thoughts."

"C'mon, man, my head hurts too much for jokes."

"I'm not supposed to tell you because your parents need to explain, but the big deal about turning eighteen? That's when you get your powers, like telepathy, or telekinesis."

"What powers?"

"I'm a Mover and that's how I threw that brick without using my hands. I Moved it with my mind. Telekinesis."

"Told you I hurt too much for that shit. What's next, the X-Men recruitment pitch?"

"Yeah, honestly. Then you Moved that mugger faster than a race car out of sight."

I stopped and tried to remember what happened, but it was blank. "I only remember a gunshot, things went dark, then you slapping me."

"You looked dead for five minutes, but you kept muttering in Russian so I didn't call 9-1-1."

"Did you get a brick to the head? I don't speak Russian."

"You're now telepathic, meaning you can listen to other people's thoughts. Everybody has The Talk first, your silent Inside Voice, and you can talk to other Grigori who've Changed. But it fades out and you can only talk to others you're close to, like parents, lovers, and really good friends. Your adult power comes in in a week or two, or you get stronger at reading minds."

My head still throbbed and clanged and I didn't catch much. "Yeah, sure, we're super teens, fighting for truth, justice and the American way. What can you do? Fly? Laser eyes?"

He shrugged. "Telekinesis. Mover. I Move stuff with my mind like I just told you."

"C'mon, my brain is throbbing like somebody's hitting a bass drum inside my head. You telling me you threw that brick with your mind? And slid that mugger away?"

"That's what I said, and you just threw that mugger with your mind. Here, watch." He pointed to three trashcans on the curb in front of a coffee shop. The lid from the middle can floated up, twirled, and settled back into place.

I watched the dancing can lid, and it made my head hurt even more. This couldn't be real! I grabbed him by his collar and got into his face. "Make is stop! This is killing me!"

"Too late, man, too late. Your parents didn't tell you this was coming?"

"I don't want any of this!" I squeezed my head again but that didn't help the pain.

He grabbed my arm and pulled to make me walk.

"What group are we a part of muggers don't want to mess with?" I asked. Mafia would make sense, but nothing else I could imagine.

"Grigori protect their own and have a long memory."

He tried to explain things on the way home, but nothing stuck because of my throbbing skull. What did stick sounded terrible, and I kept saying "No, no, no, I don't want anything to do with this shit," every time he asked if I was OK.

Back home, I threw my grimy clothes in the corner and dropped into bed like a dead man.

Chapter 5: After the Full Moon

My dreams made no sense. I floated close to wakefulness and saw Rasputin, Grigori Rasputin, the reason for the Grigori Research Associates. I rushed up to him, screamed, "Why'd you do this to me!" and hit him with a right hook. It passed through his face as if he was a hologram.

I threw off my blanket because I was burning up. A few minutes later, freezing, I scrambled to find it again.

I heard voices, similar to Max's Inside Voice, but different. Two reminded me of the Swenson's downstairs. Another woman said with an edge in her voice, "Can't believe he came home drunk on a Tuesday night."

My parents called to me, but I couldn't see them in the thick fog surrounding me. Their voices got louder and closer until it sounded as if they were standing over my bed, yelling at me.

When I opened my eyes, I saw they were sitting on both sides of my mattress. Mom smiled and said, using her Inside Voice, "*Good. You're awake.*"

I looked from her to Dad then back and yelled, "WHY THE HELL DIDN'T YOU TELL ME WHAT WAS COMING! My head exploded, I fell into a mountain of trash and thought I was dying in an alley last night!"

"Oh my god," said Mom. "You Changed? In an alley?"

I sat up. "A mugger pointed a gun at us, and my head hurt like hell. Thought I was having a stroke."

"What were you doing in that alley?" asked Dad.

"Max saw the full moon and freaked and started running to get me home and we cut through. I heard someone in there waiting for us, but Max didn't, and we kept going. A mugger stepped out, pointed a silver revolver at us, and a brick flew out of nowhere and knocked it out of his hand. He put the gun to my head and promised he'd kill me if I didn't give him my Rolex, then zoom he slid away down the alley out of sight."

"Ah, Max is telekinetic." asked Mom.

"So he says. Why didn't you warn me what to expect?"

"We tried," said Dad. "We both texted you to come home."

"You said it was late and I should go to bed. You didn't tell me why. Not last night, last week, last month, never. This is your fault. You knew what was happening, but I didn't. When I saw that gun in the mugger's hand, pain exploded as if he'd shot me. It was so intense I hoped it would stop no matter what." I checked the back of my head. It was pain free, but my hand came away sticky. "At least it doesn't hurt anymore."

Mom got a whiff of either me or my clothes. "Good lord, what died in here?"

"The torture knocked me out, and I crashed into a pile of garbage. That was the second time, after the guy knocked me into the junk when we ran by."

My Dad wrinkled his nose. "Smells worse than a rancid grease trap."

"I fell into that stink last night because you didn't warn me I was going to mutate into something from *Black Mirror* or the X-Men."

"Enough! The fox ate that chicken."

Mom picked up my blazer, then held her nose. "*All these go in the trash.*"

"Max told me what was happening to me, but I hurt too much to remember anything. What the hell did I become? What's going to happen to me next?"

She pulled the drapes back from the window. My bedroom faced Central Park, so light flooded in. Now, the light was feeble and dim. It was still early.

"*Look at that,*" Mom said with her Inside Voice. "*The moon. Last night was the first full moon after your eighteenth birthday. That's when Grigori Change.*"

Dad stood and pulled my mother toward the door. "*He needs to calm down while he showers.*"

"You know you're descended from Rasputin," said Mom. "That's what makes you Grigori. Mental telepathy is the gift his descendants inherit when they come of age. *Get your questions ready and we'll talk over breakfast.*"

"There's lots more I need–"

"Shower," said Dad. "We'll talk later, but you need to figure most of this out for yourself."

23

My parental units left me alone to take in my new situation. What I remembered most was the sound cocking a revolver makes when the barrel presses against your skull. How did Max throw that guy down the alley? Why didn't he do it sooner?

Stripped off my underwear on the way to my bathroom and put them into the hamper. Our apartment was the penthouse of the building, and the three largest bedrooms had their own private baths. The other two bedrooms shared a Jack and Jill bath between them.

My face in the mirror didn't look any different. Ran my Braun Series X electric razor over my face like almost every day. Said to myself and *"I'm shaving now"* and it sounded like my thoughts always echoed in my head. Not how my parents sounded at all.

Out loud, "Hello," seemed normal, but it all was a little crazy. I showered, washed my hair twice to get the stench out, and got dressed.

The cook put a waffle with two eggs, two strips of bacon, and coffee in front of me. "Do we have that maple syrup from Ontario?"

"Right here, sir," he said. The silver syrup boat sides were almost, but not quite, hot to the touch. He disappeared back into the kitchen.

Two bites of waffle remained when my parents joined me.

Dad raised an eyebrow. "You've got questions?"

"Yeah, the truth about my head."

"It's the hippocampus."

"Been a while since biology, but doesn't everybody have a hippocampus?"

"Technically, everyone has two. You have a third one that provides telepathic powers," he said.

"Three, thanks to Rasputin. It awakes after your birthday, triggered by the full moon," said Mom. "Every one of his heirs have mental advantages. Those of us descended from an illegitimate child of Rasputin and Madame Matej, a mystic who fled Romania to Moscow, inherit the gift of telepathy in one form or another. Your father and I have abilities. Your grandparents, on both sides. And now you," she said.

"Can I stop it? Take it out somehow?" I asked.

"That's a stupid idea," said Dad. "You got the greatest gift of all time, especially if you use it correctly."

"Why can't I hear you talk to each other with your minds?"

"Because we can block our thoughts from eavesdroppers," he answered. "Think of a wall, and a window you can look through to see the person you want to talk to. You can silently talk to them so no one else can hear."

"Max explained a few details, but the pain made it hard to focus. What abilities are there?"

"Everyone has one special power that manifests a week or two after the Change," said Mom. "Mine is tele-persuasion, and the closer I am the stronger my ability. Touching someone gives me the most influence. Telepathy, except your Inside Voice, will fade out as your other power develops."

She often leaned in and touched a person's arm or shoulder when she talked to people. "Wow, enormous advantage if you can persuade juries and judges to rule your way," I said.

"Other common powers include sensing emotions, called an empath, and telekinesis, moving things with your mind, as Max does."

Dad bragged on his ability. "True telepath. I can read people's thoughts, at least their dominant ones. Distance lowers the volume, so I need closeness as well. But no normal is able stop me from hearing what they're thinking."

"Which is why Holden has you negotiate every major deal!" Pointing to Mom, I said, "And wins like nine out of ten lawsuits with you as general counsel!"

"Thirty-seven out of thirty-eight. But who's counting?"

"Why haven't you prepared me for this? A face-plant into garbage is the worst way to get powers ever. I deserved to know."

Mom shook her head. "Not everyone in the bloodline gets an ability. One in fifteen doesn't, and nobody knows why. Our family doesn't tell children details until we verify their inheritance. Plus, it's hard to accept until you can do it. Other families may take other approaches."

They stood. "You've got plenty to figure out. Take your time. If you need to skip school, you have our permission," said Dad.

Wow, dump school? Mr. Follow-the-Rules said that? Nearly worth bailing just to see if he meant it.

"And this secret means life or death for us in certain situations," he said. "None of your friends discussed the Change, did they?"

I shook my head and the new burden weighed heavier. *This was a load dropped on me.*

"It is a load. Learn from your classmates and don't tell anyone younger. Your older friends will test you before they speak freely in front of you."

Mom put her hand on mine. "You know you can't tell any muggles any of this, correct?"

"Ha! Muggles. Perfect. Did Grigori or Harry Potter come up with the name first?" A glow filled me and made me warm and agreeable. This was important advice of the highest order.

She smiled back and leaned in to kiss me on the forehead.

When her lips met my skin, vaguely visible orders to keep this a secret floated from her to me. It looked like a color poured into clear water as the color changed the clear water to the new color.

Before I had time to react, she walked away. "Wait!" I said. "Is this how you beat that bridge championship couple on the twelfth floor?"

"All's fair."

As she turned back, she talked to Dad with her Inside Voice, *"Great day. He's strong. No need to worry anymore."*

"Don't tell him that," he said. *"But our bloodline is one of the purest, so he should be powerful."*

"Curious what skill he'll have?"

"We'll know in a week or two. I'm sure he can't hear us now because his power is so new. We'll need to block when we talk around him now."

"As a mother, I'm just glad he has something. Doesn't matter what ability he gets."

I focused on what they were saying while dawdling to the elevator foyer. *Was I not supposed to hear them talking just now?* Overhearing my parents' Inside Voices after they left the room, turned into the hall, and on to their bedroom, felt weird. They said being close is important to hear or influence someone. Was two rooms away close enough?

I face-palmed my forehead and pushed the down button. *What a great way to start my day! Inherit superpowers and fall into a pit of stupid.*

In the lobby, Darrell the Doorman tipped his cap and pointed to the Town Car that takes me to and from school. "Nice weather and I need some exercise so I'll walk," I said as I walked past. There was a ton to consider before getting to school and facing my friends. A few long New York City blocks on foot might give me that chance.

Were my parents telling me everything? They left a lot of gaps, and my questions kept coming. They discussed using a block to stop other people from listening. How could I hear their Inside Voices to each other? Close meant how close? Their bedroom wasn't close, was it? Was there something wrong with my new mutant powers?

Halfway to school, a different fear stopped me so abruptly a guy bumped my back and cursed me. Wait! My classmates were already eighteen.

That horrifying dream of going to school naked? Knowing many of my friends heard my every thought was worse. Way, way worse.

Chapter 6: With Friends Like These

Questions chased each other inside my head like squirrels around a Central Park tree. What other kinds of powers are there? What power would I develop? Did every Grigori eighteener overhear their parents' private Inside Voices? Maybe for a year then the ability disappeared? Everybody started with telepathy, but a different power dominates after a week or two? Does your ability get stronger over time? Had to, right? If you could persuade at eighteen, couldn't you persuade better at twenty-five? Why didn't I think of these questions at home so I could ask my parents?

I never knew, but this secret had shaped my entire life. My parents and grandparents took part in this before I was born, and their lives revolved around the Grigori. If this inheritance skipped me, would my folks still love me? Of course, once a son, always a son.

Did all Grigori students in school have powers? Some of my older friends started winning our chess matches the last few months. Did they cheat by mind-reading? Was my father cheating when he beat me at games, or just smarter or more experienced?

The walk in the crisp spring air did help, and my legs and shoulders were loose and warm. But answers to the questions running through my mind remained AWOL. Maybe it was because of all these thoughts running loose, but I kept looking behind me, feeling like somebody was following me. I know, stupid.

I ignored everyone at my private school, Makary Academy, but stopped on the second step when a familiar voice called my name. Through gritted teeth, my answer was as polite as possible. "Hey, Lucy."

Lucy Kilish, a petite blonde with a Cheerleading Captain patch on her school blazer, stood in front of me. If Hollywood needed another sexy teen cheerleader, they should call her. She'd been my girlfriend for practically two years.

She's the girl Mom and Dad loved and the daughter-in-law they wanted. The one they demanded me to take back for two solid weeks. The other half of our stupid celebrity name of PauLucy. Mr. And Miss Junior Sweethearts last year. My first, and so far only, intimate partner. What my parents didn't know was that she screwed at least one other classmate when we were out of town during Christmas. I knew emotional pain from losing two people I loved, and her cheating nearly matched those black holes. Months after the breakup, the knife to the heart agony of betrayal was manageable.

But based on what I learned this morning, my parents HAD to hear me thinking of why we split. And they still badgered me to forgive and take her back? Why'd they do that? Whose side were they on?

"You have a stroke or something?"

"What? Sorry."

"So," she chirped, her index and middle finger walking up my arm. "Did you notice the nice moon last night? I thought it was beautiful."

I wanted to say, "Last night? When I nearly died because I said stupid things to the guy holding a gun to my head?" But I squashed that and remained quiet.

Her rebound lunkhead boyfriend, Chip Yevgen, hurried over and draped his arm over her shoulders, as if he worried I'd throw her over my shoulder caveman style and run away.

Chip was hulking and brutish compared to my tall and wiry. Differences in our looks, personalities, and approach to, well, everything, were so opposite Max said she dated him to annoy me. It used to, a little, but no more. She suffered far more having to put up with that Neanderthal asshole than any pain it caused me.

Before I could move my arm back from her fingers, Chip moved and pulled her to the side. Her walking fingers stepped on air.

"Not doing anything, just checking." Lucy silently told Chip.

"You know I hate that jerk."

Chip took his eyes off Lucy. *"Hey putz."*

Suddenly, two drills began boring into my brain as Lucy and Chip tried to read my thoughts. By instinct and following Dad's advice, my mental wall blocked them. Hiding my new abilities from mean girls and bullies seemed a good idea. Lucy seemed curious, but Chip's attack felt darker and uglier.

"My parents said your party was a rager for the olds," she said, like nothing was happening as she tried to crack open my head. "And you never told me your middle name was Atreides."

"Atreeaadeez?" he said. "That's a stupid name."

"Guess you haven't read *Dune*," I snapped back. "Mom was a big environmentalist in college and loves that book."

"Somebody wrote a book about sand piles?" he asked. "That's really stupid."

"Could be worse. If she preferred whales, I'd have to tell people to 'Call me Ishmael' when I met them."

"What the fu-?"

"C'mon, lover boy, I'll tell you all about it." She led her confused boyfriend up the steps.

As they walked away, my focus shifted to Lucy. Her thoughts were easy to read. *"Poor Paul. If he didn't make the Change last night, he never will. Sad and basic life for him, thrown out of the Grigori and abandoned by all his friends. Genius of me to dump him when I had the chance."*

Like hell she dumped me. She called three nights in a row, crying harder each time. Came to the house twice, the second wearing only her long coat, hooker boots, and a smile. Her betrayal was horrible, but it was damn hard to close the door in her face.

Chip's thoughts sprayed everywhere. His mental drivel was tough to avoid.

"Lucy's so damn hot today. Gonna pull her into the first empty classroom and grab a handful before class." My waffle tried to claw its way back up.

I walked through the metal detector and past the statue of Elder Makary of St. Nicholas Monastery in Verkhoturye, Russia. Silent questions kept poking at my mind. Keep the wall up and act natural, and don't react.

Four arms seized me by surprise. Taylor the Guy and Taylor the Girl hugged me from both sides. Patting them on the head made them release me.

"OK, Taylors, try again," I said. "Stump the expert."

"You won't have an answer this time," said Taylor the Girl.

"Rock trio," demanded Taylor the Guy.

"Gotta narrow it some or I can give you a dozen groups that will blow your puny little almost-minds."

"Ready for that," she said. "Just girls."

"And British," he added. They plugged their AirPods in and waited for a group name.

With a snap of my fingers, I said, "Perfect group for you guys is The Faders and their one album, *Plug in + Play*, from 2005."

"Not enough," he said. "Biggest song on the album?"

"Best-performing single was "No Sleep Tonight," and it was even in an Apple commercial." I turned him to face his girlfriend.

"Most important for you, Boy Taylor, is the fourth track titled, 'Girls Can Make You Cry,' because they damn sure can." I looked around and glimpsed Lucy as she and Chip rounded a corner. Girl Taylor grinned. "Don't hurt him, OK?"

They giggled and searched for The Faders. When they found "No Sleep Tonight" they gave me thumbs up.

When heading upstairs, none of the teachers tried to "question" me mentally. Even in the Grigori Research Association Youth wing, no adults checked me.

Children of Grigori parents had some classes in the GRAY wing. Half the second story classrooms were only for us, separated by a thick wall with an entry door with keycard access.

Once inside, my search for those who were eighteen began. Before a list came to mind, someone yelled inside my head.

"*Hey, doofus, you here yet?*" That was Max, subtle as ever.

"*Yeah.*" I remembered a little of what we talked about last night. Still pissed at my parents for not warning me.

He came up from behind and caught me in one of his famous bear hugs. The surprise and pressure whooshed my breath out. Max was a bit shorter than me but thicker, hard-muscled, and remained in basketball shape all year. He was also the unofficial leader of the handful of African American students at Makary.

Max was always on my side. Who else in our telepathic world would be?

Chapter 7: Gotta Have a Posse

Escaping one of Max's bear-hugs was impossible. He laughed at my feeble attempts, then dropped me. "How you doin' this morning? Parents explain things?"

"After I finished yelling at them for hiding this and letting me think I was dying last night."

"But the word is you're not answering people, other Grigori, when they speak to you in their Inside Voice."

"Seemed smart to keep my hole card hidden."

He rolled his eyes. "You white boys and poker kill me." He stopped and pointed at me. "Your parents didn't tell you anything?"

"Dad's short on swim lessons and long on throwing me in the pool." That's almost exactly what he said this morning, but in Dad-speak.

"Shame. You blocking now? Because it blocks better or smoother than everybody else's."

"A wall, what Dad said."

He looked me straight in the eyes. "Not a terrible idea. Once you hit eighteen, people get serious. Ratchet up a level in their game. Crunch time."

"Why didn't you tell me this was coming?"

He frowned and shook his head. "You kidding? Threats, serious threats. Olds promise death and dismemberment for even a hint. My parents were on me daily because they knew I'd warn you if I could."

"My parents just told me to keep it quiet. No death threats."

We pointed finger guns at each other "Yet!" we yelled together.

As we laughed over the shtick we'd used since grade school, his girlfriend Junie came over and kissed his cheek. He said she looked like a supermodel and she said he looked like a teen Denzel. She was wrong, but he was right, and it was easy to find Junie in a crowd because her long, tight black curls poofed out everywhere.

Black students and athletes were both rare at Makary, so people began placing odds when they'd start dating back in middle school. Both were stubborn and refused. To force him to make his move, I stole his phone and texted her for a dinner date late in the summer.

He yelled at me and shook with nerves until she replied, "yes and about damn time." Just call me Cupid.

Junie winked at me. *"You in there, skinny boy?"*

"Present."

She winced. "Not so loud, man, moderate. *Control your Inside Voice.*"

"Give him a break, babe, he just got it last night," said Max.

She laughed. "You two cover for each other more than any two people I know, including my parents."

"What friends do."

"What he said," I added. "Always need friends."

We chatted a couple more minutes about class and projects, and my shoulders relaxed a bit. The tension had built up since I got to school.

A female voice caused them to tighten again. "There you are!" said Gemma Hargraves. She and Junie were best friends, but she and I were the opposite.

For years and years, she'd treated me like a cockroach. She seldom spoke to me but always gave a snort of disgust with a "Die Now!" glare when she saw me.

To keep the peace after Max and Junie hooked up, we settled into polite indifference for their sakes. Correction, I was polite. Gemma made little effort to avoid drama.

She was needle sharp and acted different from other girls. They kept every hair in place and covered up any hint of a freckle. Gemma had a Jane Austen name but Calamity Jane hair. Her red, long, and wavy hair was under minimal control at the best of times, and I bet she and Junie got together in elementary school because neither cared about controlling her hair. Behind her back some girls called her Gemma the Ginger. It didn't appear to be a compliment.

She never hid her freckles at school, or even at the formal dinners and dances. Every single reddish dot was always on display.

Gemma hugged Junie and saw me over her shoulder. When she looked at me, both corners of her mouth dropped.

"Asshole!" she thought to herself.

My eyebrows jumped.

"OK, you aren't brain-damaged. Shame. That would explain soooo much."

33

Gemma pulled on Junie. "C'mon, let's compare notes for AP History."

"I hope that means you explain the last chapter to me," said Junie. The girls left. Junie blew a kiss to Max and waved to me. She giggled when I blew a kiss back.

"Your face twisted kinda funny for a minute there," said Max.

"It sucks to hear how people think about you with no filters. How do you stay friends?"

"You found the nasty part quick. At seventeen, you can be Mr. Popular, and you were the king with Lucy. But hit eighteen and the mental gloves come off."

"It's hard to keep my mouth shut sometimes. How did you learn to keep your mind shut? You mouth off more than I do."

"Takes a while. The couples who broke up earlier this year? Bye bye PauLucy?"

"Cupid's arrows fell out?"

"One turned eighteen in every couple. You're the only one who called it quits just because."

"Because we disagreed on what exclusive means."

"I know that, and Lucy knows that, but remember the others who split? Not everyone was screwing around. Or they were. It's damn hard to hide secrets from anybody the first few weeks you have powers, so be careful."

Pulling Max off to an empty corner, I asked, "Speaking of powers..."

"The old 'I'll show you mine if you show me yours' trick."

"You said last night you're a Mover. Sounds pretty cool. Where's my phone? Oh, come here phone. And throw that brick."

"Yeah, but my big career option is a juggler in the circus." He shrugged.

A strange sensation washed over me, and Max's emotions floated in. First regret, some shame, then resignation. He didn't seem happy with the cards dealt him. Made a mental note to be careful talking to others about powers.

"Or, wait for it, knife-thrower. Pretty girl, balloons, flinging deadly daggers, cheering crowds, top billing. Max the Mighty Knife Manipulator up in lights."

"I'll take it."

34

"And Junie?"

He held up his finger. "Ask people yourself, don't rely on powers gossip. If they want to tell you, they'll tell you. Or not. Junie has psychometry. She gets information from things she touches, so I call her a Historian."

"Could be handy. I wonder what I'll get."

"From what my folks say, your parents are way powerful. You'll hit it out of the park. I saw you throw that mugger last night."

"I, ah, ah–"

"Not your fault. Blacks don't have as strong a connection to the Rasputin blood line. Plus, Mom's not Grigori."

We walked to class.

"Didn't your mom come from down South?"

Max lit up, as he always did when asked about his mother. "N'awlins. No Rasputin link, but a lot of voodoo in her family and she has powers. Says I've got some, too."

"Double-dipping at the powers buffet? Doesn't seem fair."

"Always worried about what's fair, aren't you? We're not in grade school anymore, man."

I could always snap back to Max. "You're right, fair's overrated. Back of the bus for you."

He laughed and waved his fist at me. "I'll use voodoo curses to make your butt grow together, whitey."

"Some will swear you already did because I'm full of it."

His mom did a Tarot card reading for me before Christmas. That was the first clue Lucy didn't feel our relationship was exclusive. She predicted it a month before harsh reality stabbed me in the heart.

Max was still talking about his mother. "Most people bring back a t-shirt and a hangover from N'awlins. Dad brought home a voodoo priestess he met when she gave a haunted cemetery tour."

We reached our Calculus II class and sat beside each other as usual. Max whispered, "Stay as closed as you can. Avoid dumb mistakes until you learn more about your new brain."

The rest of the day became a constant barrage of mental fingers poking at my mind. When people checked, they got a response, but nothing more. Even being careful, so many minds hitting mine made me feel like a punching bag. The pain felt so intense I checked to make sure no blood or melted brain oozed out of my ears.

As I leaned against a wall and pushed hard on my temples to ease the throbbing, Gordy and his rolling mop bucket stopped. He was the main janitor, a short guy with a nearly bald head and a scruffy gray beard, and many assumed he was learning disabled. I enjoyed the weird non-answers he gave to every question people asked.

I'd been talking to him since I was twelve because Yasmin forced me to after I made a stupid comment about a busboy. She told me to ask one of the school janitors his name and get his or her personal info, so I did. After two minutes I realized he wasn't crazy or mentally disabled, but he wasn't quite right, either. His stories couldn't be true, but who did they hurt?

"Paul, ya OK boyo? Gonna puke? Feel free, I got the mop bucket right here."

"Thanks, Gordy, just a killer headache."

"Wet banana leaves help, learned that fighting in South American jungles, but got none here sorry to say."

"Understand." His cap had a red oval with the letters DQ. Every day he had a different one. If he ever wore one twice, I missed it. "What's the DQ for?"

"Dairy Queen. Southern thing, mostly. Ever been? Probably not, since the last one in Manhattan closed during the pandemic. If ya go, get a cherry Dilly Bar."

"You're right, never been. Dilly Bar? Sounds fun."

"Cherry's the best. If ya don't need to puke, good on ya, and I'll be rolling on. If ya do, no problem, just say so pronto. Harder to mop if it dries." He rolled his bucket away, then stopped. "Your stock's up, high trading volume, new street rumors about ya, Paul. Lots to ponder, boyo. See ya."

With that, he and his ever-present mop bucket zoomed around the corner. My stock's up? High trading volume? Wasn't sure about that, but he was right because there were things to consider, and outside was the place to do it.

When the car arrived to take me home, my battered brain said no, no, no. I craved fresh air and the openness of outdoors, not a small rolling cage. Needed to figure out how to avoid all the dumb mistakes Max warned me to avoid.

Chapter 8: How Their World Works

A deep breath of spring reduced my headache. The fresh green smells of early flowers slowed my pace to enjoy the clean air. Ready to handle more thoughts? One way to find out. The window separating me from the mental noise slid open.

Too much! The voices flooded in and reminded me of a powerful wave hitting my sailboat and heeling it over. I staggered and shuffled my feet to recover my balance.

So many voices yelled that no single conversation in the flood of voices made sense, but shutting the window blocked them. My headache throbbed less, but the worries popped up again.

Did friends who changed already know my actual feelings about them? Did every girl who looked really hot one day feel ogled? Did every teacher who knocked my grade down for picky shit sense my anger? Did they care?

The last example didn't seem to count. No teacher showed any evidence of telepathy. Maybe they covered it up well, but remembering the Grigori gatherings my parents talked about, no teachers came to mind.

But the question about friends and hot girls nagged at me. If a guy figured there was a problem, he'd get in my face. Girls at school might slap me, although so far, I remained unslapped. Makary girls didn't put up with much crap from us guys. Did I just find the reason?

In AP Psychology, the teacher claimed people think about themselves ninety-four percent of the time, leaving only six percent for others. It would be tough to overhear anything interesting when listening to friends. Probably just random drivel like I was saying to myself now.

Did Grigori kids ever have true privacy growing up? If parents overheard children's thoughts, how did they not get really mad sometimes? The situation at home wasn't terrible, but mine still pissed me off on the regular. *Wish Dad would quit being a hardass. Wish Mom sparkled like Max's mom.* Those kinds of thoughts had to sting.

Darrell held the door for me with a smile and a tip of his cap, as always. "Nice day for a walk, Young Master Paul."

"Yeah, sorry, should've texted."

"No worries, sir, no worries."

I opened my window.

"*Nobody thinks about the effort I put out for them,*" he said to himself in his head. "*Work my ass off and these rich fools don't even notice.*"

The psychology teacher was right! Everyone mostly worried about themselves! Perhaps they focused on how other people griefed them, but still fixated on themselves.

It was hardly past four in the afternoon when the elevator doors opened in our penthouse foyer. My parents were never home before six or even seven, so them waiting for me was weird.

Mom stood and opened her arms for a hug. "Surprised? Your first day can be traumatic."

"You've got questions so ask us anything," said Dad.

The couch had a much softer seat than my school desks. I sank down and placed my backpack on the floor beside me, soothing the headache a little more. The maid set a tall glass of lemonade on the end table.

"Thanks. Would you get me about a hundred aspirin, too?" The first cool sip slid down with a chill.

"*What surprised you the most today?*" asked Mom.

"*If people don't like you, they can't hide it, can they?*" Gemma prompted that question because she was the person who hated me the most of all my classmates. I hoped she was the only one, but reading the thoughts of other students could change that fact. Not a fun idea. What if Gemma was but one of many, and the rest hid those feelings?

My parents smiled at each other. "It's hard to keep secrets," said Mom. "That's why Grigori members are in demand by the biggest companies and work with the smartest CEOs."

Business! Of course! Worrying about what classmates knew about my thoughts was a personal issue. The morning conversation about negotiating contracts and winning court cases was all business. Telepathy would win every time. Listeners and Pushers would dominate every negotiation and court battle.

The ninety-four percent self-absorption rule for other people applied to me, too. Lucy toyed with me to tweak Chip. I was Amina's escape hatch, while Gemma absolutely hated me. I focused on myself at school and missed the bigger picture.

"Lucy is such a sweetheart," said Mom.

Her comment jerked me back to the moment. Of course, they heard my thoughts! They'd been doing this for years! And they loved Lucy. Our parents had dinner together all the time before we started dating. Not once since we split.

"Correct, it's hard to keep secrets," said Dad. "We considered telling you about Lucy, but decided it wasn't our place."

Damn! Nothing was private! Oops!

My parents laughed again. This must seem like toddler me learning how to walk and crashing into furniture.

"We'll have to block when we talk around him now," said Dad to Mom.

"You're right. Us learning his secrets is far different from him learning ours."

A shimmer fluttered around the thoughts from my parents, like I was looking at their heads underwater. Had that been there before? They weren't talking to me, were they? Didn't seem so. Seemed they meant to talk silently only to each other.

"Do you have a headache?" asked Mom.

"I did at school, but the walk and the aspirin are helping."

"Schools," prompted Dad to Mom.

"The Mayor strongly pushed Columbia at your party. While we'd love to have you close to home, Harvard is the best choice."

"Second best," laughed Dad. "Second to Yale."

"Why?"

"Yale and Harvard have Grigori professors to help you. Columbia's retired and there's no replacement yet," said Dad.

"Harvard has three." Mom elbowed Dad gently.

"As does Yale," he said, elbowing her in return.

Mom stood and pulled Dad up as well. "You might want to spend some time alone to rest. Go relax and we'll see you at dinner."

Did the shimmer earlier mean they were blocking their conversation from me? They walked down the hall toward their bedroom. *"Pretty disciplined for being so new at this,"* thought

Mom. Again, there was a shimmer around her thoughts to Dad. I couldn't see their heads anymore, but I could still see a pastel shimmers when I eavesdropped on their thoughts.

"*Surprised me, too. He's always been smart. That should help.*" Another shimmer around his answer.

"*His thinking about Lucy was a surprise. Could he still have feelings for her? A powerful pair for the bloodline, those two. Their children would be powerful with pure lines on both sides all the way back.*"

"*Who knew he'd be such a prude about a little screwing around? I blame your mother.*"

"*Why did you say that?*" snapped Mom.

"*She never agreed with some Grigori orders and assignments.*"

"*He loves spending time with her, so they'll talk.*"

"*We better push that meeting as far into the future as possible.*"

"*I should call her, anyway.*"

On the way to my room, my mental window closed and I rebuilt my wall to keep my own thoughts private, but my confusion grew. They talked like they were alone and knew I couldn't overhear them. Were my powers stronger? Broken? What was going on here?

Dad didn't want me to talk to my grandmother? Why did they dismiss Lucy's betrayal as a little screwing around? Was there bigger screwing around going on? No, don't pick that scab and restart the bleeding. I finished the Lucy Era, period.

There was one person who would help me sort out this mess. Text to Max: "Can you hear your parents talk silently to each other?"

His response came right back. "Can't overhear any adult if they put their guard up. ???"

"Trying to figure all this out."

"Now you know why we couldn't get away with shit growing up."

"Yeah." Speaking out loud didn't answer Max, but a thumbs-up emoji did.

All this newness swirled around in my head. *Blocks on other people don't stop me from hearing them. That's not normal, according to Max. How is that possible? Why me? Does this mean my abilities are stronger than theirs? Is this good, or will it come back and bite me in the butt?*

Chapter 9: Listen to the World

The next morning, Saturday, the entry in my secret music blog featured a just-discovered CD from 1999. *They're Only Shoes*, the sole release from a band named Skasmopolitan, one of the flood of ska punk bands with horns popular in the mid-90s through the mid-00s. They buried one of the funniest rock songs ever on track 11: "A Slut Named Rachel." High school angst and snark and fun with horns. Those wonderful tunes that disappeared without notice were the gems my mentor Yasmin searched for daily. My goal was to shine a light on these overlooked diamonds as she did.

My plan: learn to control the onslaught of inner voices from people around me. With hiking boots on and carrying plenty of cash, bottles of water, and two KIND protein bars in my backpack, the test-drive began.

After crossing Central Park West, my path took me through the trees and meadows. Thoughts of everyone near crashed over me in a wave. My mental wall went up to stop the flood.

To avoid being washed away when I listened to thoughts, I needed something new, because Dad's window idea leaked. I imagined turning the wall and window into a thick door to block the voices. With the door cracked, I heard fewer voices.

How to listen to just one person? Doors have keyholes and I imagined bending to look through the keyhole. I could track a single person, but a few voices leaked through the keyhole's opening.

After walking through the park to the East Side, my control of this telepathy stuff was getting better. The wave of voices no longer overwhelmed me, but the few voices leaking through the keyhole were annoying.

Lots of doors in New York apartments had peepholes, including my friend Jaxon's. His door had a small swinging plate you moved to uncover the hole, so I tried that. Moving the plate away from the hole allowed me to target one guy who was texting.

"No babe ur the only 1 for me promise." The man finished and resumed walking. *"That will hold her,"* he thought.

42

The peephole worked! When I wanted to stop listening, the little plate swung back over the peephole, blocking voices. A cute girl walked beside me and I aimed the mental peephole at her.

"Damn I miss him. Keep avoiding him, or take him back? He swears he'll behave, but he said that last time. No, he's history."

Good for you. Dump his ass before you get in too deep! I broke up with Lucy so you can break up with him.

"But he promises that was his last mistake. OK. One more chance."

Damn! Don't fall for it! Oh well. Different mistakes called for different responses, as Mom always said. Hope she doesn't wind up crushed with a bleeding heart, but chances are she will.

With my mental door closed, it was time to check out the retail stores on Park Avenue. Most were open again except for a few that were being renovated.

My parents grabbed a major equity position at a big discount in a store somewhere close. Dad bragged he, "got them down to their absolute lowest price of past taxes and the lease contract." Now it was clear he had the inside scoop from reading the seller's thoughts.

Time for more mental exercise. A lady with a Gucci purse just like one of Mom's stopped to window shop. *"Got that. That. That. When will new models get here?"*

A man and woman in their mid-thirties came close. *"We should've gone to the Hamptons this morning. Nothing interesting in the city tonight." "Thank god he didn't drag me to the Hamptons again. So much to do in the city."*

A man my grandmother's age strolled by. *"Most of my holdings are still rising. Hope my oil stocks pay those big dividends again."*

The light stopped me just before stepping into the street. Back on the curb, the peephole swung closed since people surrounded me. A motion caught my eye.

A man with eyes glued on his phone hurried toward the street. When he was two steps from the curb, a delivery truck changed lanes and roared closer.

"Freeze!" I ordered mentally.

His foot was almost in the street when the truck driver slammed on his brakes. The driver's side mirror came within two inches of smashing his head. He struggled to get his feet under him and moved back as the truck slid through the intersection and a burned rubber cloud floated up and stung my nose.

"Watch where you're goin', ya rich dumbass!" yelled the driver. After a few loud curses, he started the engine and drove away before the light changed.

The lucky guy looked at people near him. "Did you yell at me to freeze?" he asked the woman next to him. She shook her head. "Sure thought someone yelled, 'Freeze!' before I stepped off the curb." The woman shrugged and focused on her phone again.

After the light changed, a cab stopped to let a fare out, so I grabbed it. Good idea to get away in case anyone noticed what happened. But what did? I Pushed a guy to save his life. Great! What if I Pushed him to focus on his phone and walk into the street? Shit! My Pusher ability can kill people just as easy as it can save them!

No, that couldn't be true. Hypnotists say you can't hypnotize someone to do something they'd never do for real, and a normal healthy person wouldn't follow a Push command that would kill them, right? And Pushing gets the same results as hypnosis but is much quicker, correct? That makes sense and is much less murderous.

The driver interrupted my thoughts.

"You are going to Brooklyn, sir?"

"Just across the river."

The cabbie loved to talk. Nonstop. He came from Somalia through Texas. His cousins were here now, but his aunts and uncles were too old and poor to resettle. His sixth-grade daughter was at the top of her class, even though she was behind when they moved from Texas.

"How is Texas?" I asked. "Always wanted to visit."

"You'll love it, sir. Open spaces everywhere. Friendly people."

"Where did you live?"

"Houston. Too crowded for me."

"You came to New York to avoid the crowds in Houston?"

"That does sound funny, yes?" The cabbie thought about something else instead. *Damn rednecks in Houston refused to help the rest of my family immigrate. Staff at the UN is wonderful.*

"Next, you can move to Tokyo and enjoy even more crowding."

"Ha ha, sir. Yes. More people make possible more money for us in transportation."

In twenty minutes, we were across the East River into Brooklyn and the cabbie sounded happy with his big tip. Maybe Texas wasn't a good idea because rednecks didn't sound fun.

Vernon Boulevard from Queensbridge Park was a different world and several income classes below Park Avenue. I knew eavesdropping was a privacy violation, but I needed to learn to handle all this. This time is OK, I told myself, then I'll stop. I wondered how many of my friends listened to me. Everyone who could? No doubt.

A husband and wife sat on a bench overlooking the park. *"We've got rent money for next month. After that? No clue,"* he thought.

A father held the hand of his young daughter. *"Mommy used to bring me here and push me on the swings,"* thought the little girl. *"Nobody's pushed me on a swing since the Rona got her."* When she slowed and leaned toward the playground, he pulled her faster.

An older man shuffled by. *"I can't afford insurance now. Gotta hang on until I get Medicare."* He coughed, a deep, bone-rattling explosion from the bottom of his chest.

A positive thought came to me. A girl my age leaned against a bus stop and stared at a photo on her phone. *"When you get home, I'll keep you in bed for a week. They classified marijuana stores as essential services during the lockdown. How the hell can they leave you locked up for selling two joints? Hope the parole board listens to reason."*

Not so positive, except positive her boyfriend or girlfriend or husband or whatever shouldn't rot in jail.

I grabbed a cab back and chewed on what I learned. People in my neighborhood worried over stock dividends and Gucci purses. People here worried how to pay rent and stay alive until they got Medicare. Children mourned dead parents.

Why hadn't any of the Grigori telepaths volunteered to help these guys? Sway the parole board for the innocent? Loan someone a few bucks when needed?

45

Who'd tell me the truth? The person my parents didn't want me to visit. I called and asked, "Hey, Bunny, got something tasty for lunch?"

Chapter 10: Bunny Says

Sophia Popova, my mother's mother, lived on the 10th floor of a building on the Upper East Side. It was a corner apartment bathed in sunlight.

I knocked twice and used my key to enter, and she smiled when she saw me. She put two shrimp cocktail appetizers on the table, then turned to me with arms open. As we hugged, she looked paler than she did at my party.

"*I had more makeup on, dear.*"

"Oh. Sorry. Hard to remember to keep my thoughts to myself now."

"You must control them every moment," she said. The thick blonde hair she passed to my mother was turning into a stunning shade of silver. "*Sure hope Caroline teaches him well.*"

What? Why did she tell me that? But she acted as if she was talking to herself. She just told me to control my thoughts so she must block hers as well, right?

Am I able to hear my family members, no matter what? Her shimmer didn't block any better than the ones my parents used.

"Sit, please. The lasagna warms as we speak."

Photos covered the top of her china cabinet. Me growing up, Mom and Dad, my Aunt Susanna, Uncle Roderick, and Cousin Lance at holidays. But one at the front was new, a picture of us at my birthday party a week ago.

Arm in arm, smiling into the camera, we could be an ad for formal wear. Our eye shapes were identical, but my eyes were a lighter blue.

"You got that framed fast."

"I know, I know, paper photos are for old people. But I love them and you looked so handsome."

Thinking of the party made me jangle my arm to adjust my new watch.

"Nice new car you have on your wrist," she said.

"What?"

"Don't those Rolex models cost close to forty thousand now?"

"Oh. Maybe." Hearing a price made it heavier on my wrist.

"From your parents?"

"No, it's from Holden."

"*That son of a bitch!*" She spread her napkin on her lap. "Very generous. Do you know why he gave you something so expensive?"

She couldn't have meant that first part for me. Not on purpose. "Maybe a watch is the traditional gift for a godson's eighteenth birthday?"

"Didn't you do an internship last summer in one of his companies?"

"Yeah, a software company developing collaboration tools for remote workers. He showed me around and people there were fantastic."

"I'm sure they were. *When the boss introduces you, it sends a message to everyone. And God help them if they piss off your father.*"

OK, there it was again. I've got to ask about this blocking and shimmer stuff because it's driving me crazy.

After my last shrimp, the maid brought out lasagna with garlic bread.

"I'm so glad you came to help me with these leftovers. But that's not why you're here, is it?"

Breaking a piece of bread in half, it was time for questions. "My parents aren't telling me any details on this, ah, stuff."

"*Not doing their job and asking me to lie to the boy.* They told me they want you to figure things out for yourself. Let you make your own choices."

"Mom called you?"

"*Oops.* Of course. Your mother and I talk. You come up now and again. Did you have specific questions?"

"Lots. Like what you just did. You said 'oops' with your Inside Voice but talked to me with your outside voice. Why?"

Her fork clattered onto her plate when she dropped it. "Did you hear the 'oops' before I spoke out loud?"

"Yeah."

"Did you hear me say your parents aren't doing their job?"

"Yeah. Was I not supposed to?" She sure looked upset over this. What was wrong?

"Oh, dear god!" She got up and paced around the table twice. When she sat down, she put her hand on mine.

"Did you do anything special to listen to my thoughts?"

"Same as listening to any Inside Voice. I can tell when you or my parents block, but I can still hear."

"Wait a minute, you can tell? How?"

"There's a shimmer around your thoughts, the mental version of looking at something on the other side of an aquarium filled with pastel colors. Mom and Dad have the look around their thoughts when they block." She looked so upset I worried I was doing something illegal.

She placed her hand over her heart and took deep breaths. "OK, Paulie, it's serious." Her hand back on mine, she added, "Maybe I was careless earlier. I'm going to block and think of a color now, and you tell me what I'm thinking, OK?"

"*Blue like your eyes.*" The shimmer was there, but it still didn't block her thoughts.

"Blue like YOUR eyes, Bunny." The color drained from her face and I started sweating. This didn't feel right, and I sensed a scared feeling from her and concern for me.

She covered her mouth with both hands for a moment. "No one has ever eavesdropped on me." She rose and paced between the dining and living rooms.

"*Don't jump to conclusions.*" She sat and asked, "You heard that too, correct?"

"Yeah."

"I'm not a telepath, but we're family so we can use our Inside Voices with each other. First, think of, ah, the name of your history teacher. Inside Voice only."

"*Ms. Thompson.*"

"I heard Ms. Thompson, right?"

"She's the coolest teacher I have."

"Glad you like her. Now put up whatever you prefer to block your thoughts and imagine your English teacher."

Ms. Brantley.

She shook her head. "When you block, I can't hear a thing, so your block works well. Many prefer a wall, some a door, and others a steel gate. I think of drawing thick, embroidered curtains closed. What do you use?"

"I tried a wall at first, like Dad said. He also said I couldn't block like they can for years. But I block them when I want to hide my thoughts."

"You can block your father already? Amazing progress in such a short time."

"But now I use a door."

"Why does a door work best?"

"I can open the peephole and listen to one person at a time. Keeps the noise out in crowded areas."

"You hear lots of voices around you in public?"

"Everyone around me. Even people in buildings I'm near."

"Oh, dear." She drummed her fingers on the table. "Oh, dear."

"That a problem?"

"I've known no one able to listen to that many people at once. Eavesdropping fades out in feet, not blocks."

"You're making me nervous. Something wrong with me?"

She smiled. "I'm an empath and sense emotions and intent, and can only hear words sometimes, when close enough." Patting my hand, she said, "Touch strengthens it. Now listen to as many people as you can."

How do I hear the most thoughts at one time? Visualizing my head opening and a dish antenna sticking out did the trick. Voices from the floors above and below became audible. Voices from other floors in the building flooded over me, and from people outside. Soon, I could hear people in buildings across the street in every direction.

She released my hand and put hers to her forehead. "How do you control so many conversations?"

"I tried to fight against them at first, but always lost. Now I let them wash over me like an ocean wave. To focus on a small group of voices, I imagine a cup scooping up a bit of water."

"I could feel you handle your ability effortlessly and with no emotional turmoil. What else can you do?"

"Earlier I Pushed a man to stop him from walking into traffic." A thought came to me. "I don't know why I didn't just yell at him."

"Grigori persuaders like your mother can command people do things. How far apart were you?"

"Maybe fifteen or twenty feet?"

She hummed to herself for a few seconds. "What else?"

"When my mom told me not to tell my younger friends any details of this, her suggestion felt physical. She Pushed and the visible words floated into me."

My grandmother put her hand over her mouth again. She walked to a sofa and sat, then patted the chair to her right for me.

"Your mother will die if she finds out you can see her persuade you. She's made millions with her ability, and her power fuels her ego and self-worth to an enormous degree. To discover you can see and then ignore her persuasion could crush her."

She tapped her fingers on the couch arm. "Promise me you won't tell your parents what you told me. OK?"

"OK."

"In fact, don't tell anyone. You can do impossible things that will make many uncomfortable." Her eyes glistened. "Paul, darling Paul, tell no one and stay very, very cautious."

"Will my parents get mad?"

"Yes, but they won't do anything to punish you. Repeat, please don't tell anyone else how you can read through blocks. Promise me."

"OK."

"Promise!"

"Wow! OK! Promise. Cross my heart and stuff."

She paced again. "You heard what I thought about Holden, didn't you? Of course you did. He's a nice enough guy, but his kind ruined the Grigori. We used to help people who needed it, and now we help people make money."

Waving at her apartment contents like a game show prize presenter, she continued. "The money started flowing in the 1950s and it changed our lives. Everything was glorious and there was plenty. But for leadership, plenty wasn't enough. To get more, they ignored, trampled, and trashed our scruples."

"In the 1970s, the money multiplied. We're the secret shared by the largest companies and the richest men. Never women, just men, and they threw ethics, decency, and legality in the garbage. So much pain lingers from those days, and we've gone morally bankrupt."

Picking up the picture of the two of us, she wiped away a tear. "The boy in this picture disappeared, Paul Atreides Barylan. You must become a grown man in a hurry. When people learn blocks don't stop you, many will demand control over you, like Holden. Others, including Holden in a foul mood, will want to kill you."

"What? You're kidding, right?"

"Sadly, no. I can tell you don't believe me, and that's understandable. I hope we never learn the hard way if I'm correct."

"What do I do? I hoped you'd explain and make things easier. Now I'm all nervous and paranoid." Opening my senses, a flood of feelings that weren't mine came rushing to me. Concern, no, nearer to worry with a shade of panic. Love and nervousness for me.

"Let me be clear," she added. "Just because you can listen to your parents doesn't mean you should. Everyone has things they want to keep private."

"You mean our family?"

"Yes, and all Grigori. We have positions of wealth and power now, but we gained them with heinous acts. Avoid the temptation to eavesdrop on your parents, or at least wait until you know more details of the culture, and how we bend rules in our favor."

Learn more? I was trying! My parents wouldn't help, and I scared Bunny. "Maybe friends can help me figure this out?"

"Excellent idea. Max is older if I remember." She walked me to the door. "You come from one of the strongest bloodlines, my dear. Your grandfather and I both trace straight back to Rasputin and Madame Matej with no outsiders. Power increases each generation if the lines stay true."

Kissing me on the forehead was our goodbye ritual from childhood. She leaned down to me at first, then our roles switched before my fourteenth birthday. I leaned down more than last time.

"Don't go sad on me," she said. "I don't shrink as much as you grow, so don't throw me out with the dead."

She kissed me again. "I'll do what I can to help you. Call a few friends to help you get ready."

"Ready for what?"

"When you sail, you watch for storms, right? There's a storm to starboard. A huge one."

She closed the door behind me.

At the elevator, her thoughts were still audible through her block. *"Dear god, I hope he can sail safely through what's coming."*

Chapter 11: Wish I Didn't Tele-hear That

Mom greeted me when the elevator doors opened. "Do you have some kind of Grigori radar or something and know where people are?" I asked.

She smiled. "How was your grandmother? You popped over just for lunch?"

There was that shimmer around her thoughts, making me curious. *She knew I was coming? What is she trying to hide from me now?* "That's why I'm her favorite grandchild."

She laughed and said, "And your cousin's in Los Angeles, so she sees him only at holidays. She had shrimp cocktail? Your special treat?"

I gave a thumbs up, sat, and said, "I hoped for more details on my mental change, too."

"She better not tell you anything! Really? You know you can always talk to us, correct?"

"Guess I will. She didn't say much, except she's an empath and needs to be near to sense emotions."

"Glad she listened to reason. Yes, it was a great comfort for me as a girl. She knew the support I needed based on my mood and emotions."

Dad stomped into the room with exaggerated bowed legs. "Howdy, boy! Howdy, ma'am!" He tipped an imaginary hat.

We burst out laughing.

"You called that company in Texas?" she asked. "The one Senator Kingston discussed at Paul's party?"

"Yes, ma'am!"

He patted me on the shoulder and sat beside Mom. "I'll plan to visit and talk to them face-to-face. *It remains a good acquisition if we can hide the toxic waste they've been dumping forever. That's what bothered Kingston. If we'd known how many problems they've got, we could've pushed the cost far lower."*

Maintaining a neutral smile on my face wasn't easy while listening. Illegal dumping was just a lever to lower the price. Destroying the environment? No problem.

Mom stood. "I brought, ah, a few notes home on them. Will you excuse us?"

"You can visit friends somewhere, right? We don't want to bore you with work on a splendid Saturday afternoon," said Dad. Politely, he meant I should go away.

As they walked, my senses stayed open. They thought they were having a private discussion, but nope.

"*Your mother stay quiet?*"

"*He said all she told him was how her empathic abilities worked.*"

"*You believe him?*"

"*I'm not an empath, but I felt he was honest.*"

That last comment made me smile. After learning details of Bunny's ability, adding an 'honest feeling' to my words made sense. *Once you learn to fake honesty and sincerity, you'll become a great salesperson, Holden told me once.* On the way to my room, my mental ears stayed open.

They talked out loud in her office. I couldn't hear any speaking voices, but I could hear their thoughts, and eavesdropping from my bedroom was easy. But Bunny said it was a bad idea. Why? They weren't talking secrets, just me and this telepathy stuff.

I needed to listen and learn more about how this affected me. Before I turned eighteen, I saw the Grigori Research Associates as a business and social group, maybe a different Rotary Club. Now it sounded like a crime family, such as Dad blocking while telling Mom about toxic waste. What else was he hiding?

Bunny's voice echoed in my head. "Just because you can hear your parents doesn't mean you should. We've all done things we want to keep private."

That meant no eavesdropping. But she added, "You need to become a grown man in a hurry." The best way to grow was to learn everything possible. I swiveled my desk chair around toward Mom's office and opened my mental door again.

"*... has he found out yet?*" Mom asked.

"*From his questions, he's wary. Maybe ramping up to angry.*"

What? Angry? Still talking about me? If not, listening was an awful idea, as Bunny told me.

"*... project worth ten million?*" asked Mom.

"At least."

"Too high for him to let slide."

"I hope to talk him into ruining Jenkins, not eliminating him."

"Firing isn't enough?"

What? Ten million? Eliminating someone?

"He still has a story to sell to the tabloids, even if the mainstream media ignored him," Dad answered.

"He always talks to me for legal options before doing something drastic. So far, nothing, but he scheduled a meeting for Tuesday with no agenda. It often means he plans to discuss something and keep it unofficial. Or he forgot to add the details."

Holden had rules on how to discuss illegal things? Mom was his top lawyer basically forever. Did they those meetings often? Shaking my head didn't empty those thoughts. Dad meant to fire this guy, correct? Holden forgot things sometimes, so not adding a calendar note didn't mean it was criminal, right?

"... say bury, you mean his reputation and blackball him?" asked Mom.

What was that? Bury? I could imagine Dad rubbing his chin, his tell when taking his time before answering a troublesome question.

"Get out the shovels and send flowers to his widow."

Damn! Widow? Shovels? Dig a grave? The image of Mom using a shovel, pushing it into the dirt wearing her four-inch Manolo Blahnik heels, popped in my head. Funny, yeah, but a grave wasn't funny, even with fancy shoes on filthy shovels.

Pacing back and forth from wall to wall didn't get rid of my nervous energy. Bunny said it: Holden in a foul mood meant danger, no, more. She said he might get angry enough to kill even me. But she didn't literally mean that, did she?

I should've listened to her and not eavesdropped. But my parents were so unconcerned, no more serious than if someone hit their car in a parking garage. We've got to mess with it, but no biggie. BANG! Flowers and funerals. Damn! How many shovels had they used? How many flowers had they handed to widows?

This wasn't real, right? I tried to convince myself I had it wrong, wrong, wrong. My nervous energy, anger, disappointment, and disgust at my parents and Holden collapsed in on me. The ceiling in my room pressed lower and lower, and the walls squeezed together. The lights dimmed, including the sunshine coming through my windows. I pulled at my collar, but it was still hard to breathe. Air! Need air! Had to get out! Get away before hearing something else. I left the house, careful to avoid my parents, and ran across the street to Central Park. The green, the open grass areas, the slight breeze, and the people relaxing and playing helped calm me down.

Then I made the mistake of thinking more about what I overheard. Damn! Toxic waste dumping in Texas by that company Holden just bought didn't mean a thing to Dad except he's mad he didn't get a lower price on the deal. As if saving a few bucks balanced out ruined land and poisoned drinking water and dead wildlife. A guy makes a mistake and Holden may want to kill him. Kill him! Crazy to think this was real, or at least seemed to me it was real.

I suddenly realized what being a Grigori meant: help the wealthy make more money, no matter how many people, wild animals, laws, and morals you crush in the process. My parents did this, and my grandparents, and their parents, back five or six generations to Rasputin. Bulldoze everything in the way to make sure the top one tenth of one percent live like Greek Gods, playing with humans for sport, sowing destruction, and avoiding any kind of responsibility.

Numb, I sat on a bench and stared up at the blue sky through the trees. Everything I'd learned since I fell into that pile of garbage in the alley on Tuesday night pushed me down onto the bench. Four fucking days ago, life was great. Now I was part of a global conspiracy to use these stupid abilities I didn't want to go against everything I'd been taught for eighteen years. My entire life was a lie, and my parents never warned me, never gave me a choice, and still expect me to follow orders like they do.

I was the "good boy" all my life, the son who did what they wanted, until the video of Lucy riding Brandon at his party derailed it all. My parents were still mad at me for dumping her, even though they knew why all along, and still wished I was a good boy and followed orders so Lucy and I could fulfill some bizarre Grigori bloodline plan like we were breeding cattle.

No more! The weight of all these lies disappeared as I stood up, clear about what I had to do, must do, couldn't live with myself if I didn't. When serious shit went down, there was only one person to call, or text in this case. "Hey Max, need air and coffee. Meet at our diner in 20?"

The answer zipped right back. "We'll see you there."

"We" meant Max and Junie were together. Couldn't complain because he was on the flip side last year. When he wanted to hang, I brought Lucy, so Junie could come, too. She was OK, more than OK, so talking to both of them was fine.

Figuring out what to say exactly? More of a problem. Tell my friends my parents help murder people? Giant problem.

Chapter 12: That's Not Right

Getting to the CPW Diner first let me choose the best seat. Both round corner booths were empty, so I chose the one farthest from the door.

Ruby came by and patted me on the head, which helped calm me. Max would help me figure this mess out. He understood me like nobody else.

I was thinking how to explain this when I noticed a tingling feeling. It grew like a low-frequency sound that kept getting louder. Did a Spidey-sense come with my new abilities? The tingle got stronger and stronger until Max walked in, then stopped.

He held Junie's hand, as expected. Behind them flew wild red hair. Damn! Gemma came, too?

Her block was even weaker than most. *"Let's get a snack they said. Fun, they said. Didn't tell me it was with this asshole."* My ability to hear everything sucked yet again. Her face showed exactly what she thought, so no secrets. I waved to my friends. Well, friends and Gemma.

Junie hugged me, Max and I did the man-hug of two quick back taps, and I gave Gemma a nod. Their shimmers clued me in to avoid listening to any of their private thoughts. Happy to respect their privacy, especially Gemma's.

"My idea, so get whatever you want." Coffee for me. Max and Junie got coffee and a slice of cherry pie, his favorite, to share. Gemma, different as always, ordered hot chocolate.

"What's up? Besides a nice day for a walk and coffee?" Max asked.

"Since I'm new at this, I need your help to figure out if I've gone too far." The server, one of the familiar ones, came by with our drinks and pie, but we stayed quiet until she left.

"You're not that guy," said Junie. "What's the problem?"

"I think my parents help their boss do seriously illegal things."

Max's fork full of cherry pie stopped halfway to his mouth. "You're kidding, right? Joke?"

"I wish."

Everyone stared at me for a moment.

58

Gemma broke the silence. "Reality check: they work for a modern corporation. Anything that improves executive bonuses is legal to them."

"The financial firms all hire Grigori," Junie added. "You think they're all doing illegal shit? Because my dad's a VP at an investment bank. Maybe he's doing something wrong?"

"I don't know about him, but I'm sure my parents are hiding toxic waste dumping. Maybe murder."

Everyone's eyes widened.

"OK, murder's too much. Are you sure this isn't a bad dream? How did you find out? Your parents tell you?" asked Gemma.

'How did you find out' was the big ass question. How much should I say? This critical decision could go bad in a hurry.

"First, I've got to know if I can depend on you guys."

"It's me," said Max. "Got your back like always."

Junie was in. "What he said. If Max trusts you, me too."

We all looked at Gemma.

"I've known Junie as long as you two have known each other. I trust her." She turned to me. "I don't trust you. But my mother's a lawyer too, and I wonder what she's done. My dad's restaurant fell into some deep shit and Mom met with the city and everything disappeared. I mean, is she just a brilliant lawyer, or did she cheat? She's persuaded people to get her way plenty of times. Glad she got Dad off the hook, but still."

She took a breath, paused, then leaned back.

"If you don't agree, get a to-go cup for your hot chocolate." That was meaner than I planned, but I wanted her to leave.

Her eyes narrowed as she stared at me. The waitress came by with more coffee. Everyone froze until she left.

Staring back at her, the idea of Pushing her to leave occurred to me, but I decided people should make up their own minds. Even Gemma.

"First, tell me how you know your parents are doing these things. Are you a sneak who goes through people's phones? Computers? Read their files? How?" Gemma demanded.

Max and Junie would keep what I said quiet. Bunny said not to tell anyone, but Max wasn't just anyone, and she even suggested I talk to him about this stuff. Max and Junie's emotions said they were on my side.

I focused on Gemma, who was not mad but curious, and it turned out she wanted to believe. That was a surprise. She didn't yet, but her anger wasn't against the idea. Just me, as usual.

If she didn't agree, who would she tell, and who would believe her? The idea of kids hearing adults through blocks seemed impossible to everybody. If she told someone, how could they test me?

"I can hear my parents even when they block me."

Three jaws dropped.

My stomach flipped upside down when I realized my decision came too quick, without thinking through all the details. If she reported me and a senior Grigori official believed her, they would demand I drop my block and sit there defenseless as they interrogated me.

Damn. Now if she told someone, she screwed me big time. Suddenly my fate depended on a girl who hated me. The seconds ticked by like days as no one spoke.

Gemma recovered from her surprise first. She leaned toward me across the table. "I call bullshit! Prove it!"

"OK. Block and think of a color."

She smiled at me. Not a friendly smile, but one like Michael Jordan gave players right after he dunked on them.

Clever girl. Inside the shimmer was not one color but many.

"Scottish tartan from Clan McKenzie. Dark green background. Broad light gray stripes that go white when they cross. Narrow gray stripes go white when they cross. Thick navy band with a narrow red stripe inside so it looks kinda purple."

Gemma sagged and leaned back in the booth. "OK, we're all mutants, but you're Professor X."

Junie put her hand on Gemma's arm. "You OK, girl? And where did that come from?"

"Dad's Scottish and that's his clan." She sat up in her seat and stared at me again. "OK. I don't like you, but you can do what you say. I'm in because of economics class."

Max raised his hand like in school. "Economics class?"

"Capitalism only works when markets are transparent, and everyone has equal access to both knowledge and the markets. We don't have that anymore. Our level of income disparity is worse than the Great Depression. The Coronavirus recession widened the asset gap. Sucks for ninety-five out of a hundred people."

Junie laughed. "You hate that class!"

"Makes me angry every damn day."

"So, you want to stay?" I asked.

She drummed her fingers on the table and looked at Junie. "What do you think?"

"He's got a point. Good or bad, we have these abilities, and I'd rather we all use them the right way. We can dig in and do some research and see where that takes us. If Paul's wrong, then fine. If not, well, we take the next step." She nudged Max. "You down?"

"Absolutely," he said.

Gemma stared at me. I didn't want to eavesdrop, but her emotions broadcast loudly and washed over me. Her interest finally overwhelmed her doubt. "OK. We pat ourselves on the back as the world's leader. All we're advanced at is using the government and crony capitalism to help billionaires make more billions."

I developed a measure of respect for her, something new. "You've thought on these topics more than I have. That's great."

"I said I'm in. Don't push it."

Aaaand mean Gemma was back.

Max bounced in his seat. "We need a nickname. Gang of Four?"

Junie punched him. "You not pay attention in AP History? The Gang of Four were oppressive murderers."

"Ouch. Um, Four Gang? No, sounds like 4chan."

"Maybe the Rebel Alliance," I said.

"Movie much?" asked Gemma.

I tried again. "Four Club? But then we—"

"Can't talk about Four Club," finished Gemma. Surprised she beat Max to that line.

"Right, first rule of Four Club," said Max. "How about, ah, Four the Future?"

"Lame," said Junie. "Maybe the Four Friends?"

"Sounds Amish," Gemma said.

"Um, maybe just The Four," added Junie.

"Marvel grabbed Fantastic Four," said Max.

"What about the First Four?" I asked.

"Hmmm. Those are the four lowest ranked teams invited to the NCAA Tournament," said Max.

"So, college basketball history you know all about?" asked Junie. She gave him her fake look of disgust.

"Those four teams are underdogs, right?" I asked.

"Very."

"But they sometimes win?"

"Hardly ever. VCU made it from the First Four to the Final Four in 2011."

Junie punched his shoulder again. "You remember that shit, but don't remember the anniversary of our first date? What should I do with you?"

"Kiss me?" She did. Gemma rolled her eyes while mine focused on my coffee mug.

"If the First Four had a tiny chance, it works for me," I said. "OK with you guys? But beside the name, you in for finding out what's really going on? People, including my Dad for damn sure, will get pissed. If we do it right, lots of people will get pissed."

"But more will be helped, right?" asked Gemma.

"I think so," I said, and added, "I think lots of us feel this way, but don't know what to do about things. We can figure this out and find a path forward to something better."

Everyone agreed.

"The olds won't fix the world because they trashed it. Those in charge hate change and it's up to the next generation to force change down their throats. If not us, who?" asked Gemma.

I nodded my agreement immediately. Max and then Junie followed.

I'm not into matching t-shirts or nonsense like that," she continued. "A group name is all I can handle."

"Should we get people to help us figure out what the hell is happening?" asked Max.

"Not yet," I said. "We need to get a better handle on what we're doing. Maybe have a plan."

"We should dig up some research and see what we're really up against," said Gemma. "Companies that use Grigori and how they succeed and hide their cheating."

"Good idea. Monday during zero period. Meet in the library," said Junie.

Max and Junie headed toward the door, but Gemma hung back.

"You may think you're a leader, but Max does that, not you. He's the basketball team captain and runs some school clubs. You drift along. You're not even in any clubs like Debate or Chess."

"Yeah, I like those, but have a private project I've—"

"I don't care. What I'm saying is that you're not the best choice to lead this."

"You're right."

"What?"

"You think I want to do this? Hell no," I snapped. "Didn't know about these powers and don't want'em, but I got stuck with'em. Damn sure didn't raise my hand and volunteer, but somebody has to. Take over if you want."

A deep breath helped me calm down. "Sorry. Somebody has to lead and you're right, I usually just follow Max. But I started this because of my parent's crimes, and I'll keep going. I don't know whether I'm a leader or maybe just started sooner. I don't care. But I'll keep pushing."

"That almost sounds like the truth."

"I don't lie to my friends. Ask Max. I'll never lie to you. Stack of Bibles or whatever you want."

She stared deep into my eyes for a few seconds, then turned and chased after Junie and Max.

The server brought the check and picked up my credit card. As she walked away, the idea popped up that it's not my card, it's my parent's money. We'll need our own money if we keep going. Where will we get some? How much will we need? This fight just got harder.

Chapter 13: Some Conspiracies Are Real

The rest of Saturday and most of Sunday, I researched potential Grigori influence in various businesses through the decades. The GRA certainly has complete records of every Grigori and their job and location somewhere, right? No doubt locked inside a bank vault so nobody will ever find them.

What would be different for a company helped by Listeners, Feelers, and Pushers over a regular business? Win every contract and court case? That sounded like Goldstone Equity Management, so that became my guide.

Competitors and journalists would see they always succeeded. They won most of their negotiations and court cases. Outsiders might believe they could see the future.

These were the ever-famous "X Runs the World" conspiracies. Solve for X with any of the popular options: Jews, Catholics, the Rothschilds, the Rockefellers, the Saudi royals, the Kennedys, or even little gray aliens according to some articles. Grigori-helped companies might take off starting in the 1920s.

Billionaire families made lots of people suspicious, with Rockefeller, Kennedy, and Walton leading the way. Did they use Grigori help to get so wealthy? Did Warren, Bill, Elon, Jeff, the usual suspects for conspiracy fans? The time frame works.

The Illuminati showed up in most of the conspiracy Google results. Was that a code word for Grigori? Powerful men working behind the scenes to influence everything?

* * * * *

Makary starts with a twenty minute "plan your day" study session called zero period. Kids hung out in either the cafeteria or their first period class to finish (or start) homework. Most people babbled with buddies.

Monday, the First Four meeting was in the library during zero period. Max, Junie, and Gemma sat at a table for four in the back corner by the reference books that looked sad and lonely now that Google and Wikipedia replaced them.

The only empty seat was beside Gemma. When I sat, she scooted away from me. Move her chair like I had cooties? What? Not in second grade anymore.

Junie believed, or at least fervently wished, that Elvis was still alive. She compiled pages of websites in her search history, diving into that conspiracy, and struggled to add it to every research project possible.

Max, patient with her as always, never said she was wrong. "Babe, I'm not saying he's dead."

"The four of us watched *Men in Black*, together, remember, last Thanksgiving break?" I said. "Elvis isn't dead, he just flew home."

She stuck her tongue out at me.

Max continued. "I'm saying that isn't the conspiracy that can help us right now."

"Money. Follow the money," said Gemma.

"What if many of the enormous fortunes have GRA behind them?" I asked.

"You're late," she replied. "We covered that."

"Oh. And the Rockefeller's and Kennedys and Porsche family."

"And Hearst and Murdoch and Koch and Goldman Sachs and Walton and Buffet and Bass and Ziff and Mars and Cargill-MacMillan and on and on." She shot me the same "disappointed" face as Mom.

"What about the Fortune 500 companies?" I asked.

"Ah yes, my favorite subject, corporate crimes by those powerful enough to get away with everything they want," said Junie. "But we need to get a list of GRA members and cross-reference."

"Anyone have a mutant register?" asked Max. He grinned at her.

"Human 2.0 baby, all the way," she said.

"Better question is who'll help us fight the largest companies in America?" Gemma asked, then turned to me. "Whatcha got?"

"Most markets have one leading player and a major competitor. The rest are far, far behind," I said. "Third or fourth in each market tries hardest to expand and catch them."

Thumbs up from Max. "Mr. Wall Street Journal!"

I told Gemma, "I like AP Economics, too."

She ignored me. "Who else do we check?"

"Private equity firms and the large hedge funds."

Max laughed. "The big ass Rolex gift store? Goldstone?"

"Yep. I know for a fact two GRA members are top executives over there. Bridgewater is far bigger."

"You just admitted your parents are leading a company you think is illegal," said Gemma.

My jaws clenched. Damn, she was right. I knew it, of course, but it hadn't sunk in until she challenged me.

"Soooo yes," she continued. "Who else do we have to fear?"

"Government, including the military," said Max.

"Media," Junie said.

"Private equity funds control five times more money than hedge funds," I said. "Lots of major media companies are owned by those groups."

Gemma slammed her Apple MacBook Pro laptop shut. "You want to fight every group in the country with money? Can we change our name to the Suicide Squad?"

English teachers want every paper to include a thesis statement. What was the key sentence that summed up my argument? "I hate hypocrites, and Grigori are the biggest ones ever. They preach honor and service and tell us how we're better than the normies, but we have to help them and yada, yada, yada. But they're lying with each breath."

"Do you get the 'hard work and succeed' lectures?" I closed my Lenovo ThinkPad X1 Carbon laptop. "We're so well off because we work hard? Make more effort with our focus and grit?"

They groaned in agreement.

"We never asked for this, but we have no choice, no say in what they force us to do. We can only listen to the lectures of how noble the Grigori are. But they're playing poker with marked cards, against the people we're supposed to help. They pretend they win because of hard work, but they cheat."

"You want to unmark the cards?" asked Gemma.

"Yeah, but it's different. I don't know the right slogan for our movie poster yet. Guys, want'em or not, we've got gifts. I want to use'em to help people, lots of people, live better. Not just help Holden buy another yacht."

"Markets should be transparent so everyone has equal access to knowledge," said Gemma.

"Like you said Saturday."

She gave me the first hint of a smile in years.

"It steamrolls," I added. "Once companies cheat to get a lead, they can leverage more power. Money and size distort the markets, too."

The bell rang. Everyone stood.

"You want to fight the one percent," said Gemma.

"But we're part of the one percent, thanks to our mutant ancestors," I said. "We're actually the Trojan Horse teens against the one percent."

"OK, I'm in one hundred percent. Or maybe ninety-nine since the one percent is our target."

Max winked at Junie. "Trojan Horse? I'm feeling very Greek now."

"Behave."

"When we want to meet, my grandmother said we can come over after school," I said. "She's been fighting to change things for years and is ready to support us."

"Cool," said Junie. "Two days from now?" She looked at each of us until we agreed. "Done."

We headed to our classes. I realized this was the first time I'd said those ideas out loud. They'd been festering in my mind, but never spoken. Major serious shit to go up against, including parents. Who'd be stupid enough to try this? Don Quixote was dead, so that left me.

Halls were basically empty because I'd been dawdling and thinking. I turned a corner and practically stepped into the rolling mop bucket piloted by Gordy.

"Careful, Paul, don't wanna ruin those nice shoes," he said. His cap today was from Intel, the computer chip company.

"Sorry, man, wasn't watching. Hey, where'd you get that cap?"

"Oh, you know, ya help people and they give ya little tchotchkes. That's Yiddish, ya know. You speak Yiddish?"

"I know that word. You OK, Gordy?"

"Firin' on all cylinders, just like my 1994 covert Camaro now that I tuned'er up. Rolls 120 miles per, I guarantee."

"Sounds fun. You can show me sometime."

"Not while they're watchin' ya, boyo, too much heat."

"Me? Watching me? Why?"

"Dunno yet, but you're presently the object of fascination."

Lots of kids liked to make fun of Gordy, but his comments played up the paranoia I developed after doing my research.

"Who's tracking me? Do you know why?"

He raised his cap and used a paper towel to wipe sweat off his bald head. "The most curious thing is–"

His radio squawked, and the office secretary's voice said, "Gordy, cleanup A14 please."

"Ahh, that's little Henry in eighth grade. He's a puker. Gotta go, Paul, watch yourself." Holding the mop handle, he steered the yellow rolling bucket around me quick and smooth. "Gotta go."

In a flash, he turned the corner without spilling a drop and disappeared. Everybody called Gordy crazy. I hoped they were right.

Chapter 14: One Wrong Step

The cook left early, so I figured we were going out to dinner. Nope. Parents were, but they had a client meeting.

"Sorry, Paul, search for leftovers," said Mom.

"You can go get something," added Dad, putting on his suit jacket.

When I checked, nothing looked edible, so I went to the deli around the corner. A black forest ham sandwich sounded good.

I waved to Darrell as I walked out the front. A guy to my right was leaning against the building. I ignored him as I turned left. He called out to me, so I stopped.

"Hey, are you Paul? Paul Barylan?"

I turned to face him. He was early to mid-thirties, I guess, because he was younger than Dad but way older than me. His lower-level business clothes, jeans and dress shirt with no tie and a blazer, were a serious level or two lower from the suit my dad always wore.

"Yeah? Do I know you?" The sun was low, so I put one hand up to block it.

"I work with your parents. I tried to see them, but the damn doorman wouldn't let me."

"Darrell doesn't announce people who don't have appointments. And they're out, anyway."

"Yeah, sure, I get it," he said. "I need to explain things to your dad. There's been a mistake, and I screwed up, but it's not my fault and I can fix it but need to talk to him before they fire me or something."

That sounded familiar, so I cheated and read his thoughts. He was Brett Jenkins, the guy my parents discussed. "What's the problem?"

"It's complicated." No, it wasn't. Holden told him to hold off on a trade, but he was sure he found something special no one else noticed and pulled the trigger. But he was wrong and cost the company $10 million.

"Is your name Jenkins?"

"How did you know?"

"Overheard them talk, worried you would sell a story to the news. You talk to anybody?"

"No, no, never, I'd never do that, and I won't breathe a word of this to anyone, I promise, so can you help me?"

Holden spent a lot of money on my watch, but he doesn't throw around $10 million. "I don't know what I can tell you. They're out to dinner and will be back late. When they come home, they'll park in the garage and use the elevator. Best bet is to catch him in the office early tomorrow."

"Tell them I know I fucked up, but I'll do whatever it takes to make it right. 80-hour weeks for the next two years? No problem. Claw back my bonuses each year? OK. I'll fix this, I promise."

"Sure." I watched him cross Central Park West Drive and listened to his thoughts and he was still nervous and upset and worried. Just as I turned the corner, his mind changed, as if someone else took it over and ordered him to stop. I came back and looked, but didn't see him. Then he marched a few steps up the street from a group of people and stopped.

He turned to face the street, and I saw his wide eyes and lips working around a clamped-shut mouth. I listened to his thoughts, but there was someone else in control, Pushing him.

His lips kept repeating the same words I heard in his mind: "*Help me! Help me!*" Over and over and over again.

A delivery truck, engine revving, sped up to cheat through a yellow light. The Pusher commanded him to, "*Walk.*" Jenkins lifted one foot and leaned into the street.

I yelled "No!" and Pushed him to step back, but his momentum carried him off the curb and right in front of the speeding truck. I heard a squishy thud and sharp crunch as it hit him before the driver stomped on the brakes and skidded. A tall bald guy turned and searched until his black eyes found me.

The onlookers rushed forward, but the bald guy walked away. He mentally yelled at me to, "*Back off!*" and disappeared into the crowd.

I tried to read him, but his block was bright and hard, not shimmery like most. I struggled to break through before his thoughts mixed with other people, but failed.

The thud and crunch sounds played over and over and over again in my head. You can Push someone to kill themselves? How can a Push override their survival instinct? Disgusting. I stumbled to a trash can and puked. I leaned against the metal can for balance and remembered how funny Max and I said the *John Wick* movies were because it looked like New York was full of hitmen hanging around in fancy clubs. But I just saw a hitman, a Grigori hitman, murder someone using a perfect crime no normie would ever solve. I puked again, and it helped my guts, but my head still hurt. The sounds of leg bones breaking against the truck bumper echoed in my brain.

People started looking at me funny, so I walked away. Max and my parents told me the Grigori protect their own, sometimes violently. But Jenkins wasn't fighting the Grigori. He worked for Holden and screwed the pooch as Dad said. Did he order this killing? My parents? Did Jenkins do something against the Grigori?

What should I do? Call the police and tell them someone Pushed Jenkins to walk into traffic? They'd wrap me up in a straitjacket while the bald guy walked free and killed more people.

Who should I call? Max. "Hey, man, wanna split a pizza?" I wasn't sure I could eat after that, but he would, and the offer would make sure he came. His answer was always yes. His mother was making meat with brown sauce for dinner, so tonight he said, yes, thank God, yes.

I headed to our favorite pizzeria, looking over my shoulder for that bald Grigori hitman the entire trip.

Chapter 15: The Family Business

I love researching obscure bands and great songs, but it's a time suck. My parents were already eating dinner when I joined them.

"Everything fine at school?" asked Mom.

"Yeah. You had court today?"

How did he know? I didn't mention it this morning, did I? Short pretrial hearing. Nothing big. Did I tell you that?"

Damn. She thought about it at breakfast without even blocking. "Lower heel shoes for your walk to the courthouse." I need to remember to keep track of what's overheard when eavesdropping on people, especially my parents. Can't keep blurting wrong stuff out at the wrong time.

"You getting more interested in law now?" asked Dad.

"You two mash-up both."

The cook brought in dessert for my parents. He always made key lime pie with seafood, which tonight was salmon.

"There's not a Grigori 101 class yet, so when did we connect with big companies?"

"The first child of Rasputin and Madame Matej, Krichka, was born in 1898. He went to work for a munitions plant to avoid military service in World War I," said Mom.

"Not an executive job, because he didn't go to college. Just a clerk," added Dad. "With his telepathy, he overheard suppliers think how they conned Federov, the owner, with higher prices than his competitors paid. He told him and became the primary purchasing agent, and later second in command. The owner even adopted him and left his company to him when he died."

"That was nice."

"Federov tested him, verified what he could do, and protected him from discovery," added Mom. "If he'd cried 'witchcraft' or other nonsense, authorities might have killed Krichka."

My last bite of salmon hit my stomach like an anchor. What a wonderful history. The Grigori not only make the rich richer, we started by draft dodging and making guns. Hope that doesn't become the Daily Double on *Jeopardy.*

The cook replaced my plate with a larger slice of pie than my parents got. For some reason it didn't taste so good, but that wasn't his fault.

If they had killed Krichka, he wouldn't have children to pass along his abilities. The money to help others came from his lucky break.

"*He's preoccupied. What's he thinking?*" Mom asked Dad.

I cracked open my mental door just a fraction to let him read enough not to become suspicious.

Dad frowned. "*Just about Federov and Krichka and how close a call we had.*"

"Krichka started everything? Over a hundred years ago?" I asked.

"That's right," said Mom.

"And he helped other Grigori get jobs with other businesses?"

"He's the real Grigori origin story," said Dad. "Maybe Marvel will make a comic book for him."

Laughing, I said, "You should suggest that to any GRA working at Disney."

"*I better hit the brakes.* On second thought, I'm not sure a comic book is the best choice."

I better be more careful. "Junie's doing genealogy research on Grigori for AP History."

"Who's Junie?" asked Dad.

"Max's girlfriend. We've met her several times," said Mom.

"If you say so."

"Junie's parents lack your connections, so they don't have a Grigori family tree. Do you?"

The sign I visualized on my blocking door said, "*School assignment. This is just a school assignment.*" Dad checked.

"I don't think one exists," he answered. "I'll see what I can do."

"Thanks, on Junie's behalf. Does every Grigori work for large companies and billionaires like your friends?"

"*Not sure I like his tone.* You're getting a skewed view. Many of our friends live close, and only successful people can afford these neighborhoods."

"*Maybe it's nothing,*" said Mom. "Hard work pays off, which is why you need to go to Harvard."

"Your mother misspoke. She meant to say Yale." She fake-stabbed him with her butter knife.

Their constant tug-of-war over the best college never ended. Time to push a bit more. I floated *"curiosity"* as my feeling and asked, "The Grigori I've met here or in Los Angeles work for hedge funds and enormous companies. Anybody a baseball player or violinist or sculptor or something?"

"Careful," said Mom.

Dad poured coffee from a carafe the cook had placed on the table when he cleared the dessert plates. He handed a cup to Mom and another to me.

"As immigrants from Russia, Siberia, and Romania, the Grigori faced persecution early on," Dad said. "Same thing when they arrived in America after World War I. Those who became successful could protect others and help bring more here. The more resources each person had, the safer they all were."

"There are heartbreaking stories from Grigori when they first arrived. Some welcomed, some persecuted," Mom added. "We stay hidden to all but a few normals. Most welcome our help but a few get violent."

"Protection from someone like Federov saved the bloodline," Dad said. "We make the most of our abilities to gather a cushion to protect all of us."

A little wealth? More like tons. My Rolex pulled heavy on my wrist. And for sure, no starving artists. "The Grigori have plenty. Do we ever do pro bono projects?"

"We give to charities," Mom said.

"How should we help more?" asked Dad. "We have to protect ourselves first. That means our family, our extended family, and the GRA."

Dad gave his little secret smile. *"Look out for ourselves? That's what we do best. For the last three years, we've paid a lower marginal tax rate than the cook."*

Eyes on my coffee, I pushed more. "A few of the companies GRA members work for are in the news with legal issues."

"You think we're doing illegal things?" asked Mom.

"Not what I said. You tell me to question things, right? Learn about the world? About business and the law?"

74

"I need to shut this down," said Dad. His ears were getting red, his tell for growing angry.

"He's right, we do tell him to dig into topics. Find out what he wants."

It was time for a deep breath and a leap. "So, were there GRA people at FIFA asking for bribes for soccer tournaments? In Volkswagen hiding emissions test cheating? Someone help Theranos scam billions with fake blood tests? Those Panama Papers companies caught hiding corporate and personal money from taxes from counties all over the world? Those early Coronavirus treatments that were scams? Those multi-national banks laundering money from drug cartels and terrorists under the table? The oil and chemical companies caught dumping toxic waste?"

"Where is he getting this nonsense?" Dad raged to Mom.

"No clue, but he's upset. What else, Paul?"

"Do Grigori stop companies from doing illegal things? Don't they know when execs are planning something wrong?"

Mom used her laugh that means it's time to change the subject. "Every lawyer will tell you we can only advise clients to follow the rules. We can't stop them from doing things."

The Grigori would make the ultimate whistle blowers for companies breaking the law. I don't remember one coming forward.

"We advise and consult, but we don't control the businesses we work for," said Dad. "We give owners and boards their best options, and they take our advice in most cases."

"What about Wells Fargo? Did Uncle Horatio see the illegal accounts they opened in people's names? Millions in fraud? Illegal home foreclosures? Because he'd stop that crap, wouldn't he?"

Dad slammed his fist on the table. Coffee cups rattled and Mom's wine glass fell. A blood red stain spread on the tablecloth. "Enough!" he yelled.

"That crack about pollution. Did he find out about the Texas company Goldstone bought?" Dad asked Mom.

"I don't know how. If he did, he could have heard about Holden and his order removing Jenkins."

"Let me check."

My poker face when eavesdropping on their Inside Voice conversations had gotten better. Dad stared at me so I wrote, "*I wonder what they're saying?*" on my mental door.

"*Well?*"

"*He's just wondering what we're discussing.* I don't care where you're getting all this garbage," Dad said, "but you need to let it go. We work for big companies, but that doesn't mean we break the law."

"*He won't buy that,*" said Mom.

"*He better learn to go along to get along. Or he'll get crushed and we can't protect him.*"

Standing and throwing my napkin on the table, I said, "I'm trying to find out what being a Grigori means. Nobody asked me if I wanted to join this club." I walked toward my room but stayed in the hall to keep listening.

"You don't walk out on us!" yelled Dad.

"Let him go. He needs time to cool off," Mom said, in her usual role of keeping Dad calm.

"*You didn't tell me – what happened to Jenkins?*" Mom asked.

"*Funeral is on Thursday.*"

"*Shit. So he killed him.*"

"*Traffic accident. He stepped in front of a truck. Not far from here, actually.*"

"*Right. Just as the plant manager taking files to the New York Times had a one-car accident a couple of months ago. His stolen materials disappeared from the scene before police arrived.*"

Shit! Shit! Shit! Holden gave the order to kill Jenkins! He died right after talking to me yesterday! The bald guy I saw was the Pusher he sent to kill him! And he killed someone else earlier? Shit!

Dad pounded the table when I brought up Uncle Horatio. He only goes giant drama queen when he wants to change the topic. Shit!

I sagged against the wall and tried to sort this out. Grigori do NOT stop their companies from doing illegal things. That means they help them break the law, but one step removed like Mom said. As if that makes it OK.

Worse, Holden had at least two people killed, and my parents helped. My parents helped! Shit!

Too painful to stay in the same apartment with them. I rushed past the dining room and said, "I need air. It stinks in here."

Still listening in case they wanted to tell me this was all a mistake, and they didn't help kill Jenkins, my hand shook so much it was hard to punch the elevator button. Maybe they tried to stop Holden or do something that made this less horrible? Nothing. No denials, no explanations. Shit!

"Told you he was too smart for that approach," said Mom.

"Too smart for his own good," answered Dad. *"That doesn't go well for anyone."*

Chapter 16: Central Park Confessions

Traffic was light on Central Park West Drive, and crossing on 66th Street led me into the trees. I hurried down a small trail with benches here and there.

Someone left a half-deflated soccer ball at the edge of a clearing. I kicked it so hard it hurt my foot. Looked for more things to punt and wished I could kick myself for being stupid.

Eavesdropping on my parents turned out worse than I expected, way worse. Bunny told me not to. Begged me not to. Why didn't I listen to her? I kept pushing until I heard my parents talking about Holden killing people. Junie said I wasn't a "go too far kind of guy," and she's right. Why this time?

It all seemed so stupid. Holden, basically family, ordered people killed? To save money? To avenge an employee mistake? A cover up?

None of these reasons excused murder. Hell, almost nothing was worth killing someone. But business? Another million was the reason to kill somebody? Stupid.

My Rolex glittered and sparkled thanks to the lights by the walkway. I unlatched the band and cradled it in my right hand, spotted a small pond twenty yards away, and hurried that way. Decided it was time to throw Holden's gift into the water and let it wallow in the muck with him and my parents.

One step closer to the water, I drew back my arm and aimed at the middle of the pond. A quick heave and I regain my freedom. My feet stuck to the ground and my arm wouldn't move.

I couldn't do it. Couldn't fling it away.

Shit. Could Holden be doing to me what he did to my parents? The Rolex gave me confidence and made me feel successful. I hadn't earned it, but it still looked wonderful on my wrist. Is this the first step? Get a promotion for overlooking toxic waste dumping? Another promotion for ignoring a whistle-blower who had a car accident? Promoted to vice president after helping make a manager disappear? More money, higher position, deeper and deeper into the shit? Become my parents? Is that how Holden had ruined them?

That didn't matter now. Things sucked, but I promised myself I'd do "Whatever It Takes" like The Faders song said. Just hoped it didn't get worse.

While walking and putting my watch back on, I didn't look up until I bumped into someone.

"What the hell, Paul!"

It got worse. "Gemma? What are you doing here?" Her eyes were hard and her lips squeezed so tight they were colorless.

"It's a public park, right?"

"Sorry, trying to get away from people–"

"Me too."

"-after fighting with my parents and finding out they helped... never mind."

"Trouble in paradise?"

"Paradise? If paradise is full of criminals and murderers and... sorry. Go on with your walk."

She grabbed my arm and jerked me toward a bench. "Oh no, you're not dropping criminals and murderers and walking away." She pushed me down and sat beside me.

"So, this is serious?"

"Yeah."

"OK, I'm listening."

I searched the night sky through a break in the trees. Only the brightest stars penetrate the lights of the city. None were visible.

"C'mon."

I cleared my throat. "Everything was going great. Now it's turned to shit."

"OK, this is SERIOUS."

I held up my Rolex and said, "Nice, right? I've known the guy who gave it to me my entire life. I'm his godson. My parent's boss."

"OK, so far."

"I listened and overheard my parents say he'd had at least two people killed, one just this week. Not sure how much they helped, but they didn't stop him, or seem upset. It's messing me up because I saw the guy get murdered. A Grigori Pushed him to walk into traffic."

"OMG, that's like, major serious. How do you know he was Pushed?"

79

"I tried to stop him and could tell someone else was controlling him already."

She cocked her head to one side and raised an eyebrow. "You could hear all this? Really?"

"Need another clan tartan test? Yes, I heard it all."

Her lips compressed again, then relaxed. "OK, I'll accept that. And your parents knew about it?"

"Yeah, you think you understand your parents, and wrong, wrong, wrong."

"OK, wait, you overheard them talking with their Inside Voices?"

"After we had a fight. They block, but I can still hear them."

"I didn't believe you at the diner when you said you heard your parents. Just figured you were lying or showing off."

"I told you I don't lie to friends, including you as part of the group. But show off for you? Why?"

"I don't know. Guys just do."

"Find better guys." I stared back at the ground and softly sang, "I hate myself. We'll have that in common, although I've gotten most everything I wanted."

"That's a depressing song. What's it called?"

"The Saddest Think I Know."

"You mean thing?"

"Nope."

"You listen to weird songs."

"Understatement."

"But if you can really eavesdrop on your parents when they block, it must be true," she said.

Her face wasn't angry when she looked at me, so she must mean it. "Hey, wait a minute. Show off for you? That's not me. When did I show off for you?"

She turned away and stared into the distance.

"New game now? Ignore me for years, then talk, then stop? I'm supposed to just play along?"

When she turned her head back, she leaned away from me. "You don't dare read me without my permission!"

"One quick peek and you'd never notice. But I'd rather you tell me yourself."

"Tell you what?"

"Why you hate me."

Gemma jerked and leaned away from me again. Ran the zipper up and down on her windbreaker.

She leaned closer. "OK, fine. No lies? No lies." Her eyes bored into mine. "You don't remember what you said about me in sixth grade, do you?"

"Sixth grade? No way."

"You were hitting on a girl, no doubt Lucy, since you always crushed on her. She asked if you liked me. Remember now?" I shook my head. "Of course, you don't. You said, 'nobody likes her. She's too smart,' and everybody laughed at me. Nobody ate lunch with me for weeks."

Tears glittered on her bottom lashes, threatening to fall. "Weeks."

"Sorry. Still don't remember, which makes it worse. I must've been trying to impress Lucy or whoever."

"Weeks. That's when the 'Gemma the Ginger' shit started."

Afraid of how bad it would be if she cried, I searched for stars again but they remained hidden. "I've always admired how smart you are. I recognize now that's way more important than popular."

"You're saying I'm not popular?"

"No. But, well, yeah. Not the normal popular. You stand up for yourself and your friends and always have Junie's back. You're the most real girl in school, no fake hair, fake eyelashes, fake stories. One of the few not chasing whatever's trending this week to collect more fake friends."

"Yeah? Then why do you avoid me? Since Junie and Max hooked up, I never got a clue what you thought about me."

"You haven't been nice to me in years, so why should I be nice to you? You made it clearer than clear you didn't like me. Never told me why. Thought you wanted space and for me to leave you alone, so I gave you what you wanted."

"You could've tried, for their sake."

"Wasn't your birthday before Christmas? Never try to read me?"

She stood and walked away. "I need to head home."

Took me three running steps to catch up to her. "So? Didn't read me?"

"You treated me like I was invisible. And you were with Lucy, the power couple. King and Queen of everything. PauLucy."

"Such a stupid, stupid name."

"Duh. Why did she break up with you? Turned eighteen and read your naughty little boy thoughts?"

The pain of her pulling at the Lucy scab surprised me so much my feet slowed down.

She stopped and waited for me to get back to speed. "OK, that hit a nerve."

"We were Romeo and Juliet in reverse. Our parents are, were, long-time friends. Until I begged to drink the poison and end it, and stop dating, I mean."

"Because...?"

It still hurt to admit she cheated on me, as if what we had wasn't important and I wasn't enough. But I promised not to lie to her. "Her ideas on our commitment and mine turned out to be, ah, different."

She laughed. The cheerful sound echoed between buildings. Despite everything, I smiled for a second.

"Nobody clued you in she was a slut?"

My cheeks get warmer, and I hoped it was dark enough she couldn't see me blush.

"And you broke it off with her? Because of that? Not what she says."

"Guess I was more serious than she was."

She shook her head. Her long red ponytail swished back and forth. "Mom told me first love always dies a gory death. Your parents should've prepared you better."

We walked in silence for a moment.

"I tried to read you a couple of times after my Change," she said. "I never caught more than a few words. You weren't blocking because you couldn't yet. More a lousy phone connection."

"Speaking of powers ..."

She ran her zipper up and down again twice. "Mine is almost useless. I'm a Looker, meaning remote viewing, but visual only."

"Is that where you can send an image of your body to remote places? And talk to people?"

"That's a Traveler, astral projection. I can see far away things like I'm a fly on the wall. Every other Looker can listen remotely, too. I can only see."

"Is that a problem?"

"More useless than the video doorbell Mom bought Dad for Christmas. It has a camera and a microphone. I'm just the camera."

"That could be, ah, handy."

She laughed. "My parents don't worry when I'm out at night. I can look to see if a mugger convention's waiting in ambush. That's about it."

"So, you didn't need me to walk you home?"

"I didn't ask, but you're free to walk where you want."

We walked without talking for another moment. "Sorry, again, for sixth grade."

"I'll save you the trouble of eavesdropping. Guess I don't think you're a rude, entitled asshole anymore."

This time my laugh echoed off the buildings.

"It doesn't mean we're friends or anything," she blurted. "Maybe as if we just met. Or never had a class together but get seated side-by-side at the start of the year."

"Better than being hated for something I don't remember."

She stopped in front of her building. "This is me. Aren't you around here somewhere?"

"I'm right across from the park."

"Why didn't you say something?

"Nice night for a walk."

We faced each other and shook goodbye. When we touched, there was a surge of energy and my senses extended.

"Did you notice that?" I asked.

"Just your flop sweat."

"What? Flop sweat?"

"You wanted to ask me out but didn't have the balls. Good night."

She turned and raced up the steps. My stupid hand kept waving out in front of me. Where did that power surge come from? Never felt that type of energy charge when I touched somebody. It was weird how my powers strengthened.

That comment about asking her out caught me by surprise. Didn't even occur to me because my focus is getting with Amina. But that feeling when we touched was strange.

At the door she looked back, shook her head, and walked down the stairs. My eyebrows jumped at the sight of her narrowed eyes and tight, colorless lips. Her look triggered a memory from ninth grade that had been working its way back to me.

"I see what you're doing. Act like a gentleman and watch the lady get home safe, blah, blah, blah, bullshit. You're just watching my ass go up the stairs. I don't appreciate that, and I didn't expect that from you. Again, good night."

"No, I was chewing on what you said earlier. You don't remember ninth grade, do you?"

"What about it?"

"I had the balls to ask you to the Spring Dance. You looked me up, down, laughed, and walked away. Didn't say a word."

"That's crazy, I'd remember that if it was real. Why would YOU ask ME, of all people, to the dance?"

"You reminded me of someone."

"Should've asked her."

"If only that was possible. Doesn't matter now."

She crossed her arms and tapped her foot. "You said you'd never lie to me and I thought it meant you wouldn't make shit up, either. Guess I was wrong."

Her emotions twisted around each other. "You know how people say women are complicated?"

"So?" she snapped.

"You're not. You're conflicted and angry and ashamed and unhappy and you know how to feel better, but you're too scared to change."

She didn't speak for a full minute, then put her hand on my shoulder and leaned closer. "The exact definition of complicated. Good night."

"I promised I'd never lie to you, and I haven't. And I'm sorry you're hurting so much."

I left so she could walk up the stairs unobserved. Wondered if she'd get together with the group the next time we met. Wondered whether I wanted her to stay.

Chapter 17: The Search

Two days later, my grandmother texted to make sure we still planned to meet. Max and Junie were in, but Gemma didn't reply. My next text was to Darrell the Doorman asking to keep the car out longer, taking friends home.

Max and Junie waited by the Town Car after school. I nodded and said, "Have you seen Gemma?" Max shook his head.

"You guys get inside. Need to clear something up with her," I said.

"You go first, babe," Max told Junie.

"Oh no, you're not the sandwich meat. Besides, I may want to talk to Gemma and ignore you."

"You can't ignore me." He blew her a kiss as he got in the car.

Junie leaned closer. "She said you ran into her the other night."

"Literally."

"Literally, yeah, and she wouldn't spill but wants to know if you still want her. I mean, in this crazy band of rebels."

"More than ever."

She texted, and a few seconds later Gemma walked out of the school.

"You go ahead. I need to apologize."

"Neat twist, because she's planning to do the same." She jumped into the car, laughed, and crashed into Max, then pulled the door closed.

Gemma leaned against the car and looked away from me and across the street. "Possible I overreacted. I was in the park to work out a few things myself."

"Sorry my mess had me so upset I didn't let you to talk or even ask how you were."

"Your problems were way bigger than mine."

"No excuse to talk all the time."

"You're a guy. That's what guys do."

"Not smart guys."

She turned and raised one eyebrow. "I hear smart's better than popular."

"No way I'll put THAT on Instagram. No likes on that post."

She looked across the street again. "You know that dance? I looked it up in my diary and you did ask me. I thought you were punking me or something, which is why I didn't think it was real. No clue why you'd do that." She turned and her gaze met mine. "Who'd I remind you of?"

It was my turn to look the other direction. Her question caught me by surprise, and the pain rushed back and hit me before I was ready to control it. "Long story for another time," I said after a moment.

"You OK?"

"Yeah."

She cleared her throat. "I told you I don't think you're a rude entitled asshole anymore, but I'm not sure what you are yet."

As I opened the door for her, I said, "Neither am I. But you really love to remind me I acted like an entitled asshole."

"Yep. And rude, too."

"I'll sit in the front so you can slide in unwatched."

"Yep. Over-reacted."

"You're complicated."

* * * * *

Bunny was ready when we arrived for our planning session. She gave me and Max a hug and invited us inside. "Good to see you again, Max."

"Back at ya, Bunny."

"Allow me to introduce you to Sophia Popova, my grandmother on my mother's side."

"Or you can say maternal grandmother," teased Max.

"Fine. We call her Bunny."

"Bunny?" asked Junie.

"I wanted to use Bunica, Romanian for grandmother," she said. "But Paul was young, and it came out Bunny, so we kept it."

"A lot less formal than my Cajun grandmother, Grand-maman," said Max.

"Maternal grandmother, meet Junie Johnson, Max's girlfriend, and Gemma Hargraves, Junie's best friend." Bunny hugged both girls and pointed at Gemma's freckles. "Love those. Never hide the real you, my dear." Gemma grinned and pretended to wipe off the makeup she wasn't wearing.

"Come have a seat, young friends of the son of my daughter. Snacks await." She sat beside Gemma, leaving me at the head of the table.

Plates of sliced fruit and cheese, crackers, finger sandwiches, and cookies were on the table. Everyone grabbed something as the maid brought in pitchers of lemonade and iced tea.

"Sorry there's no chocolate milk for you, Paulie."

"That's OK, kinda outgrown that."

"Paulie? Cute!" Junie reached for another apple slice. "Any more nicknames we can torture him with later, Ms. Popova?"

Bunny laughed. "Oh dear. Sorry, Paul." She gave me a comforting pat on the shoulder. "No, nothing more. No stories of thumb-sucking or bedwetting."

"Bunny!"

"And my family and close friends call me Bunny. You girls should do so as well."

They nodded, and Max grabbed another cookie.

"You told me you want to make changes, correct? What first?" Bunny asked after the snacks disappeared.

They turned to me. "You called this meeting," said Max.

I decided to wait to eat the last cookie in front of me. "I guess we've got all the same ideas as most kids our age. Stop global warming, better health care, end racism, cure poverty, and narrow the income inequality gap."

Bunny nodded. "Those are all laudable goals."

"Things we learned in an expensive East Coast liberal private school, of course," laughed Max.

"And heard from our parents, explaining the racism parts," added Junie.

"These are noble, but third-graders could come up with that list. That's not your actual fight, is it?" asked Bunny.

The silence hung over us for a moment before I spoke. "My parents are helping Holden lie, cheat, steal, and even murder. That's too much."

"We did research," said Junie. "His folks aren't the only ones."

"Indeed not," Bunny said. "The Grigori have enabled criminal activities for decades, and every Grigori has blood on their hands."

Gemma frowned and shook her head. "OK, those are strong words. My dad's a normie and owns a restaurant. Are women enablers, too?"

"Oh, my dear, all women enable the stupid men they love," she answered. "Think things are sexist now? It's heaven compared to my day. The Grigori imported a male-dominant culture from the old country that's far worse than normal sexism."

She nervously tapped the table with her index finger as she looked at Max, Junie, and Gemma. After a deep breath, she said, "If you kids are serious, I can tell you some things and help. Are you, Paul?" We all nodded. "There's a group of us women, mostly older Grigori and a few outside friends, who have been waiting for someone with the courage and tools to change things."

My grandmother took my hand and said, "Remain open and let me sense how you really feel." After a few seconds, she smiled, then repeated the process with Max, Junie, and Gemma.

She stood and said, "You four are intent on making a difference. I've got something for you, so hang tight."

After she left the dining room, Gemma turned to me. "OK, how much do you trust your grandmother?"

"All the way. No question."

"How much do we tell her?"

"Everything. She can help. You heard her, she's fed up with the GRA's crap like we are."

"He's right, my dear." Bunny sat and placed a small book on the table. "This is a list of the America Grigori families, including contact information and work details. Do I have to tell you to keep this book, and everything we discuss, secret?"

Max touched it with his fingertip. "My mother said this didn't exist!"

"So did mine," said Gemma.

"Ditto," I said.

"It becomes second nature to lie and hide things, my young friends. The information may be out of date, but still useful."

"The Coronavirus pandemic made income inequality worse," said Gemma. "Total billionaire assets in the U.S. went up by over two trillion dollars."

"My mom and dad call them 'pandemic profiteers' along with a few other words," said Max.

"But what can we do?" asked Junie. "There's just four of us."

"Five now," said Bunny.

"Good question," I said. "Not sure where to start. How do we get our parents to say no to billionaires doing illegal things? Poker with marked cards is different from killing the other players and stealing the pot."

"My mother's a lawyer who does corporate work, not just for GRA members," said Gemma.

"You sure most of her clients aren't Grigori?" asked Junie.

"OK, hmm, no. Can you take the booklet home and scan it and send it to everyone?"

The last Orange Milano cookie I spotted earlier called my name. "What pressure can we apply? I don't think saying, 'hey Mom and Dad, quit helping Holden murder people' will get me very far."

"That will not go over well with your father, that's for sure," laughed Bunny.

"So, we've got to play the long game. How would you do this?"

She drummed her fingers on the table. "There's one option if you want to keep your powers secret. More options if you don't."

Max shook his head. "Bad things happen to mutants. At least in comic books."

"Even in New Orleans, most respect folks with voodoo abilities but a few despise them," said Junie. "Sometimes they get attacked, according to Max's mom."

"We're missing the common thread that connects the things we mentioned earlier," said Gemma. "Global warming, universal health care, end racism, poverty, and income inequality."

"Glad there's nothing hard on that list," laughed Max. "Should we add world peace to give ourselves a challenge?"

"Same problem there, too." Gemma held up one finger. "Global warming is a political issue." She put up a second finger. "Universal health care is." Third finger was, "Racism's enforced by laws, meaning politics again." Fourth, "Poverty's always the result of politics." Her thumb became, "Income inequality's fueled by tax loopholes and tricks only available to the rich. Only the government can close those, meaning politics yet again. My right hand is full, so world peace, the ultimate in politics, goes on my left thumb. We need friends in politics."

"Rich people will fight tenaciously to stay rich," said Bunny.

"On a smaller scale," I said, "I'd like my parents to not help kill anyone else."

"Other Grigori are doing the same kinds of jobs for other billionaires," said Bunny.

"I don't know how to turn Holden in without getting my parents locked up too." Nobody offered me any advice. "Not ready to do that."

"Now you know the problem I've wrestled with the last four decades," said Bunny.

Everyone sat quietly for a moment.

"This is too big for us," sighed Gemma. "It's all politics, all the way."

I snapped my fingers. "Which old president was Ms. Thompson talking about the other day?"

"Teddy Roosevelt."

"The quote, 'Do what you can, where you are, with what you have,' sounds aimed at us."

"We've got an army of four teens and a grandmother," she said. "What can a literal handful of people do?"

"We recruit other Grigori our age," I answered. "If we can get'em onboard before they start work, and the money blinds them."

"Grigori may take more persuasion than billionaires," Bunny said.

"We'd have better luck if we got'em before they got rich. Other students might join the program."

"Could work," said Gemma, "but what about the adults? Our parents?"

I looked at Bunny. "Do we have any leverage except going public?"

"I don't see any right now."

"We need to think on this." I stood, and everyone rose as well. "If your parents or other adult asks, say we're working on income inequality. They'll get so mad about that they'll ignore our actual focus."

"Thanks for the snacks, Bunny," I said. The others chimed in, and we gathered our backpacks.

"I enjoyed meeting all of you, and I welcome you to the resistance movement some friends and I have been trying to organize for years and years," Bunny said, with a serious look at all of us. "You all know that line about absolute power corrupting absolutely, correct?" We all nodded. "Never more true than with the Grigori Council."

She put her arm around Max, and reached out to Junie and Gemma. "Paul has more gifts than anyone I've ever seen. Max, you've been his best friend for years and know him best. Keep him grounded. Ladies, you need to help as well, and all of you need to look out for one another. Don't tell anyone what you're doing unless you trust them completely, and feel comfortable dragging them into this fight with you, OK?"

A huge smile split Max's face. "Keep him in line, Bunny? My pleasure, got a whip I can borrow?"

At the door, Bunny held my arm. When my friends were a few steps away, she leaned close to me.

"That cute Gemma has confused thoughts about you."

"We've never been friends, but we talked the other night. Shouldn't be so much tension anymore. That's all." I bent to hug her again.

"I think there might be something else. Ever considered her more than a friend?"

That question was a surprise, and the answer was no. The idea didn't seem repulsive like in the past, just a real low priority. "There's a girl at school named Amina I'm working on right now."

"C'mon, Pauleeeee, the elevator's here," yelled Max from down the hall.

"Go with your friends. We'll generate a few ideas and do this again," she said.

After a few steps, she called out to me using her Inside Voice. *"There's something different about Gemma. Not sure what."*

Chapter 18: Accused

Getting from fifth to sixth period means pushing through the crowd in the main hall. There's never a traffic jam in the Grigori section, so the first floor crush always aggravates me.

Taylor Squared wove through the pack and each gave me a high five while going the other direction. As I glanced back at them, Chloe Jarrett stopped right in front of me. She bent over as if to tie her shoe, and bumped me with her butt.

Suddenly she whipped around and slapped me. The noise level in the hall dropped from buzzing conversations to silence. Chloe yelled, "Paul, keep your hands off my ass!"

Everyone stared at me. "Chloe, what kinda shit are you trying to pull?" I put my hands up so everyone could see them.

She ignored me and turned to the other students. "Help! Someone call Madame Polsova! Paul groped me! Sexual assault!"

This was beyond stupid. People were pointing and talking so much the noise got louder than before, then plunged again.

Madame Polsova, the principal at Makary, parted the sea of students to grab me and Chloe by the arm. "My office first thing tomorrow morning, and bring your parents and lawyers if you believe it necessary, because it might be."

She scowled at the onlookers and her voice rose above the chatter. "All done, nothing to see here. Everyone go to class."

Everyone shuffled off, and the hall emptied. I watched as everyone, kids I've known for years, disappeared while thinking or talking about me groping Chloe. They know me, and shouldn't believe this shit, but they turned on me in just a few seconds. I was so mad I wanted to punch the wall on the way to class.

I slid into my seat right as the bell clanged and ignored all the stares. What could I do? Stand up and yell 'I'm not a groper!' in the middle of class? No, Chloe's claim will stick to me until I could figure out a way to clear my name. I concentrated on a solution during that class and the next until the last bell sounded.

People avoided me in the hall as if I was a rabid dog. My jaw hurt and I realized I was grinding my teeth. Someone stepped up, and

I looked up to see Amina standing there. I smiled, but her eyes were narrow, her nostrils flared, and her plush lips a thin line.

"I believed you were a huge upgrade from C.W. but I was wrong. Better to be with a jerk than a perv."

"Amina, it's not what you think, let me explain–"

She put her hand up as if pushing me back. "Stop, Paul, just stop. Everybody saw it." She hurried off, then turned and walked backwards. "I was so excited, and you just ruined the surest thing in your life. I'm glad I found out who you were before it was too late."

"Amina, please, I'm telling you–"

She left. Her cascade of wavy mahogany hair rippled across her back as she shook her head, no doubt disgusted with herself at the horrible mistake of kissing me goodbye the other night at Junie's.

My parents asked how school was during dinner, but I didn't tell them anything. I had to figure this out, and I would, somehow. No reason to get them more upset with me than they already were.

I stared at the ceiling for a long time in bed until I developed a plan. I had no idea how to fix losing my chance with Amina, and that sadness turned to anger. I wondered what was in this frame job for Chloe? What did she have against me?

Ah, there it was. She didn't have a problem with me. But the girl she craved to please to stay in the mean girl group, Lucy, did.

* * * * *

The next day, I stood at the top of the school steps in the traffic flow so I could see who my friends were. Max, Junie, and half the Grigori bumped fists or said something like normal. Most people studied everything but me on their way into the building.

Then Gemma stopped in front of me, which caught me by surprise. She radiated emotional support and even a little concern, which added to the shock.

She stared at the ground and used her Inside Voice. *"That, ah, thing with Chloe. You didn't do it, right?"*

"Hell no. I'm guessing Lucy put her up to this and may have even Pushed her."

"Since you tell the truth, I'll try it. Never figured you for a perv. Asshole, maybe, but not a perv."

94

I smiled. *"Thanks, I guess."*

"Think this has anything to do with our First Four research?"

Damn, that never occurred to me. *"I hope you're just paranoid. I figured this was personal, but it's really strange that Lucy would pull this now. Not like her."*

"I hope it's just paranoia. Look hard enough and you'll find an answer. You're not stupid." She walked away before I could reply, but I realized what she said. Look hard enough? I closed my eyes and face-palmed myself.

I ignored people grumbling as I shoved them aside on my way to the main hall where Chloe accused me. Gemma said "look" so I studied the ceiling and located cameras in every corner of the main hallway. Two round domes hiding 360 degree cameras blended into the wood ceiling.

Chloe, two adults I assume were her parents, and another man who looked like a lawyer, glanced at me then darted into the office. I gave them a couple of minutes to get seated.

The receptionist pointed me to a small conference room. Polsova sat at the head of the table, and Chloe's team was on one side. I sat across from them, one against four.

Madame Polsova asked, "Paul, do you need to call your parents? Or a lawyer?"

I checked, and Chloe and her family were normies. "One and the same," I said, "but I can handle liars by myself."

The lawyer cleared his throat. "The Jarrett family asks that you expel Mr. Barylan for groping their daughter."

I laughed. "Expelled for touching you, Chloe? There goes our lacrosse team."

Madame Polsova slammed her hand on the table. "Mr. Barylan! That is inappropriate! You address me and me only."

I felt mental pressure and saw translucent words 'relax' and 'stay calm' float from Polsova's head to everyone at the table. None of the faculty members I'd checked were Grigori, but it made sense the principal was. I forgot to check on her earlier.

"This is a frame job and you know it," I told her with my Inside Voice.

Her eyes opened wide and her head twitched, but she regained control so fast I doubt the normies even noticed. *"How can you speak to me? I didn't initiate a connection."*

"Later."

The lawyer tried to earn his retainer. "Ms. Jarrett will not sit here and listen to this nonsense!"

It wasn't polite, but since they accused me of something serious, I listened to their thoughts. Chloe was hiding the fact that Lucy and Chip ordered her to do this. Chip must be behind it, because Lucy was petty and mean, but she'd never do something this serious to get back at me. Chip was a different story entirely, and smearing reputations was just another tool in his wannabe gangster arsenal.

"Then let's go to the surveillance console and look at the recordings from the six cameras in the hall," I said.

Chloe's eyebrows flew up, and her mouth dropped open. "Cameras?"

I laughed. "How could you not know? You're in so many Instagrams I assumed you could smell cameras."

"You're an asshole!"

"Maybe, but I don't frame people because Lucy asks me."

That jerked Chloe's mother into action. "Lucy asked you to do this? Are you kidding me!"

Chloe stared at the table. Her mother pulled her up by the arm, then faced me for the first time. "I'm sorry, Paul. I didn't know."

After the Jarrett family left, Madame Polsova asked, "How were you able to talk to me with your Inside Voice?"

"You know I just had my eighteenth birthday. I can still talk to any Grigori."

She studied me as if I was a map she needed to memorize, but she didn't Push me. "Why that remark about Lucy?"

"Chloe is one of Lucy's Mean Girl mob. She's behind this because I made fun her of half-ape boyfriend."

"Not nice to make fun of Mr. Yevgen."

"He should complain to his parents. At the zoo."

She tapped on the table with her left index finger. "Not smart to make fun of Mr. Yevgen, either."

"The rumors are true? His family is Russian Mafia?"

"I would never say such a thing."

"That's a careful answer. But if you want to expel people, throw out Lucy and Chip."

"That will not happen." She didn't tremble, but her lips did, as if the idea made her queasy.

"You know where the cameras are. You could've mentioned them yesterday and killed this nonsense fast, right in the hallway after it happened, but you let everyone think I groped her. Why'd you let this farce keep going?"

"Goodbye, Mr. Barylan. Go to class. You're cleared."

"No, I'm smeared, and this stain won't wash off for a long, long time. It's already cost me something I really wanted."

I went to the door and turned back. "Anything you want to tell me?"

She stood. "There is nothing I can say. *I wish the Council stayed out of school business. I can't believe Anton himself called.*"

I gave her a huge smile, which caused her to purse her lips like she was confused at my reaction, and left the office. Why the hell would the Grigori Council mess with me here at school?

Gordy was standing in the hallway and raised an eyebrow at me. When close, he spoke so softly I had to lean forward to hear him.

"Boyo, the market's cooled on your stock."

"Is that a real FBI cap?"

"Friends give friends things or leave them for finding." He pushed the rolling bucket, and we walked. "When the Council plays, the puppets dance."

"What?" I eavesdropped on him, and he wasn't Grigori, but he worried about me.

"Not every bald is beautiful, boyo, so put on your big girl panties."

That made me laugh. Then he grabbed my arm and looked more serious than I'd ever seen him. "What you allow is what will continue," he said.

"The hell, Gordy? What's going on?"

His rolling bucket squeaked as he did a 180 and kept going. "Watch ya six," he called back over his shoulder.

97

I watched him until he turned a corner and disappeared. Then I went to class and wondered who Gordy believed was sneaking up on me.

Chapter 19: The Enemy Within

The next afternoon, Mom and Dad picked me up at school in his Mercedes. In less than forty-five minutes, we were across Central Park and inside Mount Sinai's Functional Magnetic Resonance Imaging room. The med tech adjusted the pillow under my head and the bolster under my knees, then pushed the button to slide me into the machine.

"Paul, relax as much as you can," said Doctor Petrovich through the intercom. He was the primary physician for GRA members in New York. My parents stood beside him in the command room.

"This shielding will block any eavesdropping, so we can talk freely," Dr. Petrovich said. The fMRI unit was so noisy that hearing anything from the control room, even without the thick glass, would be impossible. Didn't faze me.

"Your group is a fascinating study in genetics," declared the doctor. "With your common ancestors, his gifts should manifest quite well."

"Don't forget the supermoon the night of the Change," Mom said. "Slightly closer to us. Stronger gravity may have increased more than just the tides."

"The adrenaline from that attempted mugging might be a factor, too," added Dad.

The tech that helped me into the machine left, leaving only the Doctor and my parents in the control room.

Time for an "Ask the Obscure Music Expert" game to stay calm. Perfect song to sing inside a fMRI? "Teenage Brain Surgeon" by the Cherry Poppin' Daddies. Before getting to the second line, the doctor interrupted me.

"OK, here we go," said Petrovich. The intercom clicked. "Paul, try to listen to us telepathically. We want to activate a particular part of your brain to make sure it's healthy."

My mental door blocked outgoing thoughts so they couldn't hear me. Listen to them? No problem. While I waited for something to happen, I sang the chorus, which fit my situation alarmingly well:

A mutant strain of DNA
Submit to my I.Q.

I am a psycho teenage
Angry young man age
Fly in the ointment youth
"What's that glowing area?" Dad asked the doctor.

"Exactly what we hoped to see, his third hippocampus. Unique to the Grigori."

What did a hippocampus do again? I meant to look it up after the Change, but forgot. Remembered it was important and maybe did something with memory.

"His two hippocampi, one in each brain hemisphere, are well-formed and larger than average. That's good," said Petrovich. "Wait a sec."

I sensed the doctor's confusion as he checked the control settings on the fMRI several times. What was wrong?

"The third hippocampus is the largest I've ever seen."

"Problem?" asked Mom.

"Usually the extra hippocampus is a small link between the two brain hemispheres. This one is much larger with much more hemispheric integration than normal."

He tweaked more knobs, and the intercom clicked again. "Paul, please listen as hard as you can."

The sign on my mental door said, "*Boring*," in case my parents checked. I opened the door a bit.

"Usually only the right parahippocampal gyrus shows activity. Telepath testing shows the left inferior frontal gyrus receives signals. But he lights up both areas, and there's more energy in the bridging hippocampal structure."

"I'm guessing that means he's better than average?" asked Dad.

"No. I mean, yes. I mean, better than average doesn't cover it. He's got the most hippocampal transactions I've seen in the fifty exams I've done."

Stupid, stupid, stupid! I slammed shut my mental door except for the peephole to listen. Don't show all your cards!

"Ah, OK, that's more normal," said Petrovich. "The machine can sometimes overstate initial response readings. This is higher than typical, but not overly active as in the early reading."

"He's not as strong as you thought?" asked Dad.

"No, no. Stronger than average, absolutely. But the original spike, if it was real, would mean an evolutionary jump in strength. In fact, so much hippocampal activity might indicate multiple abilities."

"No one has two powerful abilities," said Mom. "Although people talk about Anton on the Council."

"But you talk to each other telepathically, even if your primary ability isn't telepathy, correct?" he asked.

"It's not exactly telepathy. We call it our Inside Voice. It's a directed silent conversation you have with your blood relations or a few close people, like spouses," she explained. "Atticus can eavesdrop on Paul's thoughts because he's a telepath. I can use my Inside Voice with Paul, but we have to both engage in the conversation."

"Interesting. One day I'll convince a family to let me test that Inside Voices and cross-reference the results with pure Telepathy readouts."

Dad says he's allergic to hospitals, and I sensed he was getting itchy. Impatience was his dominant emotion. He shook the doctor's hand. "Thank you for your help."

"If you don't mind, I want to study these readings. If I find interesting details, I'll let you know," said Petrovich.

On the ride home, my parents didn't speak, but chewed on what the doctor said. Both wondered how much my larger third hippocampus would increase my power. They were more excited than they told me.

My phone beeped with a text from Max. My laughter got my parent's attention.

"What's funny?" asked Mom.

"Told Max I had a brain scan. He said they probably didn't find one."

They pretended to enjoy the joke.

"So, is my brain normal, or normal enough?" I asked.

"You're just fine. Absolutely normal. No problems," answered Dad.

"*Shouldn't we tell him more?*" asked Mom.

"*His strength is impressive, but what matters is how he uses it. Don't want to build up expectations just in case.*"

"*I still think we need to help train him.*"

101

"His powers will be stronger if he discovers them himself."

"If my mother feeds him her crazy ideas, and he's stronger than most, it could mean trouble."

"Told you I've got this under control."

Good that I heard what they really thought. "Could the doctor tell what particular ability I'll get?"

"That becomes obvious in a week to ten days. One ability should dominate by now," said Mom. "Anything seem strong so far?"

Got to be more careful before asking another stupid question. "Ah, that makes sense. I seem to read people easier now. But I can't mentally juggle things like Max can."

The shame was that testing for telekinesis had never occurred to me after the night my powers came early during the mugging. Max said I threw that mugger the length of the alley, but I didn't remember that at all. Anything around the back seat to move? Spotless as usual, except for one leaf that must've stuck to my shoe. I focused, and the leaf danced. OK, great, I Moved a leaf. Call me The Arborist and give me a comic book series. No, a graphic novel, to match my mood after losing my chance with Amina.

Max should test me. He does way more than make leaves dance.

Chapter 20: Abilities Checklist

On Saturday, I told my parents I had a workout planned with Max, so I wore sweats. I never said we were going to a gym.

After knocking on his door, it took nearly a minute for him to open it. "You didn't sense I was here?" I asked as we went to his bedroom.

"What do you mean?"

"I can ID people before they get to me, like when you were walking to the diner last week."

Max typed with one hand on his tablet. "No clue what that's called."

I shrugged and said, "I call it my Spidey-sense."

"Done."

"*I guess you can still use your Inside Voice?*" asked Max.

"*Yep, and you can understand me until I block,*" I said, slamming shut my mental door.

"Weird when you block, your head turns into granite. Can't even grab hold because it's so slick."

"Did you listen to me before I Changed?"

"Privacy and all, but I got curious. It was tough, like you were really far away. A word here and there was all I caught. I was hoping you might get lucky and avoid the powers."

"Lucky?"

"You remember your first morning? High school sucks double when you find out what people honestly think about you."

"TMI squared." To change the subject, I asked, "Can you block your Dad?"

Max typed on his pad for a moment. "I can control my thoughts so they don't leak out like a normie to other eighteeners. But if he concentrates, he can read me no matter what. It takes a couple years before you can block everybody."

"Not always."

Max checked his tablet again. "Riiight. And you can read through everybody's blocks. I haven't seen that mentioned anywhere in my research so far. You can skip college and consult as a Grigori lie detector."

"Not my idea of fun."

"Gotcha. OK, let's get back to the list. Empathy? Tele-emotions? What am I feeling, not thinking, an emotion?"

Sadness. No, contrition. "You're bummed about something."

"AP History. I got a B this six weeks and pissed off the parental units."

I remembered Junie was upset that Max's super college basketball memory didn't work for school subjects. To wrap my idea in a Push, I thought, *"Treat historical figures like players on a basketball team and memorize their stories like player stats on a card."*

Max stared off into space. "I wonder if I should treat historical figures like basketball players and make trading cards and write their stats on the back." He typed faster on his tablet.

"Add persuasion to your list."

"We haven't gotten to that yet."

I punched his shoulder. "Sucker!"

"Damn. You a Pusher, too? Is the historical figure trading card idea from you?"

"Yep."

"That's the smoothest I've been Pushed, far as I noticed. The idea is almost decent, too."

"Show me telekinesis. I don't remember throwing that mugger in the alley, so let's check if I can Move things without a gun pushed against my head."

Max didn't move, but three tennis balls on his desk jumped into the air. They flew around each other like a weave drill in basketball. Suddenly, they changed direction and zoomed right at my head.

Could I finally handle a ball better than Max? I let them get two inches from my nose, then stopped them, floated them up to the ceiling, held them there for a few seconds, then threw them at him.

"Hey!" said Max. He mentally placed the balls back on his desk. "And a Mover, because I saw what you did before you blanked in that alley. You're only supposed to have one potent power. So far I count three."

"Four with my Spidey-sense."

"Let's check on the rare ones. How about Tele-exploring?"

"What?"

"This needs skin to skin contact. You dig through people's memories like files on a computer. Most call them Creepers."

Tele-exploring? Creeping? Never heard of that, but when I focused, a long list of Max's memories appeared, same as a music play list.

"Weird. OK, last night, you and Junie–"

"Hey!"

"OK. In sixth grade we won that basketball game when I got a rebound late and threw it as hard as I could way down the court. You were snowbirding, beat everybody to the bucket, and made a layup for the win."

"Not fair. That's one of your memories, too."

"Not the part where you stayed back, too tired to play defense as you should've. You felt guilty getting all the cheers for winning the game when you were lazy."

Max typed more. "That's more of a girl power, FYI. And let's keep that between us, OK?"

"So's Feeling and Pushing, according to Bunny. There's plenty of history people hide, like how they used and abused the women for their powers back in the day as she calls it."

"Feelers and Pushers. You're right, Bunny's as mad as we are. Love to give her a baseball bat and turn her loose at a Grigori Council meeting."

I imagined my grandmother, sweet as she was, unleashed like people during *The Purge* movies. "Serious Red Wedding vibe here."

His phone buzzed. "Hey, babe, whatcha wearing?" He winked at me and held it up where I could listen.

"Stop that! You're supposed to help Paul. Is he there yet?"

"Hey, Junie."

Max put the phone to his ear. "Good timing. Are you alone, and decent? Yeah, mad skillz. Checking if he's a Traveler, too."

He put the phone back in his pocket. "Well?"

I reached out to Junie mentally and asked, *"Still got me?"*

"Yeah, but Inside Voices don't work long distance. How're you doing this?"

"You heard the man, mad skillz. I've got a great mental power everyone in the world has when they dial their phone."

105

With my eyes closed, I visualized standing beside Junie. She jumped up and down in her room four blocks away. "Crazy! You're here! It looks so solid I could hug you!" She stepped over to my astral projection, but her arms flew right through my mental hologram.

"Lot pinker than I expected," I said, looking at her room.

"Check the pink unicorn. I gave it to her last Christmas." Said Max.

She pointed to a shelf above her bed. I saw a pink unicorn the size of a house cat with a long, sparkly horn.

Max tapped me on the shoulder. "Tell her we're going to try remote viewing now."

This time I tried to be a fly on Junie's wall. With my eyes closed, there was ... nothing. The room my hologram visited was blank when Looking. The only thing I could see using remote viewing were the backs of my eyelids.

"*Paul, have you started remote viewing yet?*" Junie asked me.

"*All I see is black. Not your pink room.*" I repeated it out loud for Max.

"*Maybe we can work on that. Tell Max to study and get ungrounded. Now go away. Shoo. Shoo.*"

"Zip on the remote viewing," I shrugged to Max.

"Shame, because Lookers are rare but come in handy when you need spies."

"Gemma said she's got a problem with viewing. She can see but not listen."

"Yep, Looking is tricky. But more Lookers are around than Travelers."

"Wonderful. I can do the hard one but not the easy one." How did I manage that?

"You can't shade me for double-dipping at the powers bar with some voodoo. You're like fully loaded."

"No clue how. Kinda sucks sometimes."

"More powers suck worse than one? What the hell?"

"You know the weirdness when you overhear what people think about you, not what they say?"

"Sure."

"I can sense when people are mad, angry, depressed, replaying bad memories in their heads, you know. I don't want to eavesdrop on my friends, but sometimes I can't help it. Stuff just leaks out of people and I catch it. I worry they'll get mad if I slip and say things they didn't tell me."

Max's mom knocked twice and came into the room. "It's good to see you, Paul." As usual, she wore a conservative outfit that highlighted her tall frame and a bright scarf around her neck. She put her arms out.

Her hug completely enveloped me. "Good to see you, too."

She held me at arm's length and studied me. "Max says you can do unusual things. More than most."

"I'm still trying to figure out what's happening."

She held my right hand and turned the palm up. "Let me have a glimpse, please."

It took a moment to trace all the lines on my palm with her index finger. My creases all looked the same to me, but she studied my palm like it was a Shakespeare sonnet. Her large brown eyes in her wide face focused on learning secrets in a way that baffled me.

"You've developed a couple new lines since I last checked."

"Not on purpose. How does that happen?"

"Rare but not impossible." She traced a little more. "Your leadership path is much longer now."

"Maybe a mistake? Max is the leader, not me."

"Don't diss yourself. Things change as you grow, like it or not." She frowned.

"Uh oh," said Max. "I've seen that face."

"Maybe yes, maybe no. Your leadership line now crosses other lines. Prepare for conflict." She paused and said, "You boys take care. I sense an incoming hurricane. Understand?" Max nodded, and she left.

"Hurricane?"

"Big ass storm. Sometimes they blow over you. Sometimes they blow you over. And your house. And your city. And your world."

Chapter 21: Don't Forget Your Water Wings

Makary Academy had its own indoor swimming pool, the MA Natatorium, for PE. The rules stated boys and girls must remain at opposite ends of the Olympic-sized pool, but they never did. The male and female PE teachers had two goals. First, don't let anyone drown. Second, don't let anyone, or a pair of anyones, sneak off and get the wrong kind of physical exercise.

Max loved to swim, bragging it was another example of him smashing stereotypes. For me, swimming wasn't fun because being tall and thin made me sink, not float. When not swimming strokes, my arms and legs grow tired of treading water to keep my head above water.

It didn't help that Chip was in this class. He and his buddies gave off threatening vibes we ignored, as usual.

This morning was typical. Max smiled and joked, even though Junie wasn't in the class. He used PE to ogle the girls without her getting mad at him, saying he was helping me search for potential girlfriends. Riiiight.

School swimsuits were one-piece navy units with the school crest on the left hip for the girls and navy trunks with the crest on the right hip for the boys. Many of the girls looked far sexier than a one-piece should allow.

Max nudged me. "Hey, check out Amina over there, she's smokin' today. She's been long distance flirting with me."

Across the pool, Amina Gonzalez stood beside Lucy. They turned to face us. "Watch me piss Lucy off," he said, blowing them kisses.

I couldn't argue with Max about Amina. Her dark hair, golden skin tone, and long legs transformed her plain suit to plenty sexy. She'd ignored me with a vengeance since she called me a perv after Chloe accused me of groping her. She looked so gorgeous that sneaky trick by Lucy and Chip hurt even more. Didn't bother me a bit when Lucy gave Max the finger, but it hurt when Amina turned away.

"*Stop looking at Lucy!*" Chip blasted at me with enough oomph to make me blink, and a second later he knocked me into the pool.

The PE teacher blew his whistle. "Mr. Barylan, get out right now. You swim when I say you swim."

"Sorry, sir." Max helped me out of the water.

Chip smirked at me. *"You really are as stupid as they say you are,"* I blasted back.

He took a step forward. Two of his bullies in training stopped him.

"What's his problem today?" asked Max.

"Thinks I checked out Lucy."

"Always drama when a jealous dumbass dates a tease."

The PE teacher blew his whistle again. "Warm-up lap, so get in a lane and go to the middle rope and back. Next swimmer in line jumps in over you, so hug the wall."

Max pushed in front. "Let me show you how it's done." Always humble was my buddy Max.

The whistle blew and Max dove into the water. After three strokes, he led all swimmers. He touched the rope and returned ten seconds before everyone else.

My effort to swim as smooth as Max failed yet again. Strokes splashed water instead of propelling me forward, and my lead over the other swimmers narrowed.

Chip blasted me again. *"You want to stop swimming."* My strokes slowed and then stopped. *"You want to sit on the bottom."* I curled up and sank to the bottom of the pool.

Chip's a Pusher! Unlike Mom, his commands had a dark and ugly quality.

The Push from Chip slowed my movements more than quicksand. This became far more than a prank in a hurry. My legs and arms were numb and didn't respond.

That asshole's trying to kill me! "Stop! Stop now!" I yelled at Chip with my Inside Voice, but he didn't.

Panic never helped an emergency, Dad always said. A calm settled over me as I searched for a way out.

I looked up, saw the metal ceiling beams, and sent my Traveler hologram up there to hide but still help me see exactly where people were. Chip stood at the edge of the pool, staring at the water, Pushing harder and harder. Distracted, the teacher didn't notice Max waving and yelling, so he jumped in the pool and swam towards me.

109

Max's *Green Lantern* comic books gave me an idea, so I constructed a giant fist with my imagination and targeted Chip. I didn't have a collection of will focused by a magic ring, but I did have air and water vapor to condense into something hardly visible but solid. Still major pissed that he'd ruined my chance with Amina, I swung as hard as I could. Bam! My giant fist hit him right between the eyes!

Chip flew backwards into his buddies and slid ten feet on the wet floor. Blood poured from his broken nose, and when he coughed out more blood, two teeth bounced away.

My Traveler hologram blinked off as I broke the surface just as Max reached me. *Air! Hooray! Air!* Max tried to grab me in a lifesaving hold, but I stopped him. We made it to the edge and classmates pulled us out.

The teacher saw me with Max and ran to check on us. We sat on the side of the pool, legs in the water, catching our breaths.

"What stupid game were you playing, Mr. Barylan?"

"Sorry, sir. It wasn't my idea."

Students yelled for him to come see Chip, who was laying flat and spitting more and more blood on himself.

"What? A fight in my class! You, to the office," he said to Chip's buddy, who had blood on him from trying to help. "Yevgen, get to the nurse!" As we watched, two other boys helped Chip stand and supported him as he wobbled off with a bloody mess that used to be his mouth and nose.

"Walk him to the nurse. You GRAY kids pull the weirdest crap." The teacher shook his head in disgust and blew his whistle. "Class dismissed! Everybody get changed and get out of my sight!"

Lucy ran past Chip to grab me. *"You OK? What happened?"*

"Ask your boyfriend why he tried to kill me."

Quick as a striking rattlesnake, her right hand flew up and slapped me, hard. Guess she didn't like me shoving her back to Chip.

She went to him, but he pushed her away. Turning and scowling at me, she said, *"You'll pay for this!"*

Angry as hell but still calm, I said, *"For not letting him kill me? Have you gone as stupid as he is?"*

"You're going to be sorry you attacked him!"

"Only after he Pushed me to drown."

The teacher touched Lucy on the shoulder. "Miss Kilish, change and go to class."

She pulled away from his hand. "You need to write up Paul for what he did to Chip!"

"What'd he do?" asked the teacher. "Mr. Barylan was in the pool when Mr. Yevgen got into a fight."

Lucy pointed her finger at me. *"This isn't over!"*

"You and Chip are. He saw you blow right past him to check on me. So sweet that you still care! So sad I don't."

"Fuck you!" Her curse echoed off the tile walls of the natatorium.

"That's enough, Miss Kilish," said the teacher. "Miss Gonzalez, make sure she gets to the locker room OK." Amina grabbed Lucy's arm and pulled her away.

The teacher shook his head and walked to his office. "Always seems I'm missing something with these GRAY kids," he muttered.

Max asked. "What happened?"

"Chip's a Pusher. Told me the stop swimming and sit on the bottom."

"Man, I didn't hear a thing."

"He hit me hard and was in my head before I knew it." A belligerent bully like Chip, who was that strong a Pusher? No telling how many women he'll assault or people he might kill.

"How did you break free?"

"Pulled a Green Lantern to construct a giant Hulk fist and slammed it into his face as hard as I could."

Max laughed so much he staggered as he walked. "Funny. But you don't have it because of gamma radiation. That was your First Four Fist. And it worked, too. Did you see his nose and the giant hole in his face from his missing teeth?"

"Shame we can't bring their phones around the pool. We'd trend big all over social media by now."

"All the likes belong to us."

"Before my Change, I thought this high school was just the normal level of miserable. Now it's way worse."

"Yep. And when I get home, I'll update your powers list."

"Why?"

"Gotta add tele-punching."

Chapter 22: Road Trip Number One

I was ready to face the fallout the next day after my pool fight with Chip, but instead of a school desk, my butt flopped into a window-seat recliner in a Goldstone Gulfstream G650 corporate jet. My parents decided we all needed to go to California and "visit family."

Mom sat across from me. "It's a good chance to visit your cousins. Kind of your birthday trip."

"More a 'get away so people cool down' trip." Dad said never run from a fight, but we were running away after one.

The flight attendant brought us drinks.

"There's a bit of that," said Dad. "Your friend got his nose broken and lost teeth."

"He's not my friend, and he tried to kill me. Ask Max."

"We know," said Mom. "You were entirely within your rights to defend yourself. Nobody's blaming you or Max."

"I feel plenty blamed."

"Yevgen has obvious signs of trauma. You dried." Dad winked at me. "Next time, tell Max to hurt him without leaving so much visible damage."

"Atticus!"

The look of horror on her face made me laugh. "Next time? You saying other people are going to try to kill me?"

"I doubt another Grigori will try, but successful people attract enemies. And crazies, so it could happen."

Mom threw up her hands. "We're supposed to relax and take a couple of meetings out West. Don't start your 'go to the mattresses' nonsense."

Dad zeroed in on me. "Convenient story, Chip knocking you into the pool and Max punching him. What really happened?"

The official story was that Chip thought I was eyeballing Lucy and slugged me from behind, knocking me unconscious and into the pool. Max punched Chip, then jumped in the water to pull me out before I drowned. He was the hero.

"You don't think Max would punch him for me?"

"I do, but a right hook from Mike Tyson in his prime couldn't do that damage. A doctor and an oral surgeon both worked on that Yevgen kid. What really happened?"

I couldn't tell my parents I have multiple powers because I don't trust them to do the right thing anymore. Damn, that's hard to realize. I kept Max the hero. "OK, but you have to cover for Max. I don't want him to get in trouble for my sake."

"No problem. What happened?"

"The official story is true until the right hook part. Max is a Mover and learned a few tricks. He packed a solid ball of water and slammed that into Chip." Parts of that were true, or at least true enough. Chip started it and got hit with something, just not by Max.

"Thanks, son. Always better to tell me the truth."

I leaned my recliner back and said, "Going back to sleep if I can. Almost drowning takes it out of you." A sign saying "tired" appeared on my blocking door.

They moved as far away from me as possible. Sitting close together, they kept their voices low and let the jet noise cover their words. I still caught everything.

"*I'll deal with the Yevgens soon,*" said Dad. "*A direct assault demands a response.*"

"*They're saying their son had nothing to do with Paul's swimming problems. He's innocent and Paul and Max attacked him for no reason,*" she said.

"*They won't let anyone question the boy directly, and we know what that means. We know what they did. I'm plotting my next move.*"

Mom tsked-tsked at that. "*I heard this traumatized Lucy as much as Paul. Is she trying to make up with him? That's wonderful, and we should schedule dinner with her parents and bring that up again.*"

Amazing how every mention of Lucy got them so excited they jammed us together again. Do they just ignore what I want? Or did the Grigori bloodline mean more to then than anything?

"*One good thing to come from this?*" said Dad. "*He let people know he and his team can hit back hard when attacked. A valuable lesson for him and our community.*"

113

"He'll talk to his cousins, teen to teen, and your brother and my sister can read them later. Find out if they discussed anything interesting." Mom using my cousins against me was second level sneaky. I waited for more, but they must've figured that was enough about me. The conversation changed to work stuff concerning contracts with vendors. No need to eavesdrop on that junk.

When Max, Junie, Gemma, and I met at Bunny's, we found background info but hit a ton of dead ends. Save the world? Not so fast. Stop billionaires from cheating and murdering? No clue. Stop Grigori like my parents from helping billionaires go gangster? The only threat we had was to expose them, a real desperation play.

Mom moved seats so she could spread papers over her own table. Dad's table was full of his papers as well. Appeared that writing an action list was a good idea.

On paper? Nah. Opened my Lenovo laptop, put my fingertip on the reader to unlock it, and wrote a list of To-Dos for my California visit. First up was, "Meet gorgeous teen Hollywood movie star and start a scorching bi-coastal romance." But Mom told me, not asked me, that we were going museum hopping tomorrow. Unless teen movie stars hang out with oil paintings and statues during the school day, that plan was dead.

First for real, find out what my cousins thought of all this. Since Bunny's been talking to me, she may have talked to Lance, too. Quinn's Dad, older and even stricter than mine, probably kept her in the dark about the situation.

Second, teach them how to block their parents from reading them. My sign on my blocking door was the best plan for that.

Third, and a long shot, was explaining my ideas to them. If they joined up, and I was sure they would, what next? Fresh ideas from anyone are welcome, because mine were getting stale.

Most Grigori teens in the western half of the country went to school with them, like the teens in the east were in school with me. I wanted to learn their parent's jobs and how they felt about their work. If they hope to improve things as much as we do, new friends able to help if needed will be welcome.

It turns out almost drowning does wear you out. I reclined my seat again, and my eyelids got heavier and heavier.

* * * * *

The change in air pressure woke me up hours later when we descended into Van Nuys Airport on the west side of Los Angeles. The California side of the family was waiting as we landed. Cousin Quinn came in one limousine with her parents Horatio and Natasha Barylan. She took after Dad's side of the family with dark hair and a tall, wiry build like me.

Dad's side of the family loved heroic fictional character names. There was Atticus from *To Kill a Mockingbird* and Horatio from the Horatio Hornblower novels. Mom fought off suggestions like Sherlock (Holmes) and Hercules (Poirot) and Percy (Blakeney from *The Scarlet Pimpernel*). Paul Atreides, from her favorite book *Dune*, was an acceptable compromise. After all, Paul was the hero. They didn't consider he was the hero because he led the rebellion against the powers that be. Since Quinn was a girl, she didn't get a hero's name. Figures.

My other cousin, Lance, named for Sir Lancelot, came with his parents Roderick and Susanna Zolotov. Aunt Susanna favored Bunny more than my mother did. He was Bunny's other grandson and was so Californian he should carry a surfboard with him everywhere.

Quinn grabbed me first and gave me a full-body hug, as she always did. "Pale Boi! Time to get some sun!"

Her full-body hug was full of more body than last time. "Did you get some work done?"

She pushed her breasts up with her hands. "No, I quit eating kale all the time. That shit's nasty. Got a little curvier." She turned to the side and bumped me with her butt. "See? More junk in the trunk!"

Lance shrugged. "I got nothing extra for you, Cuz. Welcome to the land of sunshine with intermittent wildfires and earthquakes."

After greeting all my aunts and uncles, Quinn grabbed my arm. "We're getting him some decent West Coast clothes. His East Coast look is depressing," she yelled over her shoulder to our parents. She pushed me into her limo and Lance jumped in after us.

When we drove away, our parents watched, mouths hanging open. Quinn's phone rang, and she dumped the call.

"Smooth kidnapping, Quinn," said Lance.

"What the hell, cousins?"

"The gossip is all over school, at least in the GRAY wing. What happened?" asked Lance. "Story I heard was you made a play to get Lucy back and Yevgen tried to drown you. What really happened?

"Our fight made news out here?" I asked. "Here" is Makary Institute, the sister school of Makary Academy. I gave them the complete story, including my giant First Four fist made of will or imagination or water or anger or something.

"You should get back with Lucy," cooed Quinn. "She's like sexy squared. I'll go to college next year, so whooooo knows. I mean, if she's in my dorm, I don't know whaaaat will happen. I'm happy to wander into the boys bathroom or the girls'." She batted her eyes at Lance. "Wait, I do. I'll catch her in the shower, and offer to soap that dirty, dirty place on her back she can't reach, then–"

"OK!" His face glowed red. "She's saying that to grief me. After our last visit, I said she was hot. Won't let me live it down."

"Scorching, no question, but you can have her."

Quinn poked me with her elbow, which was easy since her arm was hooked around mine. "Good that you're still single, because all my girlfriends and some of my boyfriends begged me to set them up with you tonight."

"Sorry, don't know if I can handle more than five in one night." That made her laugh, so she hit me on the shoulder. I got serious and pointed to the black screen separating us from the driver. "Safe? We need to talk."

Quinn tilted her head toward the front. "Family driver, he's discrete, and the screen's closed." She turned on the stereo loud enough to cover our voices. "Double safe."

"Have you guys considered what being a Grigori means? For your future? For other people?"

"I'm going into law and Lance is going the business route. That what you mean?"

"Sounds like my parents. What if I told you they help their boss break the law and even kill people?"

I eavesdropped on my cousin's thoughts to get their honest reactions.

"Time to set Grigori on the right path," thought Lance. "I believe you."

116

"*What???*" thought Quinn. "That's disgusting."

"Good, you're as upset as I am. Let's bring you up to speed. This guy named Jenkins..."

Quinn and Lance were silent as I gave them the full story as we drove to the Tom Ford store on Rodeo Drive in Beverly Hills.

Quinn spoke first. "You sure?"

"Positive."

"Makes sense. Gotta admit I've wondered about the things my parents do."

"I'm angry since Bunny told me the same stories she told you," said Lance. "We've got to do better. You have something in the works?"

"Cooking as we speak."

Quinn led the way as we paraded into the Tom Ford store. By our second step inside, three sales advisers surrounded us, as did one of her classmates. She elbowed Quinn aside and wrapped her arm around my waist. "I've heard about you," she said, grabbing a handful of my butt. "Let me welcome you to Los Angeles in the dressing room."

"Daphne! Let go of my cousin!"

The platinum blonde who looked like she had a boob job released me. Her fingers slid over my arm to keep on touching me as long as possible. "Later, handsome." She smiled at Quinn and said, "He's a little pale, but so is yellow belly tuna sushi. And I eat that aaaalll up."

Quinn pushed her away. "Go call one of your three sugar daddies."

When Daphne disappeared, Quinn said, "She's right, you're pale," and turned to the saleswoman at her side. "He needs a suit to sit by the pool with me and get some color. And a new suit for me, too. And running-around clothes, and a nice blazer for dinner tomorrow night."

Quinn refused to let me pay for my new clothes. "Birthday present, Cuz," she said. The total on her American Express Centurion Black Card receipt could pay the rent on a New York City apartment for at least one month and possibly two. But they fit great, and I felt very West Coast.

In the car, we made more plans. Both cousins would check with their best friends and ask two questions. First, what did their parents do? Second, help the world be a better place, or let it rot? If they wanted to help, we would take the next step.

As we pulled up to Lance's house, Quinn had a suggestion. "Come to school with us tomorrow. You can tell your own story."

"Great idea," seconded Lance. "You've got new slacks and you can wear one of my school blazers."

"Hmm," I said. "Hang with my cousins and meet new friends or go to museums with my mother." I pretended to stroke my beard while pondering. "What time does class start?"

"I'll be here at eight," said Quinn. "Change and get to my place ASAP. Pool this afternoon and casual family dinner tonight. Wear the sky blue polo I bought. Makes your blue eyes pop."

Chapter 23: Hello, Cousins

One part of my Hollywood teen movie dream unrolled in front of me the next morning, but it starred my cousin instead of a sexy actress yearning for a New York boyfriend. Quinn sat in her Audi A5 Cabriolet with the top down in Lance's driveway. The District Green Metallic paint sparkled in the sun and matched her eyes.

"Paul sits shotgun," she said as Lance reached for the door.

"Why?"

"He's our guest."

"Why couldn't we meet at school like usual?" he asked.

"You can drive yourself, but I need to help Cuz with the ladies." She squeezed my knee before she drove took off around the circular driveway and towards school. "You can handle NYC females, Cuz, but the LA versions are the original Mean Girls. They're the sharks and you're the chum."

"You saw how Daphne confused him yesterday at the store," said Lance. "I can get the rest of the lacrosse team to help me keep Paul safe."

"Pretty horrible picture, but I don't think I need bodyguards from a few girls." Quinn and Lance laughed at me.

The morning sun made my cheeks tingle a little. After an hour in the pool with Quinn yesterday, my skin had a more California glow. A little pink on the nose and cheeks, but my shoulders were fine. Quinn thoroughly coated me with sunscreen three different times.

Makary Academy back home was two large three-story brownstones on a corner with underground parking. Makary Institute in Los Angeles, with more space available, followed the open campus model. Their Olympic pool was outdoors near five tennis courts.

Quinn held my left arm as we walked from the senior parking lot to about two dozen girls waiting by the door. One second they chatted with friends and the next they zeroed in on me. Reminded me of a Shark Week documentary when the sharks smelled fresh blood.

119

Daphne elbowed Lance aside and wrapped her arm around my waist like she did at the Tom Ford store. Her white school blouse, buttoned all the way up, somehow still showed her cleavage.

"Paul, it's soooo good to see you again," she chirped, glaring at Quinn. She tried to pull me away, but Quinn held tight.

"Unhand my cousin. You don't want to cover that zit before class?"

Daphne gasped and her hand flew up to touch a spot on her nose. She released me and pulled a mirror out of her purse to examine her face.

"Now I see how you understand so much about the mean girls," I said.

"You kidding? That was polite. I definitely better keep you close."

A roadblock of gorgeous young women who could all be in the final casting call as the star of their own TV show stopped our progress. Each had a perfect tan, perfect teeth, and a perfect beauty queen smile. Hair coloring ranged from light blonde to dark blonde for the majority. None were Black or Hispanic.

One girl oozed New York. She had thick black hair, dark eyes, and her complexion was less gold and more olive.

I stuck out my hand. "I'm Paul Barylan."

Her soft hand gripped mine tightly. "Isabella Costa. Upper East Side."

I laughed. "Central Park West." I mentally said hello, but nothing came back. Six other girls were silently begging for my attention. Quinn pulled me around and away from Isabella. A blonde with a megawatt smile who had to be on TV, or a working teen model, pushed her way to the front.

"I'm Emma. Good to meet this amazing cousin Quinn brags about." She wrapped her arms around me and kissed my cheek. Somehow, she molded her body against mine down to my toes.

"Nice to meet you. Maybe we could talk later and–"

Quinn pulled my arm. *"Focus! Don't get eaten by the first shark!"*

"Sounds like fun."

"Men!"

She pulled me away from Emma. "Hey, Grace, meet my cousin from New York."

* * * * *

By lunch, Quinn had introduced me to every girl and most of the guys in the building. Only a few of the names and faces stuck. I remembered Isabella came from New York and to avoid Daphne. The rest of the Graces and Natalies and Briannas and Matthews and Ethans and Ryans and Cabots all blurred together.

The lunch tables seated six, and Lance and Quinn guarded me on both sides. Emma joined us, with Quinn's silent permission, but sadly I couldn't get another hug or kiss. She sat between Alyssa and Morgan. Alyssa sat across from Lance and focused on him, ignoring the rest of the table.

"*Lance and Alyssa together?*" I asked Quinn.

"*Soon. And Emma just got dumped, so she's hunting. Careful.*"

"*Somebody dumped Emma? You're kidding.*"

"*Same reason you dropped Lucy and why I said careful. And you're on, Cuz.*"

Never considered myself a salesperson, and hated the school fund raisers I had to do, but I was ready for this pitch. I didn't use my Inside Voice because the normies would get curious, same as at home.

"Quinn said you guys want things to be better, like we do. Is she right?"

They all nodded. "It doesn't bother me to have so much," Alyssa turned away from Lance for the first time. "It hurts to see so many with so little."

It seemed like cheating, but I didn't trust these girls yet so I tuned in to their emotions, and could tell they told me the truth. Quinn's friends were as smart as they were sexy.

"My parents aren't criminals in the sense they rob banks," I said. "More like they make plans for the gang and load the guns."

All three radiated understanding. Each had the same concern about their parents.

"My group and I vowed to not use our Grigori gifts to make more money for billionaires. Do you guys think the same way?"

121

"I'm in big," said Alyssa. "My dad's firm helped that Hollywood studio guy and forced a bunch of those girls he assaulted to sign non-disclosure agreements. I'm still pissed at him."

"Didn't you guilt him into your red BMW?" asked Emma.

Alyssa held up a left wrist coated with diamonds. "My tennis bracelet, too. Still mad."

"I'm with you for anything you want," said Morgan. She had darker blonde hair and a lighter complexion than Emma, but could certainly star in any teen movie. "My dad's firm did a bunch of work for the New York guy who recruited those underage girls. All I got was a month in Paris."

They all pledged to help. Even better, they offered to find others who felt the same way. "Friends, welcome to the First Four Initiative. Not sure how or when we'll need your help, but knowing you're here makes me excited."

The four guys Lance brought to the table later were in, too. But first, the guys wanted to hear how I beat Chip down and liberated the teeth from his face. I told them Max hit him to keep the story short and my extra powers hidden. Second, they wanted details whether Lucy was as hot as the rumors promised.

"Don't let this get back home, but the average girl here rates with the top New York girls. Everyone I've met would be Top Three no question. Yeah, Lucy could make it here, but hardly any others. My friend Junie, too." She'd fit on the sexy scale but stick out like crazy on the color chart. Amina would fit in looks-wise but join Junie on the empty side of the color scale.

Lance's friends congratulated themselves on attending a school filled with tens while I buried my sadness about losing my chance with Amina. I checked, but didn't see any girls with red hair. The closest were a couple of strawberry blondes. Brunettes? A distinct minority.

"Back to business, guys. Who's the best private investigators to the stars?

They said, "Talk to Isabella."

When the subtle chimes announced the end of lunch, Isabella was in the back. I asked Lance and Quinn to wait for me outside and watched Isabella walk my way.

"Waiting for me?" Her smile almost blinded me.

"Yeah, actually. Sorry if it's rude, but, how old are you?"

"Worried about legal? Don't. Eighteen. Love to show you around tonight."

That confirmed she wasn't Grigori. "Family dinner."

"I'm available as dessert."

Focus, man, focus. "Thanks, but Quinn has me on a short leash. I've got more of a business question."

She gave me a small, knowing smile. "Parents thinking of splitting? One misbehaving? Both? I can help in New York, too. Got connections."

She radiated discretion and trust. "It's my parents, but not personal. Do much corporate work?"

She put her hand out for my phone and added two contacts. "First is me for when Quinn isn't holding your leash. You'll regret it if you don't call. Other is my parent's office. We're the second-best investigations firm in LA."

"Second best?"

"Really, we're the best, but Dragavei Associates bills more than anyone. Works constantly with the parents of the GRAY students like Quinn."

"We can't call them because that's who we suspect, ah–"

"Got it. You Grigori people are seriously tribal. I'll tell my parents you need help."

Tribal? Good word. "OK, thanks. I'll give you my number."

She smiled again, even brighter than earlier. "I help my parents in the office."

"Ahhhh, so?"

She waved her phone. "Already got it. And your address, resume, and school records. You decided between Harvard and Yale yet?"

She found this much information on me since this morning? "You know, we're going to be gooooood friends." She took my arm, and we promenaded out the door.

Quinn raised an eyebrow when she saw us together.

"Never let your guard down around Isabella," I told my cousins. *"You sure she's not Grigori?"*

"Worse," said Lance. *"Mafia."*

123

Somehow, that didn't surprise me. Or scare me. But the fact it didn't make my knees knock with fear surprised me a little. One more detail added to the truckload of anxiety about everything in my new secret world.

Chapter 24: Wealth Is a Superpower

After school, we hung out at Lance's place and they graded my day a success. "Emma's texted me three times for your number," Quinn said. "Morgan twice."

I held up my phone. "Isabella's checked twice and wants to hook up after dinner."

Quinn and Lance shook their heads in unison.

"What I figured. You were right, Cuz. Need to get a souvenir t-shirt with, 'LA Chum Boi' on it."

Lance motioned for the two of us to squeeze in beside him. "Cousin selfie!"

Quinn put her arm around my waist and gave me a little goose right as Lance took the photo. He blamed me for the result. "C'mon, quit making funny faces. Hold still for another one."

Moving to a chair out of Quinn's reach, I said, "Let's talk about dinner tonight, and how to keep secrets from your parents."

"I tried to listen to them when I got home," said Lance. "I could overhear normal stuff. When they looked at each other and used their Inside Voice I got nothing."

"Same for me."

"Can you block them from reading you?" I asked.

"That takes like a year or two," said Quinn. "You doing it now is impressive and a little weird."

"I get that a lot, at least the weird part. Here's what I do when I don't want them to listen to what I'm actually thinking. Hang a sign on your blocking door or wall that says what you want them to hear. Write 'school sucks' or 'Quinn is such a jerk' on the sign and that's all they get, at least from me."

Quinn, as expected, leaned over and hit me. "Excellent advice. But you'll pay for that later."

They tried hanging their signs and let me check them. After a few minutes, they got the idea. It should help them keep their secrets. Well, our secrets.

Quinn stood, so I did. Lance laughed, pointed, and called me a "Manners Nerd."

She kissed me goodbye on the cheek and gave him the finger. "Gotta go get ready for dinner and practice hanging out my sign. See you guys at eight."

* * * * *

Fancy group dinners are a big deal to my extended family. This time the location was Palestrina's on the top floor of the Fox Plaza in Century City.

We drove in their Cadillac Escalade ESV, the largest model. Lance's parents in the front row, mine in the middle, and "kids" in back. Lance joked the black SUV made him feel like an FBI agent when he rode in it.

When we reached the restaurant, I couldn't believe the building. "We're going to Nakatomi Plaza!"

"Don't go all Yippee-Ki-Yay mofo on us," said Lance. "The movie wasn't real."

"Still cool."

Quinn and her parents, Horatio and Natasha, greeted us with arms open. The adults had reserved a table for six in the bar area. Quinn sat at a two-top with a third chair pulled close.

I hugged my aunt and uncle and Quinn. "Daphne check, did you sweep the room?" I whispered in her ear. "Everywhere I go, there she is." She laughed and made me sit closest to her. Lance got stuck in the corner.

"Update time, cousins," said Lance. "Almost every one of the two dozen GRAY senior guys at school are interested in what we're doing. Not ready to grab pitchforks and torches, but excited about the project."

"Same for the eighteen girls, well, nineteen with me, I talked to," said Quinn.

"Good news, and thanks. If we need help, it's nice to know friends are out here," I said. "Had any luck keeping your parents out of your thoughts?"

"How can we tell?" she asked.

"You can't sense when people are trying to listen?" They shook their heads. "That'll make things tougher."

126

Quinn waved down a server and ordered a glass of champagne. She raised an eyebrow at us, but we declined.

"You can drink at eighteen here?" I asked.

The server placed a champagne flute in front of her. "Well..."

"In New York, we can't get served."

"Cuz, look around this place, it's major exclusive. Money is power here, and those with money, and their families, get whatever they want."

While my cousins tried to decide whether Emma, Daphne, or Morgan was most blatantly chasing me, my thoughts focused on Quinn's comment. Money WAS power. If that was true, it meant that piles of money, huge giant billionaire mountains of money, became a superpower.

Do something wrong and need to disappear? With enough resources, your options were endless. Fly away in a private jet. Hide in multiple homes in different countries. Hire the best lawyers to bury opponents in lawsuits. Hire a private army to bury your enemies in the swamp. You can avoid consequences. There's a reason San Quintin isn't full of white male billionaires.

Texas ska-punk band Secret Agent 8 had a song from their 1999 self-titled album that fit here: "When Push Comes to Shove." Billionaires could shove at "make or break," time.

At dinner, Susanna, my aunt on my mother's side, sat beside me. She was my favorite adult relative after Bunny.

"Do you still work in city government?" I asked her during the salad course.

"I do. Now I'm special assistant to the Mayor."

"I'm guessing there's more to it than taking calls for potholes."

She had a louder and happier laugh than my mother. "I avoid dealing with street problems, because many demand services we can't provide."

"What do you do for the city? I understand the jobs of MBAs and lawyers, but not government people."

"*Careful,*" my mother said. "*Mom's filled his head with her nonsense.*"

"I keep the peace between groups who want the best for the city, but have different ideas on the most personally advantageous approach," she explained.

Susanna's job sounded like Dad's. I wondered if she was a Listener like him or a Pusher like Mom.

"You know," said Susanna, putting her hand on my forearm. "We'd love to have you attend school out here. Pleasant change of pace and better weather."

Quinn brightened and added, "I'm trying to decide between USC and Stanford. You can come with me."

I sensed pressure and saw words floating from Aunt Susanna to me. *"Come to USC. Come to USC."* She was a Pusher, a good one. Her suggestive pressure was as strong as Mom's.

"You should come to USC," she said. "That'll get Quinn to stay closer to home."

"Isn't that where the stars bribed officials and faked records to get their kids enrolled?" I asked.

My uncle Roderick, on the other side of his wife, laughed. "Amateurs."

"It is," she admitted, "but I know people. The Mayor's office will advocate on your behalf. If you care to spend your college years at USC, I'll make it happen."

"You should," said Quinn. "Two days here and you've got much better color. You'll always have company with so many girls fighting over you, but I'll protect you."

"I don't want you to protect me from girls, I want you to recruit them!"

Natasha looked at her son Lance. "Didn't you say they voted him Hottie of the Week or something today?"

"Mom! Nobody says hottie anymore."

She focused on him. "Right. I guess 'morsel' is the new term." The way she spoke made me wonder if she plucked it from his thoughts.

"Snack, too. Tasty. Juicy. Mostly word plays on being edible," added Quinn.

"A little crude," said Roderick.

His wife laughed. "Crude? That's crude? Need I remind you what you thought about doing to me when we first met?"

Glad my blocking door stopped me from sensing emotions. Not my idea of fun to overhear the details of my future uncle lusting after my future aunt. But I knew Susanna was a Pusher like Mom.

Natasha read Lance effortlessly. Either he forgot to block, or it didn't matter. That made me nervous. How do you fight people who can read your mind and have the superpower of wealth?

Chapter 25: The First Four Initiative Grows

On the way to the airport the next morning, I texted Bunny to ask if my friends could come visit again. Her response zipped right back. Yes this evening and yes to anytime.

I sent a group text to Max, Junie, and Gemma, suggesting they tell parents I need help catching up on missing schoolwork. I put a sign on my mental door that said, "*Homework*" in case my parents checked. They told me to keep the grades up to prepare for Harvard, no, Yale, no, Harvard, blah, blah, blah. Could be the Mayor was right about Columbia, or I could escape to USC and have classes with 9s and 10s.

At 8 PM, after two knocks on Bunny's door, I used my key. "I'm here." She was waiting and gave me a big hug.

"How was your trip?"

"Great. Quinn and Lance send their love. And the rest do, too."

"Sit, I have desserts for everyone."

We sat, but before Bunny could cut a slice of key lime pie for me, I said, "Max and Junie are in the elevator."

Bunny asked. "You truly can tell where people are?"

"Just my friends. Remember, I sense people around and where they are in relation to me, but I don't know who they are unless I eavesdrop."

"That could come in handy."

"Probably." Down the hall, the elevator dinged, and Max and Junie stepped out.

Junie hugged me and Max gave me the quick and manly fast hug and double-tap back pat. When we sat down, Nydia, the maid, entered with a plate of cookies, brownies, a cherry pie, and a pitcher of lemonade. Bunny handed out snack plates.

"Why are you smiling?" Junie asked me. "Hungry for key lime pie?"

"My favorite, and Gemma's in the building."

On my way to the door, Junie said, "That knowing who's where is weird."

"Never playing hide and seek with him again," said Max.

Gemma's elevator was quick, and she beat me to the hallway.

"Find a new girlfriend in LA?" she asked.

"Six, but my cousin scared them all away."

"Sorry for your loss, or losses."

"Tomorrow is another day. None of them were exactly what I'm looking for."

"Do you know what you're looking for?"

What an interesting question. "Know it when I see it. Want me to go first?"

"Nah, I've seen your ass, and it's not that special." We walked to the dining room side by side.

"Got a text earlier from your cousin Quinn," said Max. Before he could say more, Junie grabbed his chin and wiped the corner of his mouth with a napkin.

"Oh no, what did she tell you?" I asked.

"She? I thought Quinn was a he, but she's a she?" Junie asked. She pulled Max's face around to hers again. "Why's this girl talking to you?"

"Two Christmases ago, when she and his other cousin Lance visited for the holidays, I helped her pick his present."

"*Don't tell her a thing,*" he pleaded with his Inside Voice.

"*I got you, man, but I have no interest in hearing what you did with my cousin. It was way before you started with Junie, anyway.*"

"*Doesn't matter to Junie.*"

She released him. "OK."

"As I was saying, Quinn told me you caused, a, wait a minute." He scrolled to her text. "Uh, 'He caused a wave of soaked panties all over the school.' Uh, sorry, Bunny."

She laughed and dismissed his concern with a shake of her head. "Quinn's a hoot, as we used to say." She turned to Gemma. "The blue eyes get to the girls."

"Fresh meat. The same thing would happen if Lance came to visit," Gemma snapped back.

"I'm sure, because Lance is the California version of Paul." She winked at me.

After the maid cleared the plates and refilled the lemonade glasses, we got serious. "How goes it at school?"

"Normal, if you can say that about a building full of people like us," said Max. "Chip's friends say he slipped on the wet floor, and

131

there's no reason to think was involved with you swimming like a brick."

"Slipped and fell face down?" said Junie. "Right."

"Yeah, Max, thanks for hitting him for me, wink, wink."

He kissed his knuckles. "I used my killer right cross, wink, wink."

I reported what I learned on my trip. Quinn and Lance were onboard, as were all the Grigori students. Their parents worked for different industries than ours but pulled the same crap. Record companies cheated artists out of royalties. Film studios hid profits to avoid payouts to actors and directors. Lawyers kept sexual predators, including big names in the national news, out of jail. Our new friends were as sick of criming as we were.

"We need help to make an impact," I said.

"There are plenty of my friends on your side," said Bunny. "Grigori and not, and my network has money and great connections to help. You'll need protection and support as we push on."

"Money?" asked Max.

"Not like we can ask our parents for more allowance," I said.

Max posed and smiled big. "We can get by on good looks!"

"Quinn and her girlfriends can, but you and me better find a bucket full of bucks."

Gemma shook Junie's hand. "Hi, I'm Sue Storm. Good to meetcha."

Bunny added, "One of my friends raised an FBI agent, if you can believe it. Not a Grigori, of course. But she's ready to put him to work on our behalf. And protection from outside may be important soon."

"What do they say in the movies?" asked Junie. "Follow the money?"

"One girl in LA moved there from New York. Her parents are private investigators, so she gave me her number and the office info."

"Grigori?" asked his grandmother.

I shook my head. "She doesn't like Dragavei Associates, the Grigori agency. According to my cousins, she's connected."

Junie's eyebrows knotted. "To what?"

Bunny frowned and drummed her fingers on the table. "The Mafia. Ever curious why the Mafia controls areas such as waste management, construction, gambling, and hospitality?" she asked. "Because the Grigori took most of the white collar criminal positions here back in the 1930s, like law, banking, Wall Street, management consulting, and finance. Mafia families stick fingers in those businesses as ways to launder money. But they'll kill, actually kill people, to get a bigger piece of the action."

"Most of them will help you fight the Grigori because it's in their best interest, but you jump from the frying pan into the fire." She twisted and untwisted her napkin as she talked. "Grigori spilled blood, yes, but it drenches Mafia families." She sighed deeply. "We may have to work with them in the future, but never forget the Mafia is not our friend."

Everyone sat still for a moment.

Max nudged Junie. "We should binge the Godfather movies."

"Hell no. Scare me too much."

Bunny cleared her throat. "I don't want you to be scared, per se, but you need to be aware that people, perhaps dangerous people, may notice as we gain momentum. That's one reason I want to loop in outside protection, and luckily I have a connection to the FBI we can trust."

"Scared or not, we need help to follow the money trail," I said. "Fairly sure the investigations company isn't Mafia."

"Even with options here, I don't know who can help out West," said Bunny. "You should get them started."

"Sounds like an assignment."

Gemma slid a few papers in front of me. "What are these?"

"The homework we're supposed to discuss."

"Thanks." That was thoughtful, or she covers her tracks well. Either way, it helped.

We stood and gathered our backpacks. Bunny nodded when she saw me grab two more cookies. She handed Max two as well.

On the street, Max, Junie, and Gemma jumped into a passing cab. It was a cool evening and a fine time to walk and think. My mental door blocked distractions as our discussion replayed in my head, followed by a text to Isabella. "Yes, we're ready to get her parents started on the case."

Could I trust anyone outside our group and our new LA friends? Who was this FBI person Bunny mentioned? Maybe that Klingon quote from *Star Trek* was wrong. Maybe the enemy of your enemy is not your friend. Maybe the enemy of your enemy is just another enemy.

Chapter 26: Impossible Dream

The next day at school, people asked where I'd gone and about my tan. Family stuff in LA satisfied most of them. Guys asked if I got my hands on any hot California babes. I smiled at the memories of being wrapped in the embrace of Emma, Morgan, Isabella, and four or five more, and waggled my eyebrows.

Lucy gave me the coldest of cold shoulders. Her friends followed her lead, but nothing new there. After our breakup, her crew ignored me anyway, except for the occasional drive-by insult.

Chip remained absent, and the rumors said it was to replace his teeth. His buddies were itching to attack me, but too scared to take the first step.

On the way out after school, I heard the mob bucket squeak and turned to say hello to Gordy, but it wasn't him. "Where's Gordy?"

The assistant janitor stopped the bucket and shrugged. "Dunno. He hasn't come to work, won't answer his phone in the last two days. He and his Camaro could've rolled away at 120 per out of town."

Didn't show? I didn't remember a day in years I hadn't seen Gordy during school, pushing his rolling mop bucket. But he warned me and disappeared? That made no sense. I worried about him on the way home. Did someone overhear us and do something to him because of me? That tied my stomach into knots.

I loitered by the office, mentally eavesdropping on conversations inside. After three minutes, the facilities assistant principal zoomed down the hall and rushed into the office. The entire time, he was cursing the Council for getting rid of Gordy and leaving the school short handed.

Why would the council get rid of Gordy? Did they fire him for some reason? That didn't make any sense, because he'd been here as long as I remember. Wait, last time we spoke, he said, "When the Council plays, the puppets dance." A cold shiver ran from the top of my head and down my spine. Did the Council do something to Gordy because he told me things? Did "Get rid of" mean more than firing him? That's ridiculous, right?

I talked to Darrell the Doorman when I got home and thanked him for the Town Car every day. It didn't take a mind-reader to know he was glad someone appreciated his work.

When the elevator doors opened, my parents waited for me in the foyer.

"What the hell do you think you're doing!" snapped Dad.

"What? Nothing!"

"Not what we hear from aunts and uncles. Your cousins aren't old enough to keep secrets."

"Although your trick with a mental sign on their block was clever," Mom said in her usual calm voice. "It took genuine effort to get through those stupid things you taught them."

I calmed myself to match Mom. Dad yelled, but she destroyed all the objections to what she wanted one by one. How can you out-argue a Pusher?

Closing and locking my mental door, I walked to one sofa, tossed my backpack on the seat, and sat. Mom pulled Dad's arm until he perched beside her.

"You want to save the world? Know how young and stupid that makes you sound!" Dad stayed seated, but his face was getting red from his yelling. That color change always scared me to silence when I was younger.

"What were you thinking asking your cousins to help you? Help you do what?" demanded Mom.

"Improve things? Clean up the mess of the world a little?"

"How can you be such an idiot!" yelled Dad, face getting redder. "You have everything you could ever want. We made sure of that."

"I agree."

"Excuse me?"

"You're right, I've got it made. I'm a white male with family money. Thank you."

"Why'd you get your cousins worked up?" asked Mom.

"Because of Max, and Junie, and Darrell downstairs. And the people I overhear when I'm out in the city."

"What about Max?"

136

"He's more or less me in every way. His parents have money, he's in a private school, and he gets good grades. He's ready for college, any school he wants."

Dad couldn't sit still any longer and paced. "Max being like you is a problem?"

Bunny told me to be an adult now and keep control. I tried to stay calm and make my point. "Do you know how many times police have stopped me on the street? None."

"Damn right," said Dad. "If they hassled you, we'd explain their serious mistake in a heartbeat."

"Want to guess how many times they stop Max? Six times this month! Because he's got brown eyes and mine are blue? He's shorter? He wears those weird socks? No! He gets stopped because he's Black! People follow him around when we're in a store. They glance at me but stare at Max. Why? Because he's not white! Junie gets hassled, but Lucy never did."

"Racism is still a problem," said my mother.

Dad moved nearer to Mom. "The world is unfair to your friend, so you want to make everyone hysterical? We can't fix the world!"

I couldn't control myself any longer and jumped to my feet. "But you CAN fix the world! You just won't!"

"What are you saying?"

I turned to Mom. "Who do you persuade and why?"

"I don't appreciate your tone."

"My tone! Max takes his life in his hands every time he leaves the house, and you're worried about my tone?"

"Max is a great kid and wouldn't hurt anyone," she said.

"True, but how many Black men killed by police were guys as good as Max? Lots of them, but they're all still dead."

"I'm sorry Max and his family have to worry about these issues."

"Help me improve things. Push people in power to follow the rules and the law, and stop cheating people."

"Are you back to your 'things should be fair for everyone' nonsense?" asked Mom.

"You're not eight years old anymore!" yelled Dad.

I had to convince Mom to work on Dad later. "The Mayor came to my party. Can you ask him to help more people?"

She shook her head. "It doesn't work that way."

"Then how does it work? Who do you persuade and why?"

"Your mother is not the one in trouble, young man."

"Who do you persuade and why?"

"A lawyer's clients are confidential–"

"Who do you persuade and why?"

"You won't understand all the nuances–"

"Who do you persuade and why?"

"There're many reasons to suggest people follow–"

I stepped in front of Mom and looked straight into her eyes. "Jenkins is dead, isn't he?"

Dad shoved me away from her. "Who told you Jenkins' name? What do you know?"

"I overheard you two discuss him. Is he still alive? Did you persuade Holden not to kill him?"

Mom studied her shoes. "Dad?" I asked.

"There was an accident–"

"You helped Holden kill him?"

"We did NOTHING! He tried to cross against the light and had an accident!"

I sensed his emotions. "You're lying because I can sense it. I overheard you before, just didn't tell you."

"Caroline, why didn't you say he was an Empath like your mother?"

"I didn't realize."

Dad stared at me and stomped into my head. I blocked him.

He staggered back as if I'd hit him. "You blocked me? You just got your powers a few weeks ago!"

"The Grigori are the greatest advancement in human evolution in who knows how long. You could cure cancer, at least the social cancers. But how do you use this gift? Waste it to help the wealthy make more money and cover up their crimes. You should be ashamed of yourselves! Grigori can help people all over the world, but you work for criminals and fill your pockets!"

"It's not our job to manage the world! Our job is to protect our family and the other Grigori," Dad insisted.

Hope flowed from me as the water drained out of a bathtub through the open drain. They didn't give a damn and nothing I said changed a thing. I slumped onto the couch.

"Don't create a giant problem out of nothing," added Mom. "Things are good, so don't throw away your future to chase your childish dream of Utopia. You'll screw up everything."

"What 'everything' do you mean? Convincing judges to let Holden get away with murder?"

"We can't do what you want. People told you the history of Grigori persecution," she answered. "If we're identified, we're hunted, and sometimes killed."

"There are two Grigori in Mainland China," said Dad. "Do you want the government to lock them up and experiment on them? Test them to death? There's a dozen still in Russia. Are you going to send them to the Gulag?"

I needed to stand up and move again. "Work behind the scenes like you do now! Help the Russians escape! Get the Chinese out! Push politicians to fund food programs for children here in New York City. Fight for better health care. My last Uber driver juggled whether to pay rent or get her diabetes medicine."

Mom slid her arm across my shoulders. "Yes, you want to save the world. Kids always do, but the world is a complicated place."

"Your choice isn't. Do the right thing. Help people. Free innocent people from prison. Work with parole boards to figure out which parolees are dangerous. Catch the next crazy with an assault rifle before he shoots up a school. The Grigori can contribute enormously and make the world a better place."

"If you cause more trouble, I worry we can't protect you."

"From who?"

"Grigori leadership."

"You think they'd hurt me, one of their own? Just for the money? Send that bald guy to Push me to walk into traffic like Jenkins? I saw it."

Dad jerked. "Bald? Tall? Big nose?"

I nodded.

"Did he see you?"

"Yeah."

"Shit."

Mom pulled a tissue out of the box on the end table. She wiped a tear on her left cheek. "You understand they're serious, so please stop. We'll work out something soon, I promise, just don't bring more attention to yourself."

Through their shimmering blocks, I overheard her ask Dad, "*Is there a way to protect him from Anton?*"

"*Not if he pushes the wrong people.*"

"*Will he let this go?*"

"I will NOT let this go. You had your chance. You've had decades to do the right thing, but you stayed silent and took the bribes, and followed orders. You put the blinders on yourselves."

I walked to my room. Over my shoulder, I told them, "Things have to improve. If you won't help, stay out of my way."

I escaped to my room and slammed the door, then flopped on my bed and used my pillow as a punching bag.

Chapter 27: Hi and Lo

It was spring outside our house the next morning, but inside it was chilled as deep as the coldest night in February. Nobody spoke to anyone, verbally or mentally.

At school, the normies avoided me thanks to the scowl on my face. The sign on my mental door was more terse than usual for the Grigori students: *Leave Me the Hell Alone!* They did.

At 10 AM I texted Isabella: "Call when you've got the time." My phone lit up, so I excused myself from class and stepped into the hall.

"Paul, great to hear from you," she said. Her chipper tone suggested she was a real morning person.

"I need your parents to start today."

"Oh. Lovely day here. How's the weather there?"

"Outside or inside my head?"

"Then let's talk business. How important is this assignment to you?"

"Critical. My parents hate what I'm doing on one hand but worry they can't protect me from the Grigori on the other."

"I'll have the office send our official fee list to your four email accounts. Of course, I know them. For a range to expect, let me tell you an old joke. There are three project descriptions: Good, fast, and cheap, but you get only two of those on any one project."

"Guess I should've had a second cup of coffee, because I didn't catch that."

"If you want your project done cheap and fast, it won't be good. Cheap and good? Not fast. Good and fast? Not cheap. See? You get two, but never three."

"Ah, never heard that. Makes sense. We need good as possible as fast as possible. Please."

"Done. Just curious, but if your parents are the enemy, who'll pay for this?"

"My grandmother."

"Wow. Lots of fireworks next Thanksgiving dinner."

"Not if people do the right thing."

Isabella laughed. When she got control of herself, she said, "You're adorable. If people did the right thing, my family would starve tomorrow, but I'm not worried. And I wish you the best with your fight, whatever it is."

"Thanks."

"I'll help any way I can, here or in New York. Always happy for an excuse to visit family back home, and new friends."

"Don't know if you need to come, but who knows. When will your parents get rolling?"

"Already have, the morning after we first talked. Quinn told me to start the engines. She also chose the good and fast option."

"Great. She didn't tell me." I almost hung up, but needed to add something. "Sorry for earlier. Things suck big time out here now."

"What a sweetie! You're like the second guy my entire life who's ever apologized for assholery. Yours was way minor and still you made nice."

The bell rang.

"Sorry, class change, so I gotta go. Some called me a rude asshole in the past, so I'm in a 12-step program now. Thanks for your help."

Junie came out of class carrying my backpack. "Ball rolling?"

I slipped it over one shoulder. "By the sound of it, a solid gold ball covered in diamonds."

"Bunny said money was no problem."

"Everything's a problem now."

* * * * *

By the time the Town Car dropped me off from school, I was determined to contact Senator "Big Dave" Kingston, even though his card shook in my hand. The receptionist said the Senator was in a meeting. Of course, he was in a meeting. "Will, ah, you tell him Paul Barylan called, please?"

The Senator's meeting disappeared. "Mr. Barylan, please hold for Senator Kingston."

After a minute of gooey music for old people, the Senator said, "Paul, good to hear from you."

"Thank you, sir, thanks for your card. You asked me to call if things got weird and I wanted answers?"

"Hang on a second." The sound on the line changed from speaker phone to handset. "Of course I remember."

"Well, sir, things are beyond weird."

"Such as your little dustup at the swimming pool?"

"Wow, you found out about that?"

"I keep tabs on my friends."

"That's nothing compared to other stuff. I talked with a few other kids in my circle and the GRA is way worse than I imagined. Evidence of criminal coverups, including a murder I witnessed."

"Calm down, son. Not a conversation to have on the phone."

I tried to read him, but two hundred and thirty miles separated us. Too far for me.

"I think the GRA may not always have the country's best interest at heart," continued the Senator. "Right now, there's nothing I can do. Sorry if I gave you that impression."

His refusal hit me as if it was a baseball bat to the back of my head. "Nothing you can do? But there's—"

"Now, Paul, just hold your horses. Don't tell me rumors and get everyone hot and bothered."

"But—"

"Sorry, son, I've got a meeting. Thanks for calling."

The line went dead, as deceased as my hopes for help from the Senator. Was anybody on my side? The list of who wanted me to stop, shut up, and disappear seemed endless.

Central Park glowed green and vibrant across the street. People walked by and acted normal like people in their lives were trustworthy and supported them when needed. But my life wasn't vibrant and included few trustworthy people. That's what hit me like a bat to the head. Couldn't trust my parents and couldn't trust the Senator.

No, some people were there for me. My grandmother, and Quinn and Lance. Max and Junie and even Gemma. Well, probably Gemma. Just saying that to myself made me feel better. A few friends stood by me. But many more were enemies, including the two upstairs who raised me. The two I had to face again when they came home from work.

143

Chapter 28: The FBI Visits

A few days later, the First Four convened another "study session." Bunny once again had snacks and desserts on the table for us.

Isabella's parents sent me a report that day, so I made copies for everyone and passed them out. There were lots of details on the new Texas company Holden just bought and the toxic waste issues my parents discussed. We weren't lawyers, but we thought the report exposed serious legal stuff.

"The question, Paulie, is whether these disclosures are criminal enough to cause Holden to rethink his way of doing business," said Bunny. "And your parents as well. If you want to threaten them, your evidence must stack as high as possible."

I held up my hand. "There are two people in the elevator. One of them knows you."

Junie leaned over to Max. "Still creepy."

Bunny went to the door. In a moment, a man and a woman, both in their early thirties and wearing navy suits, arrived.

"Wesley! What pleasure to see you again!" She hugged him as he grinned like a ten-year-old.

"Auntie Sophia! Been too long," he said.

She led them over to the table.

"It's my pleasure to introduce you to Wesley Turner, my friend Betty's oldest son."

"Please, it's Wes. Since I was twelve."

"Sorry, I always forget. Wes Turner. He's a Special Agent with the FBI here in New York."

We sat straight up in our chairs.

"FBI?"

"Yes, Paulie, ah, Paul." She turned to Wes. "I do it to him, too." We shook hands with them.

"This is new Special Agent Elena Martinez," said Wes. She'd pulled her dark hair back into a small ponytail and had brown eyes compared to his green ones. Otherwise, it looked as if the FBI made them in the same factory, one Model M and one Model F.

"Hello, everyone. I'm assigned to Wes, so I had to tag along and crash your party, so please forgive me."

"Welcome," said Bunny. She waved at her maid to bring more lemonade and more glasses. "Have a snack."

"You'll never leave Sophia's house hungry," Wes told Elena. He grabbed a cookie and a napkin.

"First, you two should call me Bunny. Family and close friends do. Paul, I told Wes we had intelligence on Goldstone Equity Management, so please show him the report." I slid the papers across the table. They read the papers together.

After a few minutes and a second cookie, Wes turned to my grandmother. "This shows criminality, but it's a state or EPA matter. You said there was a problem threatening national security."

Bunny sighed and looked at Wes for a second before turning to Elena. "You seem to be a lovely young woman, but I don't know you." She said to Wes, "You I've known forever. Do you trust her? With your life?" She reached out and held his hand.

He put his other hand over hers. "She's worked with me for a while, and I vouch for her."

"Yes, complete trust."

"I need to look into your eyes a moment," she said to Elena. Bunny wrapped her offered hand in both of hers. "You're proud to be in the Bureau, and white collar crime bothers you as much as the violent variety."

Elena took her hand back and laughed. "You can say that for every FBI agent."

Wes hmm'd. "I wish."

Bunny turned to me. "Tell them what we can do."

She caught me by surprise. "Wait, are you sure?"

"We need their help."

"OK, if you say so." I turned to Wes. "The people in our family tree have mental abilities people think only exist in comic books. We can read minds, persuade you to do things, know when you lie, sense your emotions, and move things with our minds. Well, each person can do one thing. I can do a little more."

Elena covered her mouth with her hand, but not before her lips curled up in a smile. Wes tightened his lips to hold his face as normal as possible.

"You're thinking my grandmother is a wonderful person, but she's gotten too little old for this type of situation," I said.

Wes' eyes widened. "Good guess under the circumstances. Not mind-reading."

"Think of your favorite sports team."

He smiled at me and waited.

Damn, had my reading ability failed me for the first time? "Why does a guy raised in New York City love the Oakland Roots Soccer Club?"

His mouth fell open. "No shit!" He reddened and turned to Bunny. "Sorry. A friend from college plays for them."

I grinned. *"You're going to get another cookie. Say it out loud."*

"I'm going to get another cookie." Wes reached toward the plate.

"Here you go," said Max. A fat chocolate chip with toffee chunks cookie floated up off the platter and landed in front of Wes.

He stared at me. "I'm full. Why'd I want another cookie? How did it fly off the plate?"

"Max did the flying. I persuaded you to want another cookie."

Elena laughed and said, "Like that was hard. Get him to eat a vegetable. But how did that cookie levitate off the plate?"

"It's called telekinesis," said Bunny.

"OK, fine, I'll look for the wires later," she answered. She turned to Junie. "What can you do?"

"Hand me your gun. Take out the bullets, please."

Elena checked with Wes and he gave his OK. "No way you touch it while it's loaded." She ejected the clip and peered into the Glock. She handed it to Junie, grip first.

Junie laid the pistol on the table and covered it with her right hand. After a few seconds, she studied the grip. "It says 'Made in America' but that's not right. Many of the parts came from Austria." She slid the Glock back but stopped and held it with both hands.

"Hold on! You killed someone with this gun. A guy not much older than us, in a convenience store almost a year ago." She pushed it across the table to Elena as if she couldn't stand to touch it any longer.

The female FBI Special Agent looked at her weapon, at Junie, and again at her weapon. "Damn. This IS real. My name was kept out of the media." She picked it up, reloaded, and put it in her holster.

After chewing her lip, she said, "I'd been in the Bureau only ten days, and stopped for gas and went in for a bottle of water. A young man came in, early twenties, seemed high. He demanded the cashier hand over the money and waved a silver revolver in her face. She cried, and he stepped forward and put his finger on the trigger. I was positive he was going to shoot."

Everyone was quiet for a moment. "Two shots," said Junie. Elena sighed.

"Agent Wes, let Junie check your phone," I suggested.

It was face down on the table. Wes turned it over, locked it, and slid it to Junie.

"It went to the same places today, but it came from Queens. You live there?" He admitted it. "About six months old. You text more than anything else."

"I know things talk to you but try talking to the phone. Ask it something," I said.

"Never tried that." She grabbed it, and after a few seconds, asked, "Who's Debra?"

"Ah, she might become a girlfriend. Not sure yet. Why?" asked Wes.

The phone vibrated in Junie's hand. The login screen flashed by and the Photo App opened. Eight pictures of a blonde woman in an elementary school classroom appeared on-screen.

"Cool!" said Junie. She showed the photos to Max, who whistled.

"Hot for teacher, Wes?"

Wes grabbed his phone back. "I locked it!"

"It told me Debra was important. I asked to see photos, and it opened the app."

"Hand me your phone, babe," Junie said to Max.

"Oh, hell no."

"What're you worried about?"

Max moved his phone from the table to his pocket. "Uh, Beyonce."

"What?"

"She wants me back. Don't want you to see how crazy she is for more Max lovin'."

After everyone stopped laughing, Wes turned to Gemma. She shook her head. "Nothing exciting. Remote viewing."

"Interesting. Can you look into the black Suburban parked in front of the building by the 'No Parking' sign?"

"Uhh, yeah."

"What paperback book is in the passenger floorboard?"

Her eyes peered up and left. "OK. I can't see the title because it's face down. The spine is against the center console. Wait, the blurb says, 'The Tomb' at the top so that could be the name."

She focused above everyone's head. "Much to the chagrin of his girlfriend, Gia, Repairman Jack doesn't deal with electronic appliances – he fixes situations for people, often putting himself in deadly danger."

Junie glanced at Elena. "Repairman Jack?"

Wes laughed. "It's a strange FBI agent who reads supernatural mysteries."

"You sure?" she asked, "Because we've got supernatural right in this room."

Wes blinked twice and asked, "Is that the national security issue?"

"My parents work for Goldstone Equity Management as a vice president and lead counsel," I said. "My father reads minds, so that could explain how Goldstone wins every negotiation. My mother can persuade people to do far more than eat cookies when they're not hungry. Is it a fair lawsuit when one lawyer has the power to change the minds of the jurors and judge?"

"My mom also persuades people," said Junie. "She's an assistant city manager for New York."

"Bunny gave us a list of Grigori members with abilities. Our goal is to research everyone. Many work in Washington," said Gemma.

"Who else knows about this?" asked Wes.

"Senator Kingston from Texas came to my birthday party and told me to call him if I wanted an explanation for the weird things going on. So, I thought he knew. But when I called him the other day, he blew me off, so maybe not. And Holden Goldstone, of course. Plenty of movie studios and record companies leverage Grigori to cheat people out in Los Angeles. Other billionaires know because they use Grigori to get away with murder."

Elena brushed back a loose bit of hair. "How much do you know about how your family uses these powers?"

I shrugged. "I just got mine. You get'em when you turn eighteen. I still have lots to figure out, and my parents won't admit anything." I turned to my friends. "You guys have any details?" They shook their heads.

Bunny patted Wes' hand. "Still read history? Go back and study President Franklin D. Roosevelt. When he started his presidential campaign, no one gave him much of a chance."

"The first Grigori immigrants from Russia came in the late teens and early twenties. 1920s. Columnist Walter Lippmann was against Roosevelt in the beginning. After two Grigori joined the campaign, Lippmann changed his mind and endorsed him. Coincidence?"

"Do you know how?" Wes asked.

Bunny drummed her fingers on the table for a moment. "I was going to tell this just to the girls, but I think you all need to hear it."

"What's that?" I asked.

"Persuasion that works quickly doesn't last. You need plenty of time and physical contact to change a person's mind. Understand what that means?" We all shook their heads.

Bunny sighed. "Persuasive powers manifest far more often in female family members." Elena nodded, but the two girls still seemed puzzled. Max seemed confused still, but I saw where she was headed.

"You youngsters need dirtier minds. Grigori men ordered Grigori women with persuasive powers to sleep with people. You need more physical contact and more time to embed your persuasion."

Elena frowned. Junie and Gemma wrinkled their noses. Max finally got it, and his face looked like he smelled something horrible.

"All Grigori women?" asked Gemma.

"All that I know about," answered Bunny.

"Does that mean–"

149

The older woman cut Junie off. "I don't want to dwell on details."

"That's unfortunately not surprising," said Elena.

"Nor illegal, I'm sure, although many of the girls they ordered to, ah, help the family just turned eighteen," added Bunny. "They were of age, even if innocent."

"I take it this was common, or at least not rare," said Elena.

"You bribed men, and back in the day it was always men, with the tools available. Some wanted money or power, but most wanted sex."

"And today?" asked Elena.

"Still true, but not so much with Grigori girls." Bunny looked at Junie and Gemma, them me and Max. "Sadly, the despicable men who want sex as a bribe now consider you too old. But any Grigori woman who can persuade or read deep emotions or memories, no matter their age, are tools for use by the leadership."

"We better come up with a smarter plan than THAT," said Junie.

"Although, with more women in positions of power today–"

She interrupted Gemma. "Not enough!"

"Agreed, but more. Should we pimp out Paul and Max?"

Junie and Gemma laughed and high-fived, while Max worked through what they wanted to do to us.

"Wait," said Max. "Do I get to choose?"

Junie grabbed his chin and shook his head back and forth. "No, Gemma and I do."

"Well, forget that!" he said. That ended the business portion of the day, so we all stood and gathered up to leave.

"Wes, so good to see you again." Bunny threw her arms around him.

She turned to Elena. "Great to meet you," and gave her a hug.

"Can you two help us?"

"I think so," said Wes.

"Yes," Elena said.

"I'll send you the information we get on Goldstone Equity Management and other Grigori-influenced companies," I said.

Wes glanced at Elena as if worried she'd overrule him again. "Great. Good job so far. The more you gather, the more we can do."

Bunny gave Wes a cookie for the road. He followed Elena out, but turned back.

"We'll do what we can. But these things always take longer than you want. And they're always harder than you expect."

Chapter 29: Cool Kids No More

School the next day turned weirder than normal as people actively avoided me. It takes time for me to become human in the morning, so I stay quiet, and not talking to anybody but Max and Junie was typical. But nobody even spoke, waved, nodded, or looked at me longer than two seconds when we changed classes between first and second period. That was unusual. Most of my classmates had been going to Makary with me since kindergarten.

Before I could figure out why, Taylor Squared ran up to me, Girl Taylor in the lead. They were the first fun thing I'd seen, so they got a big smile, but they didn't return it.

Girl Taylor was out of breath, so Boy Taylor motioned for me to lean closer. "Quick, need a song about a fight."

"How does 'Rumble in Brighton' by Brian Setzer sound? Will that work for you guys?"

"Not for us," she said.

"Be careful, man," he said.

"Word is beatdown," she added.

"We'll help," he said.

My classmates and supposed friends walked by us, and no one looked at me. Which ones were scheming against me? It appeared to be every Grigori.

"You two stay away," I told them, "serious." They didn't run off, but they hurried. At my desk in second period, I opened my mental door and listened to those surrounding me. Taylor Squared was right. People may not talk to me, but they thought about me, and not in a good way.

"*I wonder why Paul ran to the FBI and told lies about the Grigori. The Council should punish all of them,*" the girl to my left said to herself. Wonder who accused us of that?

I overheard, "*He needs a beating for what he did to Chip,*" from one of Chip's friends. That's a shame, since his lunkhead smile looked better after getting some new teeth. His friends were still mad, but that didn't bother me. I don't care what attempted murderers or their friends think of me.

"*Shame I can't talk to Junie anymore,*" leaked from the girl behind me. "*What the hell did Paul do to piss off the entire school?*" A pattern was coming into focus. Someone was spreading lies saying we were the enemy.

When the bell rang, I gathered my papers, stuffed them in my backpack, and moved to the door. On the way, Chip's running buddy hip-checked me into a desk.

Max, as confused as I was, waited for me in the hall. "What's wrong with everybody today?"

"Your Mom's storm is coming. I overheard how their parents ordered them to stay away from me."

"They must've mentioned me, too."

"Junie came up, so, yeah."

Another of Chip's gang walked closer to us. Before we knew what he had in mind, he spat at Max's feet. Basketball quick, Max hopped back to keep his shoes clean. When he moved forward, he drew back his right arm and aimed at the spitter's jaw.

I jumped in front of him to stop the fight. Chip's buddy laughed and gave us the finger as he walked away.

Junie had a "what the hell" face. "Has someone outed the First Four?"

"Ahh," I said. "My parents know my feelings about them helping Holden because of our argument. My aunts and uncles in LA know because my cousins can't block yet."

She and Max frowned. "Sorry, guys," I said. "Go to class. I'll work on this and we'll talk during lunch. Find me."

They didn't need to search in the cafeteria because classmates forced us to the back of the room. Every time I saw an empty seat, a "friend" blocked it.

Today, people spread out to fill up all the tables, leaving two open in the back. One had boxes heaped on it. The only place for us was the last table, within smelling distance of the restrooms

Max and Junie were waiting when I arrived. A moment later, Gemma came. She threw her backpack in an empty chair and flopped beside Junie.

"Something's up," she said.

"Welcome to segregation," replied Max. "Choose your water fountain with care."

"We must've pissed off everybody."

I opened my water and took a drink. "Secrets in the Grigori are rare."

"Since you told us about blocking, I tried with my mother," Junie said. "If I focus, I might sense her reading me, but I can't stop her."

Two girls walked by on the way to the restroom. Both spat in our direction.

Gemma stood and drew back her arm, so I grabbed it. "Don't, not yet. We need to know what's going on yet." She sat, but her fist stayed clenched. Again, when I touched her, my senses expanded, and power surged.

She looked at where my hand grabbed her forearm. "Static?"

"Maybe."

Junie saw an iPhone near the restroom door. She picked it up and tapped the front.

"Do your thing," I suggested.

She smiled and the phone lit up. Swiped the screen up twice and tapped once.

"Changed Hailey's password by one number. When I give it back, listen and tell us what she says."

"Do our parents know we talked to the FBI?" Gemma asked.

I poked at my lobster ravioli. "Did they read you last night?"

"Not sure I know when they do."

"How do you guys block your thoughts?"

Max preferred a door and Junie closed a window. Gemma imagined a tin foil hat.

"Tin foil hat!" laughed Max. "That's so paranoid!"

"And Fifties," added Junie.

"What my mother told me to use!" she protested. After a few seconds, she winced. "Damn."

The two girls came out of the restroom and interrupted our fun. Both spat at us again. They missed, again.

"Dropped your iPhone, bitch," said Junie. She held it up.

"You mean you stole it," snapped Hailey as she grabbed it from her.

I focused on her as she walked away. "*Not my password? Yes, it is. Damn. Still not?*" She turned around and gave Junie the finger.

"She can't get into her own phone now." I bought up my hand for a high-five and Junie slapped it.

"Good thing we're by the bathroom," said Max.

"Why?" she asked.

"If someone does spit on us, we can clean up quick."

"Not sure your natural optimism helps," she said.

I pushed my tray away with most of my lunch uneaten. "Everyone block as solid as possible."

My three friends stared at me and concentrated. Each had a shimmer thinner and lighter than the ones on my parents.

When I tried to help my cousins block, I taught them the "hang a sign on my blocking wall" trick. That added security, but not enough. I had a new idea to try.

I focused on persuasion. "When you lock the safe, your thoughts are safe. Say 'Lock the safe my thoughts are safe' when you block."

"Now imagine a bank vault, a giant steel door, and close that door."

My friends concentrated once again. Their mental shimmers were strong and tight.

"When you repeat those words, your defenses are much better," I said. "Your blocks are the same as I see on my parents."

"Can we block them from listening?" asked Gemma.

"Try it. Max, think of something. Gemma, read it."

Max grinned at Gemma, who exploded in laughter. "I'm not saying that out loud! That's for you and Junie!"

Junie may or may not have listened, but she hit him on the shoulder for good measure. "Stop that!"

"Now imagine a big steel bank vault door and say, 'lock the safe my thoughts are safe' to yourself." I nodded to Gemma, and she tried to read Max again.

She stared at him for a few seconds. "Nothing. Quiet. No more of that nonsense."

Gemma raised her eyebrow at me. "You Pushed us, right?"

"Yeah. I'll check in a couple days to see if it sticks. Your blocks are as solid as an adult's now, so I hope it holds against your parents."

"OK. I have it on good authority that persuasion takes time to affect a person permanently."

Junie added, "What she said."

Max shrugged and said, "Girls are weird."

Junie hit him again.

"Worse," I answered. "I've been told they're complicated."

Gemma actually smiled.

Chapter 30: Hammerblow

"Any clue why we're here?" Atticus asked his wife with his Inside Voice when he joined her outside Holden's office.

She shook her head. *"Try reading him through the door."*

He stepped closer to it and concentrated for a moment. *"Nothing."*

"We'll find out in a minute." They sat on one of the butter-soft Italian leather couches and waited.

After five minutes, he looked at his watch. *"He's cooling us like job applicants, giving us time to get nervous."*

She gave a slight head bob toward the blonde assistant at her desk, hinting he should eavesdrop on her.

"Rearrange the schedule! Rearrange the schedule! Why does he even have a damn schedule since all he does is change it? I have to move four meetings so he can yell at these two."

Atticus leaned toward his wife. *"Not good."* She tugged at her blouse, stopped, and folded her hands in her lap.

Seven minutes later, the intercom buzzed. The assistant turned to the Barylans. "OK."

Atticus pushed into the tall and heavy wooden doors with his shoulder and gestured for his wife to go first.

"Close it." The bright sunshine streaming through the floor to ceiling windows silhouetted Holden. A dozen majestic skyscrapers blocked the view of the Hudson River not far away. He turned to confront them. "What the hell is wrong with Paul! Why's he making trouble?"

Atticus eavesdropped on Holden's thoughts. *"Damn kid will cost me money!"*

Before he could talk, Caroline explained, "He's an optimist with the blinders of youth and doesn't understand the world of adults."

"Not good enough! It's not high school out here, even the famous Makary."

"Try to relax him," Atticus told his wife.

"He's so angry it'll take time."

"We never learned if Paul started this himself or if someone else did and he caught wind of it," Atticus said.

"I'm damn sure he did. It started right after he inherited his powers."

"That just happened, so this idea must've been in the air earlier," said Atticus. "He's smart and just picked up on what was out there."

"No, he's behind it." Holden pointed a finger at Caroline and said, "Helped by your mother."

She closed her eyes and shook her head. "Ever since that mugger killed my father, she's blamed the Grigori leadership for his death. It's warped her."

"She's warping Paul, so stop it! Now!"

She furrowed her eyebrows as she tried harder to calm their boss.

Atticus saw her effort and sought to distract him. "He loves his grandmother. She could be the problem, not him."

"No, she makes it worse, but Paul started this misguided crusade on his own. Reports say he has more abilities than anyone, so tell me what they are."

He shook his head. *"Can't tell him the truth."* Looking straight at Holden, he said, "He's shown no extra powers around us."

"And the report on his fight at the pool last week? I'm told he knocked that Russian Mafia kid's teeth out from twenty yards away while underwater."

"What? Where did you get that? His friend Max hit the other kid to protect him. Max would do that for him, and vice versa."

Holden pointed at Caroline. "I see you. Stop it!"

She held her hands up and shook her head. "No reason to get excited. Just want to keep things under control."

"I pay you to persuade other people, not me."

"I understand, and that's not happening. There's no problem here."

"No, we have a serious problem. If Paul has multiple powers, as I suspect, this mess will balloon bigger and bigger." He put his fists on his desk and leaned forward. "How do you explain the two FBI agents your mother invited to her apartment to meet him and his friends?"

Atticus and Caroline turned to each other, mouths open and eyes wide.

Holden leaned back against the thick windows. "He didn't tell you that, did he? Despite your Grigori mind tricks, it takes a mole in the FBI to give me actual information."

"I ... we had no clue," said Atticus.

"I can't believe she'd go that far," Caroline added. Her shoulders slumped. She covered her face with her hands.

"I've always treated Paul as family," said Holden. "Yet he repays me by talking to the FBI?"

"We'll work with him," said Atticus.

"I'm not the only one concerned here," continued their boss. "If it was just me, I could talk with him, make him see reason. But others at my level noticed. They don't appreciate his good points and don't have a history. They see a nail stick up where it shouldn't. I'm nearby, so I'm forced to be the hammer."

Caroline stood, followed by her husband.

"I understand what we need to do. We'll fix this," she said as she turned to go.

"Do it fast, dammit," said Holden, looking at the skyscrapers again. "Get out so I can decide how to defuse this shitstorm."

"I think it's hit the fan," Atticus said as they walked away from Holden's office.

"*Inside Voice. If he's got FBI spies, he could've bugged this office.*"

"*Got it. You've got to persuade him to ignore this. You may have to sleep with him again.*"

"*No, not again. You screw him this time.*"

"*That's not the way it works.*"

"*Maybe Paul is right and the Grigori need to change. Let's start with their misogynistic attitudes,*" she said. "*We women talk, and we're damn tired of the fact we get no voice in decisions, but have to clean up every giant mess caused by the Council's stupidity.*"

They reached a hall and turned to go to their own offices. "*We need to get Paul to understand he'll cause a major problem. And help him find new areas to focus on,*" she said.

He squeezed her hand. "*If not, I don't know what will happen to him.*"

159

Chapter 31: Shut Up and Smile

During my last period class, Isabella from LA emailed with lots more details on Goldstone Management. I forwarded it to the others and Bunny, and offered my friends a ride home. After the hostility we received at lunch, none of us should be out alone. We gathered at the front steps after school and other students elbowed and bumped us as they passed, so we moved off to the side.

"OK, everyone think of a big red panic button," I said. "Like on a cartoon or something."

"What's up?" asked Junie.

"In physics class we learned focused beams of light and radio waves go farther than unfocused. What if that idea works with telepathy? What if we can't read people from a distance because the signal spreads in every direction, making it weaker as it goes? If we create a 9-1-1 alert from each of us to the other three, we may bypass the distance problem."

"I would've called you paranoid this morning," said Junie. "Now I'll pay for an alarm button."

I faced my friends and started Pushing. "When you imagine a big red panic button, and you hit it, everyone in this group will hear your distress signal. Try it."

Max laughed, did a quick mime search for the button, found it, and hammered down his right fist.

Alarms rang in my head and Junie's and Gemma's. "Damn, bae, you're loud!" said Junie.

None of the other Grigori students reacted to the alarm. "It needs volume to carry. Hit it, Junie." She slammed her hand down like Max. Gemma and I scrunched up our faces, while Max shuddered as if we'd splashed him with freezing water. No one around us flinched.

"My turn," Gemma said, and punched her imaginary button. Max and Junie winced, but I staggered backwards.

"What's wrong?" asked Gemma.

"It started a jet engine inside my head."

"Hers had less volume than Junie's," Max said.

"Quieter than Max's to me," added Junie.

I rubbed my temples. "That sure hit me hard."

The Town Car drove up, and I asked if it was OK to give people a ride home. Gemma, Max, and Junie got in the back, leaving me in the front passenger seat. After they gave their addresses, I turned back to talk.

"We should keep a low profile in school, at least until we figure out the situation."

"We're not making problems," said Gemma. "Not since you knocked Chip's front teeth out."

"Should've knocked them all out," Junie muttered.

"If our friends mess with us because their parents tell them to, being nice to kids at school won't stop them," added Gemma. "No matter how much we smile."

"You're right, and I'll work on a plan. New subject, Isabella's research dug up a bunch of skeletons."

Max waved his phone. "Why is that Texas company so important?"

"Holden's most recent acquisition, so it's higher in the search engines."

The car stopped in front of Junie's building. She gave Max a quick kiss on the cheek and scooted out. "Stay safe, guys!"

"*Holden has lots of bodies stacking up,*" said Max.

"*I bet my parents enabled every one,*" I answered.

After Max left, Gemma spread her arms wide. "Ooh, nice. I've got a driver and a bodyguard."

"Bodyguard? You're the one ready to rumble at lunch."

"I was! Bitches spit at us! Girls I've known for years!"

"They may have spit towards me, not you."

"I didn't think of that. Ha! Never mind, spit away," she laughed. "OK, OK, I'll protect you from those mean girls."

The driver stopped at her building. I asked him to make sure she got inside. "She gets mad if I watch."

* * * * *

Outside my building, I sensed my parents were ready to fight. They paced around in front of the elevator, and anger blasted from them like heat waves. I gritted my teeth and got ready.

Dad yelled as soon as the elevator doors opened enough for him to see me.

"You talked to the F-B-fucking-I!"

I stepped back and stayed still so long the doors almost closed. He stuck his arm between them to force them back open. Then he grabbed my arm and dragged me into the great room and flung me onto the sofa.

"Atticus!" yelled my mother. "Too much!" She sat beside me.

"Answer me!"

"Bunny called them. I didn't know."

Mom snapped her fingers. "The Turners! What's their son's name? Walter? William? He's FBI."

"Wes."

"I don't care what his damn name is. What did you tell him?" Dad loomed over me. I sat up straight and looked him in the eyes.

"They've killed seven people, counting Jenkins, the reporter, and five more in Texas."

"Who told you that?" asked his father.

"We had someone research suspicious deaths."

"You shouldn't have done that. Not your place!"

I had to escape the weight of my father's anger, so I stood and forced him to take a step back. "I know it's not my place," I hissed. "It's yours! But if you help Holden kill people, you're in too deep to see it's wrong." I turned my back on my father and paced the room.

"These things are more complicated than you understand," said Mom.

I stopped and stared at them. "Complicated? You persuade people to do things and call that complicated? Riiight. But saying Jenkins pissed off Holden and the next week he's dead is way past complicated. It's murder."

"We didn't kill anyone!" Dad insisted.

"Because you didn't pull the trigger? You helped plan, or at least didn't stop Holden." I said to Mom, "Did you find some loopholes? Hand envelopes of cash to a shady guy? Send a bank transfer to Dragavei Associates–"

She gasped at the mention of Dragavei. "They kill people for you and clean it up, don't they?" I asked.

She shook her head but refused to face me.

"Did Dragavei cover up the toxic waste dumping? Help smooth over the five deaths? Hide the two major citations for toxic waste disposal on public lands?"

"Oil and timber are dangerous industries," said Dad.

"Everything around Holden turns deadly."

Mom stood and tried to hug me, but I stepped back. "If you keep pushing, we can't protect you."

"Who have you protected?"

"We didn't love any of them. You're our son, but that may not be enough if you attack Grigori business relationships."

"You don't understand how far this goes," added his father.

"I bet way further than Holden."

"Correct. Over three hundred billionaires have access to a member of the Grigori."

"What a surprise, billionaires cheat. Do they also murder?"

Dad shrugged. "Yes, and each one will squash you like a bug to keep their secrets."

I stared at my parents as if they were strangers because that's what they'd become. The people who raised me disappeared. In their place stood two people who turned a blind eye to murder, and may even help. Too mad to talk, I turned my back on them and walked out.

"I can't believe he talked to the FBI," I heard Dad say.

"Blame my mother because she's made him so angry over this. I wish I could persuade him to let it go."

"So do I. But even if you persuade him to stop, he may have gone too far."

Chapter 32: Beatdown Reversal

I jumped out of bed, dressed, and escaped the house before my parents were awake. Darrell wasn't on duty yet, so I left a note canceling my ride.

What the hell should I do now? The yelling replayed in my thoughts as it did during the night. Should I stop? Quit? Run away and hide? Were Mom and Dad serious, they couldn't protect me from Holden? Naw. Impossible.

But maybe Jenkins thought the same way. Crazy to think Holden would kill him for a mistake. He'd get demoted, sure, even fired, but murdered? No matter what he considered, he wasn't answering questions. A gross idea made me shudder. Could Junie's ability to read the history of objects work on corpses? Creepy.

I sat on the steps of the school and watched students trickle in. Most avoided eye contact and glanced away as if I was a rat in the street. The vibe was more hateful than the day before. Every friend who ignored me made the back of my neck tingle more.

"You're here way early," Max said as he sat beside me.

"Big fight at home, so I left before Round Two."

"Ah. They bang on you for the FBI visit? They say they can't protect you if you ruin the wonderful world the Grigori have built?"

"Yep."

"Not awful at my place," said Max. "My mom's pissed at Grigori doings over the years. I think she halfway agrees."

"You accuse them of helping their boss murder people? And they covered it up like good little soldiers?"

"Nope."

"You're smarter than me."

"That ever in doubt?"

I figured out what kept nagging at me. "Wait a minute. How'd your folks know? Are our parents texting each other? Somebody telling them what we're doing?" Who was watching us? I didn't need more anxiety.

"How'd they learn about the FBI? None of us or Bunny would talk. It had to be Wes and Elena."

"No, I checked their emotions. Perhaps they have to tell people where they go."

"Mole?"

"Special Agent Rat."

"Shit." Max stood and waved when he saw Junie coming.

"Things are weird," Max said as she got close.

"Are we dog poop?" she asked. "Everyone looks at me all disgusted and turns away."

"Stay alert," I told them as we walked into the building. "It feels like hunting season today."

"Quack," said Max.

* * * * *

When the third period bell rang, I stayed in my seat. People elbowed and bumped and pushed me in the halls between classes, and I was sick of it. Why hurry and get beat on more?

Suddenly, the shriek of an eyeball-bursting alarm went off in my head. I realized it was the panic alert, and Gemma was pounding it again and again. My heart racing, I shot out of the room and into the hall, pushing and plowing through students myself for a change. I tore past the cafeteria into a section of unused classrooms and storage at the end of a long hall. As I rounded the corner, I saw a half-dozen guys and three girls surrounding Gemma. Ashley banged her against the wall while Logan tried to pull off her school blazer.

Running as fast as I could, I barreled into the group attacking her. Logan lost his grip on her jacket, hit the floor, and slid a few feet.

I stepped in front and pushed Ashley away from us. Gemma grabbed my shoulder and pulled to get ahead of me. She drew back her arm and loaded up her fist.

I grabbed her and dragged her toward the end of the hall. The others stood and watched. Guess they worried the odds had changed.

"What the hell?" she yelled at me.

As I tried to catch my breath, I held up her hand and touched the fleshy part on the side below her little finger. "Hit with this part." I made a fist and banged the wall three times to show her.

While I held her arm, I received a charge and visualized Max and Junie within ten steps of turning the corner. Another group of students were on their heels.

Gemma pulled her arm away from me as Ashley reached for her. Like pounding on a door, she smashed Ashley's nose twice. Blood burst out and she stumbled backwards. She grinned at me. "Didn't hurt a bit!"

Logan reached for Gemma, grabbing her left shoulder and pulling her towards him. That gave her fist more momentum as she swung sideways and clocked him hard in the temple. He dropped like a full trash bag.

Max and Junie arrived and punched, pushed, and kicked people in the mob away from me and Gemma. The crowd reformed and forced Max and Junie toward us. More students came, and they blocked the hall, trapping us.

"Are they stopping?" Max asked.

I eavesdropped on our attackers. "Chip wants to start the beatdown."

Max bounced on his toes in a boxing stance. My adrenalin surge made me clench and unclench my fists, but we needed something more than our hands or we'd never get out of this alive.

"Does your mother use voodoo needles in dolls?"

"What? You wanna talk cliches now?"

"Imagine a voodoo needle and use your power to shoot it into Logan's leg."

Max stared at Logan, who was still struggling to his feet after Gemma's punch. He rubbed his fingers together as if rolling a needle between them, then flicked it at Logan's left leg.

Logan screamed as if Max shot him. His leg buckled, and he fell again, hard.

"Damn!" said Max. He twirled his imaginary needle, threw it, and another attacker dropped to the floor crying.

More students arrived, so we retreated as far as possible into a dead end. A solid wall of angry classmates trapped us, so we'd have to fight through at least fifteen people to escape.

I spotted Chip's head above the crowd. "Get'em!" he yelled, his new teeth flashing white as he pushed the pack forward.

A few swung and grabbed at us. I blocked one wild swing with my right forearm and hammered my fist down and crunched a nose way over to one side. Brandon covered his face with both hands and fell back, crying.

I looked over at Max as someone hit me in the face, and I wobbled and dropped to one knee. I twisted to catch who hit me but saw Chip throttling Gemma. His arms shook with the effort to squeeze the life out of her. The world burned raging red, and the only thing I could see was him crushing her slim, freckled neck. I bulldozed through the mob, backhanded a face without even looking at who it was, and rammed him at full speed. He let go of her throat and she collapsed, gasping and coughing. He staggered back a few steps but stayed on his feet.

I looked at my fist, imagined Chip's broken nose and new teeth, and a shimmery green outline flew from my hand and smashed into his face. The huge bully yelled and fell backwards. He sat up and shook his head, flinging blood everywhere.

I yelled, "You assholes stop this now!" The mob grew louder and surged forward. Junie backhanded one boy just as a girl hit her in the jaw. She dropped but bounced up again. Max howled and threw needles into two guys reaching for her. Both stumbled backwards, screeching from the pain. Behind the mob, lacrosse sticks waved in the air. It looked as if the entire team came to join the attack.

Gemma was still on the ground, and I elbowed a girl in the forehead before she kicked her. "This is your last warning. Back off!" I yelled. I helped her to her feet and absorbed the jolt of energy between us, stronger this time, with a welcome shot of extra anger.

I looked at my hands and imagined my huge First Four Fists and banged them together to make a crash louder than the screaming mob. With my giant left shimmery fist I bludgeoned two classmates pummeling Max from each side. I used my right hand to grab a girl as she pulled Junie's hair with one hand and punched her with the other. The fist lifted her into the air and threw her into the crowd. Two guys fell as she banged into them and they slid backwards on the tile floor.

That left an opening large enough for a few lacrosse players to attack. Preston swung his stick right at Gemma's face. My green hand grabbed the weapon from his hands, and I used it to crack him in the head: bang, bang, bang, bang. He slumped, tripping Jacob, who dropped his stick and put his hands out to break his fall.

My giant hand caught him and used him like a baseball bat to knock the next three lacrosse players sideways. The four of them slammed into the wall and sprawled in a heap.

Chip, bleeding from where his new teeth had been, screamed and lunged at me. I grabbed him with both green hands and smashed him to the floor. His breath exploded out in a spray of blood from his mangled nose and mouth.

I was so pissed I didn't care who got in my way or how badly I hurt them as I threw him right into the screaming mob. Chip became my bowling ball, crashing through the pins. I made a strike, sweeping the bully from side to side, wall to wall, scattering everyone attacking us. Then I slid him, cursing and crying the whole way, as far down the hall as I could. He slammed into the wall at the corner so hard a metal-framed poster hanging above him fell, missing his face by two inches.

Three assistant principals came running, blowing whistles at ear-piercing volume. One stayed with Chip while the other two checked on the students I'd flattened.

More teachers arrived. The principal, Madame Polsova, picked her way through the prone bodies of moaning students. She stared straight at me. *"What do you think you're doing?"*

Still breathless, I raised an eyebrow. *"Defending ourselves against the mob you sent to kill us!"* I yelled back.

"I ordered no one, and I'm calling the police to arrest you."

I pointed to three round domes with 360 degree security cameras inside spaced along the hallway ceiling. *"Remember our meeting with Chloe? Ready to show the videos in court to explain how four of us crushed the two dozen people attacking us?"*

I sensed her barrier go up and could see the shimmer around her thoughts. *"I better get to the office and delete these videos before I call."*

"You can't get to your office fast enough to delete the files. Good luck explaining telekinesis in court."

Her jaw dropped. "You can't do that!" she said out loud.

"And yet I did." My pulse still pounding in my ears, I picked up my backpack and stepped around a girl moaning on the floor. Max, Junie, and Gemma followed me.

"You either told these people to attack us or turned away to make it easy for them. I'm guessing the Council gave the order, and you followed like a good little soldier," I thought to her.

"There's no truth in your accusations!"

I walked to her and got in her face. "You're scared of what's on the video. So are the bastards who ordered this attack. You always tell us to stand tall and make moral decisions. Time for you to do the same and tell the Council to leave us the hell alone."

It was easy to walk through the crowd since our attackers lay on the floor or slumped against the wall. When I got to Chip, he was groggy but awake, propped in a half-sitting position. I drew back my leg as if I was going to kick him. He whimpered and cowered and gasped in pain with the sudden movement.

The assistant principal standing over him grabbed my arm. "His new teeth are missing, and I believe you broke several of his ribs."

I flung him away from me. "He was choking my friend to death. He's lucky to be alive." I squatted in front of the bleeding brute. "This is the second time you tried to kill me and lived to tell about it. Next time you won't." I watched the blood drip onto the floor from the holes in his gums as he avoided looking at me. "One more thing. If you ever touch Gemma again, I'll bury your body parts in each of the five boroughs."

The four of us marched through the hall past stunned students and headed toward the front door. Classmates from the cafeteria followed, and students poured from their rooms to gawk but stayed against the walls out of our way. I felt my cheek and my fingers came away bloody. Max and Junie bled from cuts on their faces and hands as well. Gemma's split lip was bleeding.

I pulled out my phone. "Bunny? Got any bandages? Great. We're on our way."

"What the hell was that?" croaked Gemma through her bruised throat and bloody lip. I held her arm as she wobbled.

"The Grigori Council just declared war."

Chapter 33: Caroline's Choice

We were quiet, numb, and shocked on the ride to Bunny's apartment. When we arrived, she and her maid looked over each of us and tended our cuts and bruises.

"Nydia was an EMT back in Mexico," Bunny explained.

"You put cream on Paul and Gemma's cuts," Nydia told her, so she swabbed Polysporin on my cheek and closed the cut with two butterfly bandages. "Your eye will go black then full Technicolor in the next few days," she said, patting my face.

"Technicolor?"

"You kids need to read a history book."

She checked Gemma's split lip. "Sorry I can't put a bandage over your mouth."

"Mom might pay you to do that."

Bunny laughed. "The cuts aren't much, but they'll hurt for a while. Here's an ointment you can apply."

Nydia wrapped Max and Junie's right hands. "You two are lucky. People often break these bones." She touched the top of Junie's hands.

Gemma made a fist and hit the table with the fleshy part of her hand. "Paul showed me. You pound just as hard with this part of your fist, but you don't mess up your hand."

Max held up his wrapped right hand and struggled to make a fist with the tight bandage. "Yeah, but you do serious damage with the knuckles."

She put her fist against his. "One short chop and I broke Ashley's nose. It cracked when I hit her."

"Brunette Ashley or blonde Ashleigh?" asked Junie.

"Brunette Ashley."

"Good. Bitch deserves a beating."

I pounded the table with my hand as well. "I mashed Brandon's nose sideways, and backhanded somebody this way. They dropped like a rock."

Max turned to me. "Yeah, but at the end, how did you do it?"

"What?"

"Throw everybody around like dolls. I know you're a Mover, but kids went flying."

"Excuse me, did you say he threw students telekinetically?" asked Bunny.

He nodded, along with Junie and Gemma.

"If I hadn't, they would've killed us." I didn't dare tell them my heart was pounding when I tried. Hitting Chip at the pool was one thing, but fighting off an angry mob? No clue if it would work.

"I've never heard of anyone able to throw another person."

"I can't move more than a few pounds," Max said.

My phone rang as I shrugged. I saw it was my mother, frowned, and rejected the call. "I guess the school called Mom."

Bunny's phone buzzed a few seconds later. She answered. "Yes, Caroline, he's fine. In fact–" She listened and turned to look at me. "Which hospital?" She hung up. "Someone attacked your father. Mugged. Stabbed. He's at New York Presbyterian Lower Manhattan. This was how the Grigori killed your grandfather. They disguised it as a mugging."

"But my parents aren't on our side. They want to stop me."

"This is a warning, or he'd be in the morgue. I guess Holden or the Grigori leadership believe they should do more to derail your efforts."

I hurried to the door, then turned back and asked Gemma, "Can you ... whatever?"

"Of course," she said.

Bunny put her arm around Gemma's shoulder. "I'll make sure everyone stays safe and gets home."

"That was one helluva fight," Max declared as Paul left.

"That's for damn sure," Junie added. "Did I see Paul knock Chip flying when he choked you?" she asked Gemma.

"Just in time, too. Things were going black, and I thought it was the end."

"My man comes through when it counts," said Max. "But I wish he'd turned them all into bowling pins before somebody knocked me brooly."

Gemma coughed, and Bunny got her a glass of water. "Thanks."

She put her hand on Gemma's. "You have odd emotions concerning Paul. Conflicted. Angry sometimes."

"There were a few angry years. Me at him."

"He mentioned you two had reset or something. Now you're more positive but still nervous and worried about his feelings for you."

"Wow, he promised he'd never lie to me and always be honest. He must've gotten that from you."

"Paul means what he says, period" said Max.

"He doesn't give little bullshit excuses and shade the truth like some people," said Junie. She bopped Max on the top of his head.

"I knew that was coming. Maybe I can predict the future now."

"Nydia, could you bring these tired kids the lemonade, please?" Bunny asked.

"Who said get over the sixth grade crap and find somebody decent for a change?" asked Junie.

"You just want us to double," laughed Gemma. "Like going skating back in middle school."

Junie pulled Max up from the table. "Let's go get that lemonade."

When they were out of earshot, Bunny put her hand on Gemma's. "You're an interesting girl. If you accept how special you are, you'll become a fascinating young woman."

Gemma didn't react for a moment and took a deep breath. "I'm not sure if that's the best compliment I've ever gotten, or the worst insult."

"Sorry, I get carried away sometimes, and I'm more protective of Paul since this started. Before, you thought he was weak. What do you think now?"

"Chip is at least fifty pounds heavier than him, but he threw himself into him and knocked him off of me."

"You and Paul have an interesting dynamic. Your emotions tangle together, and that means a strong bond." Bunny wove her fingers around like she was knitting.

"When he grabbed my arm at school, there was an electrical charge. It happened again today when he helped me up, but it was stronger."

"I've never heard of that."

"All I know is, if Paul wasn't way tougher than I thought, plan my funeral. I guess some guys talk tough and other guys just are."

"Oh, my dear, the guys who talk tough always fold in a crisis. The quiet ones corner the market on courage."

* * * * *

I burst through the Emergency entrance, searched for my mother, and found her as a doctor holding a tablet walked up. "He's our son," Mom said.

The doctor tucked a strand of long brown hair back under her cap. "Your husband is lucky, or his mugger is new at this. There are two wounds. One is a lengthy cut on the right side, from below the armpit to the hip. Odd, and we never see cuts like that. The blade didn't penetrate when the laceration reached the abdomen, so the attacker did it on purpose."

She checked her tablet. "There's a stab wound on the outside of his left thigh. In his vastus lateralis, the big muscle on the side, but it didn't hit any arteries."

"So, he's not in danger?" asked Mom.

"Neither injury is life-threatening, but both will be painful for a couple weeks. I'm going to keep him overnight just in case."

"Of course."

"We'll get him upstairs in the next hour." She left through a door labeled Staff Only.

I took Mom's arm and led her over to the waiting lounge chairs. She stared into the distance for a moment before noticing my bandages.

She touched my left cheek. "Oh my god, what happened?"

"Big fight at school."

"Chip again?"

"Him and two dozen others. They cornered me, Gemma, Max, and Junie. We were lucky to get out alive. They were trying to take us out."

"You mean hurt you?"

"Hurt? Way more. Chip choked Gemma half to death. They were attacking and trying to kill us."

173

She turned and stared into the distance for a moment. "This is a nightmare."

"Yeah." Thinking of the fight, and Dad getting attacked at roughly the same time, made me more determined to make Grigori leadership pay for their crimes. I hoped Mom was ready to help me now.

She turned and grabbed my chin with one hand and forced me to look at her. "This is the nightmare you caused!"

I pulled away. "Me? Bunny says they're sending a message."

"Not so loud. Of course. They're telling you to stop your nonsense before someone gets killed."

"Before? Should we ask Jenkins?"

She closed her eyes and exhaled. "Your father's not here so there's no reason to get angry."

"I think I can damn well be pissed at whatever Grigori leader has tried to kill me two different times!"

"You need to stop your crazy crusade before they succeed. I don't want to lose you and I don't want to lose your father. I demand you stop this nonsense right now."

"No."

"What?"

"Hell no. Demand all you want, but I'm not stopping."

Her eyes narrowed and she slapped me, hard, across my newly-bandaged cut.

"Hey!"

"This is more serious than you realize, so don't make snap decision like a soft-brained child. The wrong choice will force other people to make decisions you won't enjoy."

"People like you and Dad?"

"Yes, and others."

"Who's giving you orders? Grigori Council? That who's been spying on me?"

"I can't say, but you have to end this."

"No way."

"This is serious, Paul. Stop, please. You must stop."

"I already said no."

She stared at me for a moment, biting her lip. The she nodded to herself, stood, and pointed to the door. "Go away. Get out of my sight!"

"OK, OK. See you at home later? Or will you stay in the hospital with Dad?"

"You don't understand. Go home, pack a bag, and go the hell away. Get out of our lives."

"What?"

"I have to choose a side, and I choose your father."

"Wait, what?"

"You are no longer our son."

Chapter 34: Home Invasion Reversal

The pile of clothes on my bed wouldn't fit in my gym bag. I needed to steal a larger one in a tiny act of defiance.

The elevator bell dinged as I grabbed the bag from my parent's closet. That made no sense. Both my parents were in the hospital twenty minutes ago, with Dad still in the emergency room. The doctor said he'd be there overnight. Why were they home?

I sensed their emotions to check how angry they were, and my discovery sent chills down my spine. The two in the elevator were NOT Mom and Dad.

Something muffled the two men's mental activities, as if their brains were distant and wrapped in barbed wire. There was intensity, but no clear thoughts or emotions.

A single burst of three gunshots blasted from my room, chased by three more shots, loud as hell. Shit! I dropped to the floor and crabbed away from the door, gulping air like crazy.

I heard the intruders kick open my bathroom and fire six more bullets. Each three-shot burst made me jerk and hug the floor. As loud as those shots were, my heart pounded even louder.

I knew there was a baseball bat in the closet, but assault weapons always beat bats. My only chance to escape alive were my First Four fists.

Crawling back to the bedroom door, I stuck my head past the door frame. I saw two figures in black and crawled back as quick as I could. Six more shots slammed into the wall and floor where my head was seconds ago.

I scrambled as fast as my fear-heavy legs allowed and dove behind the bed. The hit men burst into the room, automatic assault weapons blazing.

I Moved their gun barrels up, so the bullets hit the wall above me and stitched holes up to the ceiling. I smashed a giant fist into each of them. They flew backwards out the door and slammed into the hallway wall. I grabbed one in each huge hand and hammered them to the floor once and twice and again and again for good measure.

I waited and watched for two minutes, hiding behind the bed, until I felt safe enough to crawl closer. The pause helped my heart rate slow, but the cold sweat down my back increased.

Both wore black military clothes, with bullet-proof vests and belts hung heavy with magazine clips and lethal-looking items I'd never seen. The gunpowder residue stung my eyes and burned my lungs as I struggled to breathe. I kicked their assault rifles out of reach, and my overwhelming fear twisted and flipped to anger.

"Bastards!" I screamed at the unconscious attackers and kicked the helmet of the man closest to me. He didn't move. I booted him again and his helmet flew off and my heart raced.

The helmet bounced off the wall and careened through the hallway. After my heart rate slowed, I retrieved it. Something struck me as odd, but I wasn't sure what. Wes and Elena might investigate these weapons for evidence that could help us. Once my legs stopped shaking, I got the large gym bag and gloves from my parent's room.

Both helmets and assault rifles fit in the big bag, as did two handguns the men carried. One was a Glock like Elena showed us, while the other was larger and heavier.

I heard a rustle behind me as I was closing the bag. Whipping around, I saw the man without his helmet pull a knife from his boot and leap towards me.

My green fist backhanded him into the wall, then scooped him up and slammed him to the floor three more times. He lay motionless, bleeding from cuts on his cheek and out of his nose. The knife fell from his unconscious fingers. I put that one and one still sheathed above the other killer's boot in the bag.

I tied the men to a column in the elevator foyer using their own plastic handcuffs. Both were so out of it I probably gave them concussions. Tough luck. They were still breathing, and that was more than they deserved.

The small gym bag had room to hold the few clothes without bullet holes I had left. What type of bag would EMTs zip my body into if that pile of shirts and pants had been me? That thought made my heart pound again. Mental powers or not, bullets beat bodies every time. Luck was on my side, at least so far, but that didn't keep my knees from shaking.

177

When I dropped the two bags by the elevator, I realized what I saw that bothered me on the helmet. I pulled one from the bag and held it up to the light. There was a fine metal mesh woven into the transparent plastic face shield. It was a Faraday Cage, and we just studied those in AP Physics. The wires blocked electromagnetic signals such as telepathic connections.

There was only one reason to wear a helmet with that type of protection: to block mental signals from their telepathic victims. If my only ability was to Push, the helmets would block my commands, and the assassins would send their three-shot bursts of bullets screaming into my body as I Pushed them in vain to stop. The only reason I was alive was because the mesh in the helmet didn't block my Mover power.

Who sent these men? The Grigori Council, the group my parents served their entire lives. The people my mother refused to admit were giving her orders. My legs became numb, and I fell back against the wall and slid to the floor. Classmates attacking us were depressing enough. Trained killers assigned by the Council to stop me? This attack ramped up my fear and nerves to a crazy new level.

I took photos of the bullet holes and verified the men were still breathing. It hit me I might never walk into my apartment again. That caused my blood to run cold. Banned from the home I grew up in?

Never have dinner with my family in the dining room again? Or my aunts and uncles and cousins? I remembered how Lance and Quinn and I, when we were little, ran giggling through the house and piled in one bed together trying to stay warm during the winter. Not count my presents next to Lance and Quinn's under the Christmas tree in the corner? The Grigori killed my remembrances of growing up surrounded by a loving family, because they no doubt leaned heavily on my parents to stop me. They trashed my hopes of ever returning home again and ruined the memories of my childhood. I wiped the corners of my eyes and pushed the elevator button for the last time.

In the lobby, I called 9-1-1 and reported two burglars breaking into my apartment and gave my address. If the police didn't believe me, my parents would have a big surprise to deal with when they got home. Then I texted Max, telling him people had attacked me, and asked him to warn everyone else to be extra careful.

When I passed Darrell's office, I noticed a few red spots on the floor, and his always-open door was mostly closed. I walked over and found larger red spots. I held my breath and pushed the door open.

Darrell slumped motionless against the wall. Red splotches in the front of his uniform had long cuts in the middle, so my attackers must've used their knives on him. His eyes were wide, staring at infinity. The smell of blood and death invaded my nose, and I dropped the bags. There was nothing I could do, that anybody could do, for him.

I balled my fists and hit my thighs over and over. Dead, right in front of me. Dead, as I'd be if I didn't have more powers than anyone guessed. Dead, never again able to tell me to have a splendid day, welcome me home after school, and ask if I needed help every single time I saw him. Dead, in a cramped office he occupied ten hours a day, surrounded by delivery boxes for residents. Just. So. Dead.

Numb, I called 9-1-1 again and reported that someone attacked our doorman and please send an ambulance. With a handful of clothes in one hand and a handful of death in the other, I zombie-walked out and past the steps into the darkness and stood motionless, with no idea what to do next.

Chapter 35: End of the Night

I don't know how long I stood there, brain-locked and motionless. A couple strolled by, then a guy with his dog. I saw them, kind of, but couldn't move or smile or wave.

A woman walked up and stopped in front of me, but I just stared past her. Then she shook my arm.

"Paul? You OK? What's wrong?"

"Gemma!" I dropped both bags and wrapped my arms around her, holding tight to keep myself steady.

"OK, OK. I need to breathe."

"No, it's not OK, they killed him."

"Who killed who? You're talking crazy."

"The guys upstairs, it's, it's, not OK, they, they must've murdered Darrell on the way up to me."

"Who's Darrell? Somebody's dead? Are you OK? Did that bag clank?" She kicked the larger bag, and it clanked again. "What's in there?"

"What I'm trying to tell you that just happened in my place." I pulled the zipper open. Even though the assault rifles were black, the metal reflected the streetlights.

"Shit! Where'd you get those guns?"

"From the men who tried to kill me ten minutes ago. The ones who killed Darrell."

"What? Who's Darrell?"

"Our doorman." A police siren wailed in the distance. "We've got to disappear. I can't talk to any cops."

She grabbed my arm. "C'mon."

After we turned a corner, she asked, "Two guys came to your house carrying those guns?"

"Yeah, and knives."

"We must've pissed off lots of people. Hope that means we're doing the right thing."

I stopped. "Shit. How'd they got the elevator code?"

"Your doorman has it, right?"

That was a kick to the head. They killed him because of me! My chest was so tight it was tough to talk. "Shit."

"Anyone else know your code?"

"Holden."

"How did you get away from them? Those barely visible fists you used at school?"

"That's twice today they saved me."

Her phone buzzed, and she showed me the text. "Max says I should be careful because people are trying to 'hut' you."

"That's why I help him on his English papers."

"Ah, not chicken or whatever, but should we worry a hit squad will come for us?"

"No, I've heard Holden's ideas on this stuff over and over. Cut off the head off the snake and his other *Art of War* crap. He's after me."

"And the doorman?"

"Just in the way, I guess. Damn, that sucks."

Suddenly, my knees buckled as my adrenaline rush drained away. She caught me before I fell to the sidewalk and steered me to a bus bench. "You're shivering. Cold?" She sat and put her arm around me. "Deep breaths. Relax."

Her arm circling my waist and her body against mine helped. Breathing became easier.

I pulled up the photos for her to see. "These bullet holes are from the two men Holden sent to kill me. Or someone ordered."

"Damn! Glad you got out of there in one piece."

"Gonna send these to Mom."

"You don't want to add anything?"

"Like what?"

"Like, 'Say hello to my little friend,' or 'Yippee-ki-yay-motherfucker,' or something?"

"Funny, but Mom's not big on movie quotes." I typed, "Tell him if he tries again, it'll piss me off."

She moved my hand so she could read the text. "OK. That works. Do you know which 'him' is after you?"

"Holden, I'm sure, but what matters is that she knows." I took a few more deep breaths and stood. "I can walk now."

We walked slower than earlier. "How's your Dad?" she asked.

"I didn't get to see him. Doctor said the long cut down his right side, over his ribs, was strange."

181

"Not stabbed? Cut?"

"Yeah. Stab wound in the big muscle of the left thigh, but not near any arteries. Back to normal in a couple weeks."

"Maybe what Bunny said, a warning?" she said. "Cuts on both sides? I sleep on my side. If your Dad does, he'll have trouble sleeping."

"That's pretty devious. Remind me not to piss you off if you've got a knife."

"Try not to piss me off no matter what. Hey, what's in the other bag? Grenades or something?"

"Oh, yeah, that. My clothes that aren't full of bullet holes. Mom told me to leave and never come back, and I'm not their son anymore."

She pulled me to a stop and looked into my eyes. "Thrown out? Disowned? No shit?"

"Her exact words were 'You are no longer our son.' Ordered me to clear out before Dad gets out of the hospital."

"OK, that sucks big time. Like, damn, double cold."

"I'll go back to Bunny's," I said when we reached her building. "I have stuff in her guest room."

"You're not going anywhere alone." She took my small bag from me. "It's OK. Parents are at a chef's retreat until tomorrow afternoon. And you're still shaky. Eaten anything since school?"

"Can't remember."

"What I thought. My family feeds people. C'mon." Before I could protest, she cut me off. "No arguing."

Her apartment was smaller than mine but had a homey quality. Once inside, she warmed up some pizza, and we ate without speaking, both too overwhelmed to talk.

I swiped the last piece of crust left on her plate and chewed on it.

"Better?"

"Yeah, but, well, no. A few weeks ago, everything was great. Now it's all gone to hell."

"That night in the park you were all sad dog because you had a fight with your parents. Oh, damn, sorry."

"Right, back in the good old days when I had parents."

"And groups of people didn't hate us."

"Listen to me whining about my problems while you sit there with bruises around your neck after Chip almost killed you. Sorry I dragged you into this." Remembering his hands squeezing her throat and her hitting futilely at his arms hurt deep down in my chest.

She touched her neck. "A little concealer and it's gone. And you didn't drag me into anything, because you never wanted me in the group. I saw your face when I walked into the diner with Junie and Max. But things have to improve and I believe in what we're doing."

"When we talked in the park, I told you what worried me, how I struggled with the mess I was in. Why'd I do that? We weren't friendly. Why tell you tonight I'm scared this fight I started will turn into a giant dumpster fire? Get people hurt or worse? I almost got you killed earlier. All of us killed."

"You can handle this. Broad shoulders and all that." Her voice sounded confident, but she touched her bruised neck.

"I never realized how deep that Beatles song is. Yesterday all my troubles were, well, zero. Today I'm in deep shit, dragging my friends with me." I focused on my shoes. "People still want to kill me. Kill us. How do I handle this?"

I shook my head and stared into her eyes. "I don't tell people how I feel. What've you done to me?"

"Helped you grow? Mature and get in touch with your emotions?"

"Growing up sucks. Had no clue what I was getting into when I started this. Now I'm Indiana Jones in the tunnel and that round boulder's rolling toward me, but I'm caught in a bear trap and can't run away."

"Hey, look at me." I did what she ordered. "Your grandmother fought all of society for her rights as a woman, while she rebelled against the idiot men running the Grigori. Bunny didn't give up and neither can you."

She stood and grabbed the smaller of my bags. "C'mon." I followed her into her bedroom where she stacked both bags out of the way and waved toward a small desk with a chair. She sat crossed-legged on the bed.

"Hard to believe Mom threw me out. My mother? My father, yeah, I can see that. But Mom? Can't get a grip."

"You said she picked your father over you?"

"How could she do that?"

"Mom says some Grigori women prefer to let the men do their thinking. Others can fend for themselves."

"What about you?"

"We've met, right? I can take care of myself. Except against an angry mob. That's when it's good to have friends." She rubbed her bruises. "Real good."

"Yeah, friends are great. Better to have friends who don't get you attacked by mobs."

"But you came when I needed you." She patted the bed. I moved and sat close. We looked into each other's eyes for a long time. She shifted closer and her breath caressed my cheek. Her eyes were the deepest green I'd ever seen. Glad I was sitting, because my knees went wobbly.

She finally grabbed my shirt, pulled me to her, and kissed me. Her lips, warm and inviting, erased my fears.

"Ow, ow, ow," she said. "Sorry." She patted her split lip.

Great, more guilt for getting her involved. "Relax and let me kiss you." I pulled her close and kissed her chin, her forehead, and last, her nose. She laughed, deep in her throat.

She kissed her index finger and touched it to the bandage on my cheek. I took her hand and held her palm to my lips. She uncrossed her legs, lay back on the bed, and pulled me down beside her.

"Didn't say you could stop," she whispered.

I brushed her lips with the pressure of a butterfly landing, and her cheek twice. I raised up on my elbow and grazed her beautiful lips again, kissed her cheek several times, before moving to a spot just under her ear. Made a trail of soft, soft kisses down her neck, careful to avoid her bruises, and reached the little hollow at her collarbone. She shivered and matched the flutters inside me.

"OK," she said, shifting away a bit. "You better rest, because I don't know how you're still going. Fought off a mob at school for lunch and two armed killers at home for dinner."

"More tired than forever." I put my head on the pillow and my arm out. She turned on her side and put her head beside mine, facing me. Her neck warmed my arm.

"This is nice," she whispered, and kissed my cheek.

She put her hand on my chest, patted me twice, and left it there. I said, "More than nice. This is amazing," but I'm not sure the words made it past my lips before I fell asleep.

Chapter 36: The World Is New

In my dreams, or nightmares, people attacked me on every side. Fellow students, men in military uniforms, people who used to love me like my parents, and even Holden. I struggled to wake up, like a man underwater desperate to reach the surface. Things were different, more than the strange bed and the leg laying against mine. Stronger than ever, my powers stretched out, sensing people throughout the building and in buildings near me. I sensed scores of people planning their day, and I closed my mental door to block the noise.

Most important, Gemma was near, mentally and physically. Memories of kissing her made me smile and open my eyes.

"About time," said a face so close it was out of focus. She was up on one elbow and smiling.

Her green eyes sparkled brighter than emeralds in a forest of red hair and freckles. "The light shines through your wavy hair and gives you a red halo," I said.

"I'm an angel now? I'll take that." She smiled, leaned closer, and kissed me.

"Maybe."

She kissed me again, then slid over and lay on top of me. After a moment, she sat up, straddling me, and kissed me again. Her lips were softer and more inviting than last night. I tugged her shirt.

She kept kissing me, her long red hair making a curtain around our heads. The red-tinged darkness made my heart race. She sat up, unbuttoned my shirt and spread it open, and my heart skipped a few beats.

"Yesterday was the worst day ever with the fight at school, and your day was even more dangerous. Let's celebrate living through that shit, OK? Make this a better day?"

She locked her eyes on mine, unbuttoned her shirt, and threw it in the corner. Her bra followed. She leaned over to kiss me again, her breasts warm on my chest. Staying on me, kissing my neck, she pulled a condom out of her nightstand drawer.

When she sat back up, I only managed a hoarse whisper. "Can, uh, I–" I tried to keep looking at her eyes, but kept looking lower.

"Ms. Brantley would object and tell you to say 'May I' but we're not in class. And I'm on top, so ... I guess I should ask."

"Yes. Whatev–"

She put her finger on my lips. "Talk less, sex more."

* * * * *

We lay still, legs intertwined, deep breaths making our chests rise and fall in sync. I decided I'd face armed killers every day if this came afterward.

My excitement refused to stay bottled up. "I was stupid not to talk to you. We should've been together for years. I wasted all that time with Lucy when I could've been with you."

"What? One time and I belong to you? Are you Cronk the Caveman?"

"No, no, I just meant–"

Laughing, she said, "Teasing you is way more fun than hating you."

"I like it better, too."

We lay still again. She ran her fingers through my chest hair.

"Oh, oh, oh." She propped herself up on her elbow again and grinned at me. "You've only had sex with Lucy, right? You think we're steadies because that's what happened with her!"

I tried to stop my blush before it showed on my face, but failed. My lips tightened and my cheeks flushed. She laughed at me, but in a friendly way, and her smile lingered when she stopped.

After my cheeks cooled, I cleared my throat. "We were sixteen when we started dating. Hooked up on my seventeenth birthday. I thought it was sweet, but found out she forgot to buy me a present. She was more fun to unwrap than a shirt, so it worked out."

"That's almost funny."

"Thanks. I wondered about her, us, seven or eight months later. I was unhappy but hated to cause any problems and disappoint my parents. Just thought I'd ride it out and make sure we picked different colleges."

"You were seventeen! It's your job to disappoint your parents!"

"Heard some rumors she was, you said it, a slut."

"Saw her myself at Brandon's Christmas party."

"We were with family in Los Angeles, but I saw the video. Stabbed me in the heart and the bleeding didn't stop for a loooong time. Breaking Brandon's nose yesterday felt great." I smiled, then stopped. "Sorry, that's a terrible thing to say."

"No, no, not at all. Made me happy to bash a few people, too. They deserved it. Especially Brandon, because he knew he shouldn't hit on Lucy, but he did anyhow."

"I blame him some, but I blame her more."

"Sometimes girls make stupid mistakes."

"They shouldn't. But I'm still scared of what we're doing. Put you and Max and Junie in danger." I shook my head. "Man, I just have to tell you things I never tell anybody. But talking to you is so easy." I poked her on the shoulder. "Sure you're not a witch or something?"

"Only when somebody pisses me off, and I told you that's a terrible idea." She sat up and grabbed a three-inch tall Raggedy Ann figure on top of a circular base from her nightstand.

"See this? My grandfather gave it to me, the non-Grigori one. He always taught me that when you fall..." she pushed the bottom of the base. The strings holding the doll got longer, and the figure collapsed into a heap ... "you get up again." She released the bottom, and a spring forced the base down and pulled the figure upright. She did it two more times. "Fall down, get up. Fall down, get up."

She walked to the bathroom. "I'll shower first. Your turn while I make breakfast."

* * * * *

I came out of her room wearing clean clothes and damp hair. My nose led me to the kitchen.

She put two plates of scrambled eggs and bacon on the table beside glasses of orange juice. I took a forkful, and the taste exploded on my tongue. "These are incredible."

She shrugged. "A few spices."

"Right. Your dad's a chef and owns a restaurant."

"You actually listened and remembered what I said? Nice."

After finishing my last bite of bacon, my worries returned. I looked at my shoes and asked, "Why me?"

"Aaahhh, well—"

"Why did I get all these extra powers?"

"Oh, powers."

My shoes didn't answer, so I looked at Gemma. "I never asked for any of this. If I didn't hear my parent's Inside Voice through their blocks, we wouldn't be in this mess. Nobody told me about any powers and I got'em all. Why not Max? Junie? You?"

She pulled her chair around to face me and held my hands. "I don't know how this happened or why you won the telepath lottery. But of all the Grigori at school, you do the right thing most often. Corny, yeah, but true."

"Max would do better. You said yourself he's the leader, not me."

"I did say that, but I was, I was, well, wrong. About that, and about you. I love Max, but he doesn't have your honesty, basic decency, and self-control. Not Junie, either. Sure as hell not me. You're the only one of us who can carry this load."

How could I stay sad after hearing that from Gemma, of all people? "Amazing. I'm beginning to think you almost like me now."

"We've gotten a lot, ah, closer. And if you tell anybody I said those things, I'll call you a rat-faced liar."

That made me laugh loud enough to silence my doubts. I squeezed her hands. "What are we going to do today?"

She squeezed back. "Just like every day, Pinky, we're going to try to take over the world!"

"You're the Brain? Cool. What's next, boss."

"I remembered how scared Madame Polsova was about the video."

"Yeah. What scares the Grigori leaders?"

"Being discovered." She poured me more juice.

"They've been hiding crimes left and right, but they're always worried of news of us getting out."

She put the dishes in the sink. I stood and shook my head.

"What's wrong?"

"Earlier I felt stronger, like my powers were turbo-charged. Not now."

She patted my cheek. "Did I wear the poor boy out?"

"There it is again!" I said, and she jumped back.

"It's gone!" I reached for her hand. "I can't believe it! When I touch you, it makes my powers stronger. Like I'm Super Mario and hit a power-up star."

"Multi-power showoff," she said, staring into the distance.

Suddenly I was standing in the lobby of a building. I couldn't do remote viewing before, but that was her power. She had visuals only, but I heard people talking.

"Damn," she said. "I can hear while remote viewing when I touch you!"

"I can see and hear. Remote viewing is bonkers!"

"This is amazing, no, better than amazing. I don't feel like a half-breed anymore! I've got a full power! Not a great one, but at least it works."

"I couldn't do it at all. Max said it's handy if you want to spy on people."

She looked at me. "OK, something happens when we touch, right?"

"I like it, but it's more than just fun. And the feeling gets stronger every time. When I shook your hand after we met in the park, it was faint." I gave her an eyebrow waggle. "You called it flop sweat."

"That it wasn't, based on the last twenty-four hours."

I counted on my fingers. "Killer mob at school, Dad attacked, no longer have a Dad or Mom, assassins. Believe me, you're the best part of my week no contest."

She smiled, but it thinned out and disappeared. "We need to work out a few things, OK? At least I do. Please don't make a big deal out of this yet, OK?"

My chest tightened and my happiness vanished. "Ah, well, I hoped for something more positive. Is this kinda weird for you?"

She sighed. "I mean, I don't regret it, at all, but there's a major roller coaster going on inside me right now."

"Hope it doesn't make you puke. That would really ruin the mood."

"Where's that funny guy been hiding? I like him. But what do we do now? I damn sure don't want to set foot in school."

I squeezed her hand again. "We try and take over the world."

"Let's go see your grandmother and start making plans."

Chapter 37: Forget the Media

On the way to Bunny's, I got a text from Max and Gemma got one from Junie. We agreed to meet there.

Bunny greeted the two of us at the door. When she saw us together, she gave us an enormous smile.

"Do I smell coffee with a dash of cinnamon?" Gemma asked.

"Her Dad's a chef," I said.

"That explains her clever nose. Come have a cup."

Gemma sniffed the coffee before she drank it. I followed her lead. The cinnamon added a pleasant twist.

"Wes and Elana are coming," Bunny said. "He wants a report of your, ah, fun at school."

"They'll love what's in that big bag, too," added Gemma.

Bunny held up the pot. "More coffee, dear?"

I said, "Max and Junie are in the building."

Nydia changed Max and Junie's hand wraps and bandages while Bunny put new butterfly bandages on me. Nydia soon brought in fresh-baked cinnamon rolls. Max and Junie hadn't taken time to eat, so they grabbed some. Gemma said she was fine. I wavered and finally took one.

"Hungry, huh?" she said as she poked me on the shoulder.

"Girl!" yelled Junie. "You two totally hooked up last night!"

I held up my hand. "No, we did NOT hookup last night."

Gemma seconded. "Nope. Nothing happened."

"It was this morning," I said.

Junie clapped her hands and bounced in her chair. Bunny kissed Gemma on the forehead while Max waggled his eyebrows at me.

"OK, don't make a major deal over this. After all these years of hating him, it feels weird to like him. And maybe admit I blew dumb kid stuff into something serious and stupid," she said. "There's this strange mix of feelings, but mostly good."

"I'm happy she's not giving me her Die-Paul-Die glare anymore. Turns out she has a gorgeous smile."

"Stop it! Too nice to me too soon! I need time!"

After we stopped laughing, I turned to my grandmother. "What do we do? The only thing we came up with before is to go public, or at least threaten. Now that they're trying to murder us, we have a story we can tell that will get plenty of attention."

"Can we give them a juicy story without explaining why they're trying to stop us?" Gemma asked. "Keep our powers out of the news?"

"Ahh, yes? No, probably not," I said.

Bunny took the pot and warmed up her coffee. "The Grigori leadership responds well to leverage. Exposure is their biggest fear and your best lever. The attack on you kids adds more details and increases your position."

"My parents say that leads to being turned into lab rats for the military," said Max.

"That's always been the bogeyman story they tell. But more people know about us, because there's more of us. We ourselves told Wes and Elena. Some in government know, and many top-level global business leaders work with us. No lab rats yet."

"But they're still scared of being outed?" Gemma asked.

"Oh, yes dear. You don't get a seat at the high stakes poker table when people know you cheat."

"So, losing money worries them the most?" I asked.

"Always." Bunny poured more coffee in Max's cup.

We all sat and sipped coffee, thinking about what to do next.

Junie caught Gemma's eye. *"Tell me everything."*

"Not sure—"

"Talk girl!"

"OK, OK. I promised Bunny I'd check on him, so I went by his building. While I tried to decide what to do, call or whatever, he came out, shaking, from guys trying to kill him."

"Damn."

"Worse. He had his clothes in another bag because his parents threw him out."

"Daaaaaaamn."

"Maybe we better check out the media companies and see if we can trust them," said Max.

Gemma nodded in agreement, then used her Inside Voice with Junie again. *"He was jittery and shaky and wired and exhausted all at once. Grabbed me like he was drowning. I had to hold him up and catch him one time before he fell. A mess. Just a giant ball of need—"*

"You hate that."

She thought for a second. *"Not needy like guys I date. They need attention, well, adoration, but Paul went through hell and just wanted someone there for him."*

"So, you took him, ah, where?"

"My place. Parents went to a retreat."

"Wait a sec, if he needed help last night, why did you wait until this morning?"

"He could barely walk, wrung out and overwhelmed after everything. Major upset they killed his doorman to get to him. We made out some, and he gave me shivers. That surprised me."

Max waved his phone. "I see lots of Grigori-type names in the list of tech executives, too."

"I'll bet" Junie replied.

"I woke up first, looked at him, and, well, he'd been through so much, and he saved my life..." She shook her head. *"Not that I owe him or something. But he was so cute asleep, so sweet. He's Mister Everything at school, everybody loves him, so why was I so focused on hate, hate, hate, for years and years? Since we started this crazy project, he's been more than nice. He treats me, and you, as equals and doesn't ignore us to make plans with Max then order us around after. Never talks over us or interrupts."*

"Hmmm, you're right. Hadn't realized that."

"At the diner he promised he'd never lie to me—"

"Never to his friends."

"Which makes him the first guy I've ever talked to three times who hasn't lied over something. So, I thought perhaps the problem was me, not him."

"Smart."

Gemma took a deep breath. *"First guy who ever touched me somehow, not just my body."*

"Wow, that's ah, interesting."

"And sex in the morning's a great way to start the day, right?"

Junie stifled a laugh like it was a cough. *"So, how was it?"*

"OK. Not bad at all. More shivers."

"High praise from you."

"You love this, don't you?"

"Told you he was a brilliant match and to give up whatever your grudge was. But somebody here is awful damn stubborn."

"You just want me to get with him so we could hang together."

"Of course! Best friends dating best friends is so symmetrical."

"It's not geometry class, it's love."

"Love!"

"Have you kids tried the newspapers?" Bunny asked.

Gemma shook her head vigorously, red ponytail flipping back and forth. *"We've got this weird connection and amplify each other's power. It's amazing. But don't say 'love' or I'll get my tennis racquet and backhand your face."*

"Old people social media?" I teased. "I'll look."

"You're right," said Junie. *"Not love at all. Nope. Nothing to see here. Wait, aren't you with that Italian guy from uptown?"*

"Don't think so, but he's ghosted and come back twice. Who knows?"

"Since I've been with Max, I know Paul way better. Warning, he's not the drama-filled asshole you usually date. Not his game."

"Sounds boring as hell. Can't wait to escape." She gave Junie a sly grin.

Junie pulled her laptop out of her backpack to join the search. When Gemma saw Junie's laptop, she got hers.

Junie also brought out the Grigori address book Bunny had given her. "Every big media company I've checked has a Grigori vice president."

After a few minutes, and multiple checks of the address book, I said, "Mainstream media sources have us on the payroll."

"Social net companies do as well, but only the biggest ones," added Gemma.

"Mind-reading posts are everywhere on Twitter and Instagram," said Max. "We could post there and the censorship bots won't catch all of them."

"You can leak little bits here and there," said Bunny. "In my day we spread things through gossip. Seems most social media is just evolved gossip."

"That makes sense." I looked at Gemma. "Make sense to you?"

"Yep. OK, we're here to make a plan, so let's go."

I stood. "You guys start. Wes and Elena are near the building."

Bunny got up as well. "Wes likes his coffee. I'll make more."

From the door, I said, "Hey, Max, check the Justice Department."

Bunny hugged Wes and Elena when they arrived and put coffee and cinnamon rolls in front of them. Elena took one and Wes grabbed two.

After a moment, Wes said, "Police reports have you guys started a riot in school yesterday."

"Does the report say how we could escape a mob? Including the lacrosse team with their sticks?" I asked.

"You sucker-punched those innocent children with baseball bats," said Elena.

"All two dozen of them?"

"No doubt we used our mad ninja skillz," said Max.

"What excuse did Makary give for no video?" Junie asked.

"They turned some over," Wes said. "We could tell at once they doctored it. Tried to fake a camera failure in that hallway."

Everyone sat quietly for a moment and sipped coffee.

"Did you get a report of what happened at my place last night?" I asked.

Wes and Elena shook their heads.

Did that mean a police cover-up? Not good. I told them my story of the two attackers in my apartment and dropped the bag of weapons between their chairs. Wes opened it and whistled.

"Heckler & Koch MP7, a NATO weapon. Armwest LLC M4, an improved version of the standard Army M4. Glock 17 and a Colt 1911."

"Nice combat Ka-Bar," said Elena, as she pulled on a latex glove to pick up a knife.

"Not when it's coming at you." The memory of that angry guy, with teeth bared, lunging toward me with that blade made me shudder.

With his gloves on, Wes studied a helmet. "Why'd you bring these?"

Pointing to the fine wires criss-crossed inside the plastic of the face shield, I said, "I couldn't read their thoughts or Push them to stop. These helmets have a Faraday Cage to block electrical, meaning telepathic, signals. Plus, you might get DNA or trace the radio or something."

"If they block the signals, how could the radios work?"

Max leaned over and pointed to a fin on the back of the helmet. "Looks like an external antenna to me. Dad's Audi e-tron has one."

Wes and Elena looked at each other. "Serious weapons and premeditation," he said.

"I called 9-1-1 for the two guys I left tied to a pole. You can call the cops and see if they have them."

"If not," said Bunny, "that tells you something important."

"Wait a minute," said Wes. "Two men armed with these weapons attacked you and you only have a black eye and a cut on your cheek?"

"That was from the mob at school. These guys didn't touch me."

"They fired these guns," said Elena. "Easy to smell the residue."

"Lots of holes in the walls, ceilings, and my favorite clothes." Wes and Elena stared at me. "What Max said, our mad ninja skillz."

"We'll dig into that later," said Wes.

"You need to find the mole in your office before we give up more details," Gemma answered.

"Mole?" asked Elena.

"My mother knew we talked to you and was plenty pissed."

She looked at me, Max, and Junie. "Your parents know we met?" We nodded. Elena flashed Wes a grim smile. "You buying me lunch today or tomorrow?"

Bunny took the Grigori address book from Junie and tore off the top right corner of the cover. She threw the paper into her remaining coffee.

"They numbered these and tracked who got them. This may slow them down if they find it. We checked, and embedded Grigori are everywhere, including the DOJ. Careful, kids." She handed the book to Wes. "You did scan this, right Junie?" Thumbs up.

Wes and Elena's phones buzzed at the same time. "Excuse me," said Elena. She stared at it and slumped.

Wes sagged as well. "The NYPD put out arrest warrants on the four of you for school vandalism and violence."

He turned to Bunny. "In the Bureau, we call this deep shit, pardon my language."

Elena asked, "How do we handle this?"

He studied the four of us. Max and Junie leaned together.

"We report how Bunny, ah, Ms. Popova, found this bag of weapons left for her during the night by her grandson. That's why she called me, an old family friend."

Bunny nodded. "You see what we're fighting. Do you have friends you trust to help you?"

Wes nodded and looked at Elena. "A handful I bet will help," she said.

"Make sure," I told her. "Because you're betting with our lives now."

Chapter 38: A Friend Appears

A few minutes later, my phone buzzed with a text. "Senator Kingston is outside school and wants to meet. At Makary or he'll come to my place."

"He blew you off last time, right?" asked Max.

"Yeah, but he's in the city and ready to talk. He could've changed his mind." I texted him Bunny's address. If he was interested in helping, great, although I didn't expect miracles. But if a Senator calls, you answer, right?

Wes stood with the bag of weapons. "We'll log these in and come back." Bunny walked them to the door.

"What do we do now?" asked Junie.

"I have something for you," said Bunny. "Sit tight." She returned with four credit cards and pulled the top one from the stack and handed it to me.

"What's this? It has my name on it from a company I don't know." She gave a card to each of us.

"One of my friends owns a trucking firm. She issues cards to her drivers for gas, hotels, food, and so forth. This hides your names among hundreds of others. Anyone trying to track you will find thousands of transactions, and her company has no connection to any of you."

We pulled our parent's cards from our wallets and backpacks and put them on the table.

"This is way smart," said Gemma.

"I've learned a few tricks over the years. This will give you some breathing room."

Everyone stayed quiet for a moment as we considered our position and what the credit cards predicted about our future. I said, "We may have to leave town and hide somewhere. With arrest warrants out for us, we can't go home."

"My parents are a little unhappy with me," said Junie. "Well, major pissed."

"Ditto," Max said. "When they find see the warrants? Ouch."

"Forget arrest warrants," said Gemma, looking at me. "I'm scared of more commandos. Mad Ninja skillz or not, they could've killed you last night."

"Where do we go?" I asked. We started researching, but before anyone found the perfect escape, I went to the door. "Senator Kingston's in the building."

After a moment, Senator Big Dave Kingston, wearing a suit and a Stetson, stepped out of the elevator. "Good to see you, Paul," he announced as he shook my hand. "I need to explain our last conversation."

"Come meet the First Four Initiative," I said, and led the Senator to the dining room. "Hey, Gemma, what's the Watergate term for Nixon's buddies?"

"Un-indicted co-conspirators," she and Kingston said at the same time.

The Senator shook my grandmother's hand much longer than necessary. "It's wonderful to see you again, Sophia. I enjoyed our visit at Paul's party."

"That was one of the last nice evenings I've had," she answered. "This situation grows worse every day."

"So I understand."

"And please call me Bunny. The kids do."

The Senator sat and looked at my battered face and whistled. "Impressive black eye. I should see the other guy, right?" he said with a smile.

"No sir, you should see the other two dozen," said Gemma.

"Two dozen? Sure you aren't part Texan? With that story I persuade the Governor to make you an Honorary Texas Citizen."

"Better get the Governor to sign four papers because we all got slammed, and it took all of us to fight our way out. Just hope we don't wind up like the Alamo, sir."

"I'm guessing the report I received on the school fight was inaccurate. Fill me in, please."

I did, and the others added extra details.

The Senator studied each of us, then turned to Bunny. "I'd only discovered Grigori mind-reading and persuading. There's that much more?" She pointed to me.

I told the Senator about Dad's mugging, Mom's rejection in the hospital, and the attack by the two commandos.

He shook his head. "This level of violence surprises me. These FBI agents, can you trust them?"

"Yes," said Bunny. "I've known Wes since before he was born."

"Speaking of Wes, he and Elena just parked outside," I said.

"How does he do that?" Kingston asked Bunny.

"He's got more powers than any Grigori ever. Two strong bloodlines mixed well. Many of the things Paul and his friends do I didn't believe were possible."

I let in Wes and Elena. They stopped when they saw the Senator.

"It's OK, agents, I'm here to support the efforts of these young people. In fact, that brings up the reason for my earlier rudeness."

"For years I suspected the Grigori have orchestrated corporate misdeeds and worse. Not doing them, although the attacks on you kids indicates a more aggressive approach. I just found out this morning more info about abilities than I thought possible. What I hinted at when we spoke at your party were your coming powers and the activities of Grigori leadership."

Bunny poured Senator Kingston more coffee, and he took a sip. "They installed a new staffer I didn't request. Turns out she hears thoughts and is there to spy on me. When you called, she came into the room and watched. Didn't even hide what she was doing, so I had to convince her I had no interest in you."

I checked the Senator's emotional state, and he spoke the truth. "I believe you. But these attacks may mean you didn't fool anyone."

"True enough. That's why I invented an excuse to come to New York. The only person with me is my security chief, so I could leave her in DC. He's been with me since well before I made the mistake of jumping into politics, so he's rock solid."

Big Dave swirled the coffee in his cup for a moment. "There are arrest warrants out for you four. That right, Special Agents?"

"Local PD only," said Elena.

"I need to ask a favor. Our friends must leave town because powerful enemies want them silenced. I've got my jet over at

Teterboro, ready to take me home. Can you help me get them out of here and somewhere safe?"

"What do you need us to do?" asked Wes.

"Help them get a few belongings, small bag only, and avoid any local LEOs."

"*Leos?*" Junie asked Gemma with her Inside Voice.

"*Law Enforcement Officials,*" answered Gemma.

"*How do you know that?*"

"*Mystery novels.*"

"I can take Paul and, ah, Emma?" said the Senator.

"Gemma."

"Sorry. Gemma and Paul to get their bags, and you take the others."

"No need for me," I said. "My parents threw me out, so I packed a bag last night."

"Sorry to hear that."

"I'm good," said Gemma. "I saw Paul's bag, so I packed one myself just in case."

"Smart," said the Senator. "I guess that leaves you two."

"We'll take them," said Elena. "If a local sees us, we'll claim new orders."

Wes drummed his fingers on the table. "You're asking a lot, Senator."

"I know. But I give you my word that I'll protect you. I don't know where you're from, Special Agent, but in Texas, a man's word still means something."

Wes raised an eyebrow at me. "Can we trust him?"

"He doubts his protection could break or get bypassed. Slim, very slim chance. Any problems that crop up he could fix after the news cycle moves on. As a senior member of the Judiciary Committee, he's got more clout than the average bear."

"Damn, Paul, that's freaky," said Kingston, shaking his head. "Just what I thought but didn't say, including the bear. I see now why all the billionaires have Grigori work for them but keep them hidden behind the curtains."

Kingston gave Wes and Elena each a business card and took theirs in return. They gave me their cards, too.

"Paul, you and Gemma grab your bags. Wes and Elena, I'll see you at Teterboro Airport, Hanger J7, in an hour if possible. I want to get home before too late."

Wes, Elena, Max, and Junie left together. Gemma redid her ponytail in front of a mirror in the hallway. That gave me a chance to hit the bathroom.

The Senator stood, as did Bunny. He shook her hand and put his other hand on top of hers.

"There's plenty of room for you to come and take care of Paul and his friends."

Bunny chuckled softly and smiled. She put her left hand on the Senator's.

"I just stepped in it," he said. "You can read minds, too! Of course you can!"

"Technically, I'm an empath, and read emotions and intent."

"Ah. Guess I'm still in trouble."

"No, Dave, not at all. I'm touched you want to help Paul and the rest, and I appreciate it immensely. But my place now is here, to gather support for his efforts. Run interference with locals, such as Max, Junie, and Gemma's parents, and the Grigori leadership who killed my husband ten years ago."

"That's a sad story for another time. You're being gracious with me, but I'm a bit shaky here all the same."

She slipped her arm through his as they walked to the door. "As for the rest, yes, I look forward to seeing you again, and I'm flattered as to your intentions. I accept your invitation, but for a later date."

Gemma and I came back into the room. "Date?" I asked.

"We'll talk soon, my clever grandson." She kissed my forehead, hugged me and gave Gemma the same goodbye. "Listen to the Senator. I told you there are people on your side. Dave is one, but many others are behind you. Learn from him and don't fight the entire world alone."

"A little dramatic, Bunny?" I asked.

"No, son, you'll soon think the whole universe wants a piece of you," said Kingston. "Because they will."

Chapter 39: Gone to Texas

In the elevator going down, I warned Kingston, "There're cops with descriptions of us are waiting outside the building."

Gemma stared off into the distance for a second. "A cop car faces this way, half a block up."

"Should we go out the back?" I asked.

She checked. "Two waiting there as well."

The doors opened in the lobby. "Cal Ray can talk himself out of tight spots, and I'm a Senator. We should make it."

Cal Ray Reynolds, Big Dave's security chief, waved us into a black Suburban. Gemma and I ran with heads lowered and looked away from the police car.

As soon as everyone was in and buckled, Cal Ray pulled out. Before he drove twenty feet, the police car rolled up, lights flashing, and forced him to park.

"Howdy, Officer," said Cal Ray as he rolled down the window. "How can we help you?"

"Please step out of the vehicle. We're serving warrants for four individuals. Two are in your back seat."

Big Dave leaned over Cal Ray and showed his Senate ID card. "Officers, I'm on official Judiciary Committee business and can't afford the time to prove my passengers are my niece and nephew on our way to dinner."

"Sorry, sir, please exit the vehicle now." The second officer moved to the passenger side and peered through the window at Gemma.

I opened my door and stepped out into the street beside the first officer. I smiled and said, "Gee, officer, I think you made a mistake. The guy you want has dark hair, and the girl is a redhead. As you can tell, my hair is red, and she's blonde."

Gemma rolled down her window and waved her ponytail at the second officer. "Blonde."

"Oh, sorry, Senator. Thought we located these other, well, never mind. Drive safe and enjoy your dinner."

Cal Ray pulled around the patrol car and drove away as fast as he could. Stopped at a light, he turned and introduced himself. He said to Kingston, "You were right. That was amazing. Never believed 'these aren't the droids you're looking for' worked in real life."

"Trust me," said Big Dave, "you ain't seen nothin' yet."

* * * * *

In Kingston's Gulfstream G500 headed from Teterboro, New Jersey to Shreveport, Louisiana, Gemma asked Max and Junie how they handled the cops outside the building.

"We noticed them pull up as Wes came out of the garage. Guess they didn't see us, or didn't dare stop an FBI car," she said.

Cal Ray opened a heated cabinet full of something that smelled delicious. "I loaded BBQ and sandwich fixin's as well. Want hot BBQ or cold ham or turkey on white bread?"

Gemma, Junie, and Max looked at me. "Since we're bound for Texas, we better try the BBQ."

"Good choice," said Cal Ray. He passed out sliced beef, ribs, and sausage along with cans of Dr Pepper sodas. Sides were beans and cole slaw.

Kingston swiveled his seat around to face us.

"We're headed to Jefferson, Texas, Bed & Breakfast capital of the world. If asked, you four are studying the town's post-Civil War heyday when it was a major port comparable to St. Louis and New Orleans. Rich kid school project. I'm staying twenty minutes south at home in Marshall."

"Richard White'll put you up in his Haunted Grove B&B. You can trust him, and he'll help you with your cover."

"Relative?" I asked.

"High School football teammate," he answered. "Since High School football is a religion in Texas that meets every Friday night in the fall, we're kinda related."

Kingston looked at Max and Junie leaning against each other, while Gemma and I weren't sitting that close. "I suppose we better discuss sleeping arrangements. There are six bedrooms upstairs and three bathrooms, each linking two bedrooms. I figured everyone gets their own room, the way I would arrange things for young students.

But Max, it looks like you and Junie are together. You guys want to share a room?"

Max winked at Junie and she winked back.

"So, I guess–"

Gemma interrupted him. "Paul and I'll share a room."

"What? We will?" I wanted to ask her but hadn't worked up the nerve.

The Senator laughed. "As a soon-to-be Honorary Texan, let me explain something Texas men know from birth. If a gorgeous woman asks you to share her room, and you're not otherwise encumbered, you tip your hat and say, 'Yes Ma'am' with a smile."

I turned to Gemma, mimed a tipping a Stetson, and said, "Yes, Ma'am." She tipped her imaginary hat in return.

"The reason we should stay together is that when we touch, both our powers are stronger," I said.

"I know what powers are stronger," said Max.

Everyone laughed. "OMG, Paul's face," said Junie. "He's blushing!"

"It's adorable, isn't it? He does it a lot," Gemma said. "Poor naive thing."

"You'll fix that."

Kingston searched his napkin for a space not stained with BBQ sauce. He used that spot to dry the outside corner of each eye.

"My late wife and I were your age when we had our first date."

"Late?" asked Gemma. "Sorry."

"Two years ago. Cancer according to her doctors, but she hated Washington and I believe politics killed her."

I didn't understand. "Why didn't you leave?"

"She said we had to stay and fight. The corruption we found, perverting the people's will, must stop."

He finished his can of Dr Pepper. "When you have horses, you've got to shovel the barn now and then. Before, I thought someone else should lead, and I'd help. She made me promise to do more. Now I'm that shovel."

"Shovels and manure sounds yucky," said Junie.

"It's dirty and disgusting, but necessary."

"What if the only way to get rid of criminals like Holden is to get rid of them literally? Shovel them out, the hardest way possible?" I asked.

"If you killed the two who attacked you last night, no one could blame you," said Cal Ray. "Self-defense clear as day. You could've persuaded them to kill each other."

"I don't want to kill anybody. If we do, we aren't any better than the guys after me last night and Holden. We've got to label them as criminals without exposing the Grigori connection."

"How do we release enough details to make the authorities close in on billionaires, but not our parents?" asked Gemma.

"Think deeper," said the Senator. "In politics, I learned the best course is to tell the truth but not all the details."

I snapped my fingers. "Forget the telepathy, but focus on the crimes. How can people get results similar to mind-reading and persuasion?"

"We need synonyms," said Junie.

"English class again?" groaned Max.

"Yep. How else can normal people get results Grigori do?" asked Gemma. "Without powers."

"They could use intuition or insight," he droned as if in school.

"A mentalist," added Kingston. "People used to call it mentalism, and Kreskin did it on TV."

"OK, whoever that is," said Gemma. "And hyper-intuitive, with concentrated persuasion techniques."

"Correct!" said Junie. "These tricks and techniques stayed within the Grigori family generation after generation."

"The way a chef guards secret family recipes," added Gemma.

"Concentrated persuasion techniques would help in politics," mused Kingston. "Wish you could teach me a few."

"We will, I promise, but now we've got to push the word out." I poked Gemma's shoulder. "Why aren't you a big famous Instagram influencer?"

"Who'd take fashion tips from me? My only makeup trick is all dots all the time."

Makeup triggered an idea. "I'm an idiot! We have influencers on our side," I said. "My cousins and their friends in LA."

Max picked it up right away. "Quinn must have a bunch of social media heavy-hitter influencer friends."

Junie frowned. "Her again? Why do you follow her?"

"I know her, and she tells funny things on Paul sometimes. Calls him her pale cousin and East Coast Boi. And LA Chum Boi since you came back from your visit. What's that?"

Gemma glanced at me, so I waved it away. "Family joke."

"Anyway," said Max, "she and her friends are in LA, and a few must be huge with millions of followers. I'll call her, but only because we need the help."

"Riiiight," said Junie.

"Should've thought of them earlier, way earlier." I texted my cousins my idea, the hashtag #BillionairesCheat, and tapped on my phone. "Texts aren't going out."

"They take longer in the air," said Kingston. "They'll go soon."

"Good. And billionaires waving piles of money as their superpower naturally have concentrated persuasion techniques."

"Don't order me a cape," laughed the Senator. "Not yet in that club."

"Many people are," said Gemma. "I hope we can get a few on our side in this fight."

That triggered a way forward. "You're a genius!"

"Just now figuring that out?"

"Maybe, but I wasn't paying attention. Our goal is to stop billionaires from criming, Grigori or not. I looked at this only from the Grigori angle. But making companies behave better means no crimes for Grigori to enable."

"Will reforming billionaires be easy?" she asked. "What would it take to make your buddy Holden go straight?"

"Need to think on that."

Kingston said, "Interesting idea, but you'll require a huge carrot, or an even bigger stick."

"Don't know if there's a carrot big enough. He always wants more and more and more." Twisting my wrist made my Rolex sparkle in the plane's lights. "We need an enormous stick." What will it take to change Holden's mind? Convince him to behave? "A Texas-sized stick."

Chapter 40: Welcome to Jefferson

The Gulfstream landed in Shreveport and taxied into a hanger. A Ford F250 pickup was the only vehicle. Big Dave led the way and Cal Ray put the luggage in the bed.

"You drive a truck?" Junie asked.

"Most do down here," said Cal Ray. "But this ain't a work truck." He opened a back door for her.

"Nice leather." She stepped on the running board and into the seat and made room for us.

"Sorry it's tight back there," said Kingston. "We'll be in Jefferson in well under an hour the way Cal Ray drives."

As the light faded and the trees got thicker on the sides of the highway, boredom lulled Gemma and Junie to sleep. I texted back and forth with Quinn and Lance. Many of their friends were, as expected, social media monsters. Attacks on billionaires and companies like Goldstone Equity Management for illegal acts and disgusting behavior trended up quickly.

* * * * *

Richard White met us on the porch of the Haunted Grove B&B. He slapped Kingston on the back and shook everyone's hand.

"You folks need to eat?" he asked.

We shook our heads. "BBQ earlier," said Gemma.

"Your BBQ, Dave? Any left for me?" he asked.

Cal Ray waved an insulated bag. "Course."

"You guys get hungry there's water, drinks, and snacks in each room. If you want more come down and help yourselves." Rich led the way to the bedrooms upstairs. "Y'all can use our rooms over the butterfly garden."

"Why do you call the place Haunted Grove?" asked Max. "Build it over a cemetery?"

"Dave didn't tell you? Ghosts live here. That a problem?"

"Cool," said Junie. "Ask'em to let us sleep tonight and we'll talk to'em in the morning."

Our room was full-on country, done with period furniture, a seating corner, and a four-poster queen bed. The chair had a pillow with a rooster embroidered on it, and a small ceramic cowboy boot held the TV remote.

I locked the door and said, "So you can't change your mind and escape." She smiled, so I pushed my luck and opened my arms. After a few seconds, she stepped into them. Amazing how much nicer she fit than the girls in California, and way better than Lucy. My heartbeat got louder.

We separated and put our bags in the closet. Gemma turned and stared at the bed for a long time. I wondered what thoughts churned around inside her head. I could listen, but violating her privacy would piss her off. I didn't dare eavesdrop without her permission, no matter how jangly my nerves.

"Let's talk." She pulled me to the small sofa, leaned against the arm, slipped off her shoes, and put her feet in my lap.

I grinned and held my nose. She laughed and kicked me.

"Ow! I'm wounded!" I began to massage her left foot. After a few minutes, she half-closed her eyes and relaxed.

"OK, since I've injured you and you're massaging my feet anyway, the floor is open. Anything on your mind?"

I inhaled slowly, looked at her, and refocused on her foot. "This morning was, well, great. A surprise and gave me these feels I usually ignore or bury. But again, I've got this scary urge to tell you everything, no matter how personal."

"OK, I–"

"Let me say something first." I switched to her right foot. "We haven't been friends for years and years. At all. And I've had the two worst slams of my life when I found out my parents were helping Holden murder people, and yesterday when they told me I'm now an orphan."

"Both are horrible, and I'm sorry."

"Horrible and they still hurt like hell. But somehow, some way, you were there both times. I mean, you were there for me as a person and a friend, even before we were friendly, and helped me more than I can ever explain. Kept me from falling too deep into that black hole. No matter what happens, I'll never forget your help and, well, kindness."

She pulled a tissue from the box on the end table and wiped her eyes. "That's so nice it's not even fair to tell me. I was kinda mean after we met in the park."

"You explained. I promised I'd never lie to you that day in the diner. Maybe because of this Grigori power connection we have, I've got this compulsion to be completely honest. Or, it's because you're just that special."

"Damn it, I can't enjoy this massage if I'm crying."

"Sorry. Pleasant weather in Texas, yeah? Warmer than I expected."

She kicked me again. "Now I have to be honest. Damn, I hate telling guys the truth. Never been my style. Ever, no matter the guy. OK. Um, OK. No details, but I've got more experience with, you know, more people than you."

"I figured that out."

Her eyes popped wide open. "What? When?"

"You had a condom ready, making you way smarter than me."

"OK, yeah, right."

I stopped the foot massage and searched my memory. "In fact, I can't remember a single guy you ever dated."

"If you wanna talk, you gotta rub." I started again. "There are lots more cute guys in New York than at Makary Academy."

"Oh? How many cute guys?"

"None of your business and you shouldn't even ask. But I'll give you a pass this time for two reasons. First, I know who you were with because they're all girls at school. Unequal knowledge balance, and, honestly, a lack of imagination on your part. Second, Lucy's screwing around really hurt poor little naive Paul, so I see why you're sensitive."

She jerked as I hit a tender spot. "How'd you learn to do this?"

"Dad does it to Mom when they watch TV. You know, those people I used to call parents."

"Smart boy to learn that lesson. Just by watching?"

"Quinn decided we should practice on each other last Christmas. A lot. She bought us books, and we watched videos."

"My stomach's gurgling!"

I pressed a small knot in the arch of her foot. "Because of this."

After her stomach settled, she said, "Don't worry about who I was with before. Be happy we're together now."

"Together, huh? No boyfriend back home? Nobody looking for you?"

She thought for a second. "Not sure. I think I had one last weekend, but no texts or anything lately. The position is open."

"Soooo, accepting applications?"

"For intern boyfriends with potential. Foot massages jump you to the top of the list."

She relaxed for a moment while my hands worked on her feet. Then she looked at me and grinned. "On the other hand, you skipped town right after we hooked up. That kinda thing can hurt a girl's feelings."

Her grin made me echo with my own. "On the other, other hand, I brought you with me."

"Mmmm, a tender spot."

"Sinus pressure point. Grab a tissue."

"Yeah, right. My feet affect my sinuses?" Three minutes later she blew her nose.

"You were with Lucy two years, right?" she asked.

"Twenty months."

"I usually get bored after two weeks."

"Guess I better make this an interesting two weeks."

"Fleeing the state after a school mob tries to kill us is far more exciting than necessary, FYI."

"Noted. No more homicidal mobs. Will that buy me more time?"

She closed her eyes and breathed deeply. "Keep this up and me and my feet will forgive almost anything. This gives you an extra week just because."

Suddenly she sat up and pulled her feet away. "If you read me to find out about old boyfriends, I'll know. I'll get my baseball bat, wait until you're asleep, and break your kneecaps."

"Already decided I won't listen without your permission."

"Good. A girl's got to have a little mystery. Stay honest, even though it still feels weird. And rub my feet."

I pulled her feet back onto my lap and resumed massaging.

"I'll respect your privacy. And I apologize in advance for all the stupid things I'll do to get another week."

After a few more minutes, I stopped and shook out my tired hands.

"That was nice." She sat up, kissed me on the cheek then pulled the comforter down on the bed. I stayed on the sofa.

"You coming?"

I wanted to yell "Yes!" and run to her, but she already meant far more to me than a hookup. I swallowed my nerves to keep my voice steady. "You still seem, ah, unsure about us. I don't want to, you know–"

"You saved my life during the fight at school. I was nearly gone when you knocked Chip off of me."

That didn't match the feelings I had for her. "I don't want that to be the only reason we're together."

"It's not. Don't get me wrong, I thank you with every breath. But the sexy part? Makes me warm and tingly inside when I think about it? You threatened to dismember him if he ever touched me again. Not Max. Not Junie. Me. No other guy ever thought I was worth fighting for. You not only beat him to a pulp, you turned downright gangster threatening to bury his body parts in each of the five boroughs."

"I don't know where that came from, but I stand by it." Her description of warm and tingly inside was exactly how I felt.

"Well, Mr. Honorary Texan, didn't the Senator say if a pretty girl asks you to get in her bed, you say, 'Yes Ma'am' and smile?"

"No."

"What?"

"He didn't say pretty. He said gorgeous. And you are."

"Get in bed."

212

Chapter 41: Field Research

The next morning, Gemma and I thought we were up early since we were still on East Coast time. But Max and Junie were in the kitchen with Richard and his wife Tanya when we got downstairs.

A timer dinged. Tanya said, "Biscuits!" and shook hands with us on her way to the oven. Our hosts danced around each other in a well-rehearsed breakfast routine. They poured juice, turned bacon, flipped sausage patties, and stirred scrambled eggs.

Gemma sniffed the cooking smells. "May I rev up those eggs a little?"

"Course, sweetie," said Tanya.

She went to the spice rack, pulled out thyme, and sprinkled some into the eggs in the frying pan. "You're probably used to pepper and salsa down here, and I don't see wasabi. We need something stronger than dill."

Richard scooped eggs onto each plate Tanya prepared and everyone ate. After a bite, Tanya asked, "Did I hear your name right? Gemma?"

She nodded as she chewed on a bacon strip.

"These eggs are great. We're updating our Haunted Grove B&B cookbook. I'll add this as Gemma's Eggs if that's OK with you."

Junie laughed. "A named dish? Does your Dad have any dishes named after him?"

"Several, and two are decent."

"Something funny?" Tanya asked.

Gemma shook her head. "No, ma'am. My Dad owns a restaurant in New York."

"What's it called?"

"Hargraves. Our last name."

"I'll call these Gemma Hargraves' eggs so he'll know his daughter has a named dish, too."

"Amazing," I said. "Gemma's here one night and she wins Texas."

"You guys hear any ghosts last night?" asked Richard.

Gemma and I shook our heads. "We were, ah, talking," I said.

213

Max and Junie laughed. She explained, "I fiiiinally got Gemma over being mad at Paul. Now she sees how perfect they are for each other."

"This giant mess kinda threw us together, so we had to start over," said Gemma.

Junie asked me, "You get the baseball bat warning?"

I turned to Gemma. "You threaten to kneecap every guy you date? And here I thought I was special."

She patted my hand. "You are, babe. I was just teasing the other guys. I really mean it with you."

"How long is that list of other guys?" I asked Junie.

Gemma waved her hand. "Tanya, do you have any sports equipment? Baseball bats? Golf clubs? Maybe a shotgun?"

"You kids are fine," she said. "If you can tease and laugh together, you can weather any storm."

After breakfast, Gemma showed Tanya the ways New Yorkers upgrade scrambled eggs. I contacted my cousins. Max and Junie explored the town.

* * * * *

Max and Junie rushed into Haunted Grove and yelled, "Party tonight!"

"We need local clothes," said Junie.

Gemma and I stuck our heads out of the parlor where we monitored Twitter, Instagram, Facebook, TikTok, and other services for #BillionairesCheat mentions. Tanya walked out of the kitchen with a basket of fresh cookies. "Let's check the Closet of Orphaned Objects, otherwise known as Lost and Found."

"It's OK," I told her. "We can go buy some."

"Nope, you need jeans. New ones look stupid, and they'll laugh at you."

"They laughed at us 'Yankees' plenty already," said Junie.

Tanya opened a hallway closet door, stuck her head in, and came out with a t-shirt that read, *Well-behaved women seldom make history. Laura Ulrich.* "I knew I'd find someone who deserves this." She held it up to Gemma. "It's yours."

I clapped until I had to catch a pair of faded jeans she threw at me. Max got the next pair.

As she dove back into the closet, Junie said, "I've got to wear a dress. I'll explain later."

"Another one I've been saving for somebody special." She pulled out a black t-shirt tunic with a deep V mesh insert with "The Girls Rule" in white letters where the V stopped.

"That's yours because I don't have the boobs for it," said Gemma.

"The girls'll show the locals which Junie I am."

"What?"

"We need to try these on," she said as they ran upstairs.

"Cookies, boys?" asked Tanya.

"Always," Max said.

Richard came from the back of the house. "Do I smell chocolate chips?" After his second cookie, he said, "Big Dave called. Time to head home. He'll pick you up at nine in the morning."

* * * * *

After dinner, we changed into our "new" clothes. Junie was right, and the mesh insert put her 'girls' front and center. Gemma tied off her t-shirt on one side and turned it bare midriff but kept the quote readable.

"It's ten before eight. We better roll," I said.

Tanya shook her head. "Eight doesn't mean eight. It means eight-ish. Don't leave for at least thirty more minutes," said Tanya. "Now, Big Dave said you guys have powers. What did he mean?"

I checked Richard and Tanya's emotions and found they trusted Kingston and accepted us, but curious about what they'd agreed to protect. "It's OK."

"Take this dress," Junie said, and adjusted the mesh insert. "A woman named Laura, pregnant with a son she planned to name Milo, left it here."

Tanya dropped the candle in a jar she was lighting. "How did you know that?" Before it hit the floor, it stopped and floated back up to her. Max smiled.

"No wonder people are after you guys," said Richard.

215

"The ones who want us dead are the billionaires using descendants of Grigori Rasputin, like us, to use our powers to help them get away with crimes, including murder," I said. The rest of the thirty minutes zipped by as we explained why we were on the run.

"While you're gone, I'll dig up info on the Akme Johnson Company," Richard told me. "That's the local firm bought by Goldstone that's caused so much trouble."

* * * * *

Max and Junie led the way to Eager's Coffee Shop. Someone opened the door from inside. "Hey," said a Hispanic girl in overall shorts over a yellow t-shirt. "I'm Carli."

"Max stole a workin' man's jeans," she laughed, patting his face. She checked Junie's outfit, gave her a thumbs up, and turned to Gemma. "Lookin' good."

Max introduced me and Gemma just as the other Junie came up. He was Black like Max, but a head taller and twice as thick. "He's Junie Johnson, too."

"Two Junie Johnsons?" asked Gemma. "Double the fun!"

"Looking good, new Junie," he said.

Carli smacked him on the shoulder. "Settle. You've seen boobs."

"Not those," he said, winking to Junie.

Carli hit him again. "From now on, she's Sexy Junie and you're Ugly Junie. Everybody'll figure out who's who." She loudly announced to the other people there, "The Yankees are here. Come say hello."

That kicked off a parade of unknown faces and names, starting with the eight people already there. When new people came in, Carli or Ugly Junie brought them to meet 'the Yankees' right away.

"*I can't keep everybody straight,*" I said silently to Gemma. "*Is that Joe Bob or Bobby Joe?*"

"*I think he's Jim Bob.*"

"*He's not Carlen?*"

"*The girl in the green top is Carol Anne.*"

"*I give up.*"

Carli and Ugly Junie sat down with us. "This a bit much?" she asked.

"People treat us like celebrities or something," said Gemma.

"You are, famous or infamous. The Senator put you up at Haunted Grove, right?"

"Bingo."

"That's where he hides witnesses for his Senate committee," said Ugly Junie.

"Last year a mafia hit man was here for a couple months. Real New York City asshole." Carli covered her mouth with her hand. "Sorry."

I laughed. "New York's biggest export is assholes."

"He called everybody putzes, so he must be the real putz," said Ugly Junie.

"What part of New York City is Bayonne?" asked Carli.

"That's in New Jersey," said Gemma. "He's definitely a putz. That's where New York exports most of the assholes."

Carli nodded. "We send ours to Dallas."

"How long're y'all staying?" asked Ugly Junie.

"We leave tomorrow morning," said Gemma. "We can only fight this stuff up close."

"Not long enough. You'll be back."

"I'm sure everything's getting sorted out at home."

Carli and Junie shook their heads. "We'll see y'all again," Carli insisted.

Someone called his name, so Ugly Junie left.

Carli leaned in closer to us. "Forget the glory days of Jefferson. Do your report on the Akme Johnson Company and their workplace deaths and toxic waste dumps and the cancer clusters across East Texas. Akme Johnson was a slave owner, and his ancestors have the same attitudes."

I checked her emotions as she spoke. There was serious intent, truth, and loss. "You've lost people because of them, haven't you?"

"One uncle died in a work accident and my auntie got a shitty little check. My granddad retired early so he could die from cancer caused by Akme at home and not run up more hospital bills."

I put my hand on hers. "It's hard, and we researched what they've done." I sensed her anger subside. She glanced at Gemma

217

quickly and back to me. Thoughts of sex with me popped up, so I used that hand to pick up my Dr Pepper.

"If you want other stories on Akme, just ask. Everybody has two or three." Carli gave Gemma a half-smile as she left.

Gemma put her hand on mine. "Guess you were right about Akme Johnson."

"Great. Another reason for Holden to make me dead."

Chapter 42: The Federal Hammer

At 9 AM the next morning, Senator Kingston arrived at Haunted Grove with Cal Ray at the wheel. Richard and Tanya said they hated to see us leave, but Gemma got the most attention. Why didn't I notice her these last few years? What else did I miss that others saw?

Once on the highway, Kingston turned to look at the four of us squished together.

"You guys want the bad news or good news first?"

"Bad news," said Gemma. "The good news can make us feel better."

"Makes sense. This morning, the Securities and Exchange Commission filed insider trading indictments against all your parents." He looked at Gemma. "Except your father."

"You mean they indicted the Grigori members?" I asked.

"Exactly."

"Is that dripping with irony or swimming in it?" I asked.

"Dripping's the usual term," he agreed, "but I think swimming is more exact. And so far, the law firms run by Grigori refuse to represent them."

"That a problem?" asked Junie.

"Nah. There's more lawyers in New York City than rats, many with SEC experience. They'll find good representation."

"It sends a warning to other Grigori that if you help us, you'll get punished," I said.

"Sucks for my parents," said Max. "They charged my mother as well? She's not technically a Grigori."

"Babe, she's got powers and works with them," said Junie. She turned to the Senator. "Even though our folks don't want us to do what we're doing?" He shrugged.

"This will distance us from our families," I said. "And warn other families to control their kids so they don't help. Oh, any news on my aunts and uncles in Los Angeles, and my cousins?" He shook his head. "This really sucks."

"I know. But the work your California friends are doing made a serious impact. My PR team says #BillionairesCheat opened a vein of anger and resentment that's flooding social media."

"But they still have tons of money and influence to use against us."

Kingston agreed. "As Gemma said, there's good news. The police dropped the charges against y'all, so that should help you feel better. That's why you can go back to the city, although maybe not your parents, depending." He looked at me when he said that.

Relief washed over me, and I could sense my friends relax. I leaned toward Gemma, which wasn't far since she was almost in my lap in the cramped back seat.

"Still like me if I'm not a bad boy?" I whispered to her.

"Better get a neck tattoo to regain your street cred."

After a moment, Junie said, "We better tell our parents." Max and Gemma agreed, and they all texted. I didn't move. Gemma put her phone away, frowned at me, and patted my knee.

Everyone chewed on their own thoughts the rest of the ride to Shreveport. On board the Senator's jet, the mood remained somber. Max and Junie sat apart from us. Big Dave and Cal Ray were at the front of the cabin.

After takeoff, Gemma pulled my face around from the window. I smiled and kissed her.

"Nice, but I wanted to ask about Carli last night."

"What?" I remembered what I sensed. "Oh. You knew? How?"

"I don't need powers to catch a girl hitting on you."

"It caught me by surprise."

"Saw that, too."

"She was sad and angry for her family, and suddenly there was this hot attraction. I let go of her hand and ... wait, you saw?"

"When you were with Lucy, you never realized when other girls rubbed on you for attention, did you?"

"I think I'd catch actual physical rubbing."

"No, you didn't. I noticed lots of touching and crowding and flirting. Full on attempted seductions a few times."

I raised one eyebrow. "Why'd you watch?"

"We had that anthropology section in AP History, and personal interactions between social groups interest me. It's what my Dad does when planning restaurant flow, but doesn't know why."

"Maybe a tiny bit jealous?" I teased.

She took a quick breath as if she was going to snap back, held it, and slowly exhaled. "OK, here's that damn honesty thing again. So weird. I had this twinge, but it wasn't quite jealousy. You were King of the World, but I thought you were an asshole. Did they know something I missed, or did you fool them? I wondered if I made a mistake about you."

"You never said anything."

"Why would I? Besides, Lucy owned you. Then I met a guy at a party and focused on him." She grinned and waggled her eyebrows. "Never gave you another thought."

"Another guy, huh?"

Her grin faded. "Go ahead."

I peered through the peephole in my mental door. "That's a big baseball bat."

"Only the best for you, babe." She grinned again and patted my cheek. My smile fell. "Hey, what?"

"Honestly? That joke is getting old."

She held my hand and kissed it. "I can't undo my past and I don't want you to change how you think of me because of the stupid things I did."

"You know the dumb stuff I did with Lucy and other girls, right?"

"At least some."

"And you still like me?"

She took a deep breath for a snarky reply, but stopped. "Damn this honesty."

"Give me the same chance."

She kissed her fingertip and put it on my lips. "Some mistakes are stupider than others."

"I don't care about any of that."

"Real stupid." She turned away from me.

* * * * *

221

We rode in a black Suburban from the Teterboro Airport into New York City. Cal Ray slowed in front of Bunny's building near an open parking space, but changed his mind and kept going. He circled around and parked a half-block from the entrance.

"Wait here."

He walked toward the entrance and stopped by a parked car. The two men inside the black Ford Taurus focused on the door and didn't notice Cal Ray until he tapped on the window. They startled, and Cal Ray held up his left index finger. The driver rolled the window down halfway.

"Gentlemen, my Smith & Wesson Model 627 says it time for you to leave."

The passenger put his hands on the dashboard as the driver started the car. Cal Ray took a picture of the license plate as they left.

Wes and Elena were inside with Bunny when we arrived.

"Seems like you were in Texas forever," she said as she hugged us and shook Kingston's hand for a long time. "Thank you for keeping them safe."

"My pleasure. They're now the talk of Jefferson, Texas, Junie and Gemma in particular. Maybe they'll tell you how Yankees charmed small-town Texans."

Cal Ray texted Wes the photo of the car out front. "Two armed tough guys had this place staked out."

Wes and Elena looked at each other. "Told you," said Elena. She turned to Cal Ray. "We'll get someone to watch this location."

"Thank you," said Kingston.

"Dragavei Associates purchased the guns Paul recovered. Rifling matches bullets found at other crime scenes," said Wes.

"And bullets inside a couple of bodies," said Elena. "We found matches for the DNA in the helmets in the ex-military database. Alerts are out. The men who attacked Paul never arrived at a station."

Bunny handed me a large envelope. "Your little friend Isabella is a real talker. You made a strong impression on her."

"I knew she was flirting and so I flirted back," I told Gemma. "I needed her help, and you still hated me."

"When you were visiting your cousins? OK, I thought you were an asshole then."

"You don't think so now, right?"

She struggled to keep a straight face and held her thumb and index finger an inch apart. "This much." She laughed at her own joke and Junie joined in.

"Laugh now," said Bunny. "The envelope contains evidence showing Holden's shipping company added human trafficking to their services."

She held another envelope up for Wes. Kingston intercepted it.

"Agents, I need to read this first. If you make this an official case, it could blow back on Paul and the rest."

"Understood, Senator, but we need to see it," he said.

"We'll talk soon."

Wes left Elena to guard Bunny until a protective detail arrived. I turned to the Senator. "We can't go home, and there's not enough room here. We'll get a hotel nearby and can come back tomorrow and stay together."

"You need protection," said Kingston.

"I'll go," said Cal Ray.

"Than it's Penn Station for me to catch the Amtrak direct to D.C." said Kingston. "Get home tonight, no problem. Nobody's mad at me yet."

I turned to my friends. "Somebody, either Holden or the billionaires or the Grigori, waited to ambush us here. Tomorrow we lay out our plan to take the fight to them."

Chapter 43: No Sleep Tonight

After a few minutes on the phone, Cal Ray gathered everyone.

"I turned up a hotel a couple blocks away with a two-bedroom suite and a pull-out couch. Your bags still in the car?" We nodded. "Let's roll. Elena, I'll let y'all know where we are when we're situated."

Max and I carried the suitcases to our suite at the Upper East Manor. Junie and Gemma dove into a conversation, deciding which couple gets which bedroom.

"*Did you see any differences in those rooms?*" I asked Max with my Inside Voice.

"*Did one have blue curtains and the other beige?*"

Cal Ray dropped his bag by the couch. "What's the holdup with the girls?"

"You didn't know? Girls are complicated," I said.

"True dat. I'm going to look around, find the exits, reconnoiter."

The girls described which bedroom they wanted when the door banged open. I held up my hand and said, "That's not Cal Ray." Gemma yelled as two men holding Glock handguns slammed the door shut behind them.

Max and I jumped in front of Gemma and Junie.

"Who's Paul?" asked the first intruder.

I Moved the guns to point at the floor and away from us, then Pushed each guy to aim his gun at the other.

"What the hell!" said the second guy.

Max made his rolling finger motion and flicked the voodoo needles at the intruders. Both screamed and collapsed. They thrashed around with the intense pain, but kept their guns aimed at each other the entire time.

"You gonna knock'em out?" asked Max.

I stepped closer to our attackers. "Last guys I knocked out got concussions."

A Smith & Wesson entered, carried by Cal Ray. He watched them thrash and moan from the pain.

"You guys shoot'em?"

I pointed to Max. "Magic voodoo throwing needles. No bullets needed."

"That's a new one." Cal Ray went to his bag and pulled out plastic restraints. "Let'em go enough so I can cuff'em around this column."

After he handcuffed them on either side of the pole, Cal Ray found their phones and tried to unlock them, but failed.

"Hey, Junie, sweet talk these phones, please." I said.

She took the phones from Cal Ray. "These both belong to Dragavei Associates. They followed our car from Bunny's."

Cal Ray shook his head. "Sorry, I spotted one car and didn't look for more."

"If you got brains, you'll let us go," said the second guy.

"I oughta shoot your ass right now and call it self-defense," said Cal Ray. "Sucker punch me, will ya?" He punched him in the kidney. "Shut up."

"No reason to hurt them more than we have to," I said.

"You're a smart kid and still believe people are decent because you are. One day you'll learn certain people just aren't. Hope that lesson doesn't hurt too much."

"I think we've learned certain people aren't decent over the last week. But Max hurt them enough." I pulled Cal Ray's arm to move him away from the two bound men.

"Should we ask them questions or something?" asked Max. He poked one of them. "Who sent you after us? What were your orders?"

"Go to hell."

"Needle'em again?"

"I have an idea." I focused on the "Go to hell," guy and searched through his recent memories. Ambushing Cal Ray in the hall, following our car here, seeing us arrive at Bunny's, a call from a burner phone. That was the one I needed. "Someone named Anton called and ordered them to follow us from Bunny's and hold us at gunpoint and contact him."

"At least they didn't come to kill us," Max said.

"Or Anton wants to do it himself." I answered.

"Cheerful tonight, yeah?"

Gemma thought to Junie, *"He can read memories, too?"*

225

"Seems so. You still hiding secrets?"

"Aren't we all?"

"Let's skedaddle out of here," Cal Ray ordered. "Leave these bastards for the FBI."

I used my phone and booked a two-bedroom suite at the ParkView Suites using the credit card Bunny gave me.

After we checked in and trooped upstairs, Max and I put the bags in the bedrooms without asking Gemma or Junie which one they wanted.

"I'll stay outside the door," said Cal Ray. "And call Elena to report those other guys. You guys catch a few Z's now."

Max and Gemma took the first slots in the respective bathrooms. When they left, Junie pulled me into the far corner.

"How are you two?"

"I think it's great, but she doesn't seem so sure. Touchy about her past."

"Don't you dare sneak a peek!"

I held up my right hand like taking an oath. "Decided it was a bad idea before she gave me the baseball bat-to-kneecaps speech. I promised her."

"Here's the situation: She's my red-headed sister, but she falls for the worst guys I've ever seen."

"I feel special."

"You're the exception that proves the rule. She always picks assholes and tries to change them, and they never do. They're better at being an asshole than she is, and they treat her like shit. She hates it and poof and tears and late night calls when I need to sleep."

"She told me two weeks."

"That's about right. Some a week, don't think any guy lasted a month." She looked to make sure we were alone. "You treat Gemma as your equal and a woman and she's never had that. She expects guys to treat her like a girl, but you keep doing what you're doing because she'll learn that's way better. You've got to undo crap other guys did to her. Not fair to you, but she's worth it."

"I agree. Any of them massage her feet?"

"Hell no, because that's something only a great guy would do. You rub her feet?"

"Yep."

She gave me a sultry smile and licked her lips. Squeezing my bicep, she whispered, "Baby, have I told you how sexy you are? You ready to pull my shoes off and have your way with me?"

I laughed. "I don't know if Gemma'd care, but Max sure would."

"She'd care but won't admit it because she doesn't think she deserves a nice guy. She usually blows up relationships and runs. You're a firm guy two levels up and that's new for her."

"I'm not that firm a guy."

"Not before, but you're the man now. I'm serious."

"Never was with Lucy. I let her run things."

"See where that got you?"

"Ouch. What do I do when she tries to blow it up and run?" Her "two weeks and bored," comment nagged at me.

"You hold tight or tie her to a pole if necessary. Call me, and I'll bitch-slap some sense into her."

Max and Gemma came into the common space while Junie and I still huddled in the corner.

"Hey, Junie–" said Max.

She waggled her finger at him the entire distance as she walked up and poked him in the chest with it. "You need to learn how Paul keeps Gemma happy at night."

"What?"

Gemma rushed closer. "Hey!"

"Take notes, Maxy Baby. When they're alone, when the moment is right, the lights dim, the stars come out, Paul goes lower, and lower, and lower, and finally, when she can't stand the suspense any longer ... he massages her feet."

"The hell?" Max looked at me with eyebrows knotted. "Foot massage?"

Gemma put her arm on Junie's shoulder. "OMG, it's wonderful! I just melt."

Junie resumed finger waggling at Max. "You'll learn or I'll dump your ass and steal Paul from Gemma."

"Hey," said Gemma. "I'm not through with him yet!"

"Tell you what," I promised. "When things settle, we'll get together for a foot massage party."

Junie grabbed Max's head and nodded for him.

"I'll teach Max and the both of you, too. Foot massages go both ways."

"I have to give them?" asked Junie.

"Worth it," said Gemma.

Junie thought to me, *"She's not through with you."*

"Yet."

Gemma yawned. I put my arm around her waist as we walked to our bedroom. "Sleepy?"

"Every time I close my eyes, I see those gun barrels pointed at me. Not restful."

I locked the door when we got in our room. "Long day. Pretty tired myself."

"Not me. Wired. Nervous. Guns. Angry. Everything rolling around inside my head."

She was asleep four minutes after her cheek hit the pillow. I stared at the ceiling for hours. What's the best way to fight to Holden and the Grigori? I was sick of being "Steamrolled," because I was too nice, as the Cherry Poppin' Daddie's song said. Did I want to turn the other cheek or go eye-to-eye, as the chorus said. Guns pointed at you over and over will change a guy's approach in a hurry. No more turned cheeks.

Chapter 44: More Friends and Enemies

The next morning, we returned to Bunny's. NYPD stationed two officers in front of the building, two in back, and two between the elevator and her door.

Elena stayed there overnight, and Wes beat us there. Bunny hugged Gemma extra long. "How are you, dear?"

"Shaky. Guys burst into our room with guns. I tossed and turned and didn't sleep at all last night."

"She fell like a chainsawed tree and slept like a log," I thought to Bunny.

She smiled at me over Gemma's shoulder, but got serious again to comfort her. "Paul and Max are real, what do you say, badasses, aren't they?"

"That they are," said Cal Ray. "When I came back, the bastards were on the ground, squealing like they'd shot them."

Wes turned to me. "How did you do it?"

I pointed to Max.

"Paul figured it out and told me what to do."

Elena braced herself. "I've gotta see this, so do it to me."

"I don't want to hurt a, you know–"

"FBI agent?" He shook his head.

"Girl?" asked Junie. He looked at his shoes.

"Get over it. Half of the people who attacked us at school were girls. You didn't hit any of them, and one knocked me loopy."

"You sure?"

Elena gave a thumbs up.

He twirled his thumb and forefinger and threw the imaginary needle. She gasped and crashed to the floor. Max waved his hand to stop the voodoo pain.

"DAAAAMN that hurt!" Wes helped her up. "Like he stabbed me with a burning knife and it bored all the way through my thigh."

"C'mon, it can't hurt that much," Wes laughed.

"Do it," Elena said.

Max twirled and threw. Wes yelped as he thudded on the carpet, grabbed his leg, and groaned louder than a dying cow. Max stopped the pain.

After he struggled to his feet, Wes said to Elena, "More of a drill covered in acid feel for me. I can't believe a gunshot hurts that much."

"At least it's not deadly," said Elena.

I noticed Max's face. "Max?"

"What if I hit someone in the head? In the heart? Would that kill them?"

Elena went over and put her hand on his shoulder. "We're trained to protect the innocents. If you or your friends are in danger, aim at the torso since it's the largest target. Think of it like a contract: if they try to kill you or yours, they agreed you're allowed to defend yourself and kill them."

"I don't throw the needle so much as decide where I want it to hurt," he replied. "But if someone else points a gun at Junie, I'll send a dozen needles into their head."

"On a lighter note," Bunny said, "breakfast."

Wes and Elena waved off the food. "Back to the office for us," he said.

"These are for you." Junie handed the intruders' phones to Elena. "They came from Dragavei."

"How do you know?"

"Things talk to me, remember? I unlocked them for you."

"Since you took them away from the crime scene, we can't use them in court. But we've got plenty on those perps for attempted murder. And these may give us background info for other cases."

"Look for someone named Anton. He called from a burner, but you can track other calls and texts."

Elena turned to Cal Ray. "Our plan is to paint you as the hero. You came back and karate-kicked the men from behind."

The FBI agents waved as they left.

Everyone sat at the table for breakfast. "Guess I better learn some fancy moves before the trial," said Cal Ray. "Can you pass the bacon?"

After breakfast, Bunny said, "Some reporters wish to speak to you guys later this morning."

"Why?" I asked.

"Your cousins and their friends did an outstanding job spreading the news. Reporters want your side of the story."

230

"That Quinn's something else, isn't she?" said Max. He noticed Junie's face. "And Lance is great, too, right?"

"Not sure I'll like this Quinn girl," Junie said.

"She's a sweetheart and you'll get along fine," said Bunny. She touched Gemma's hand. "You might take issue."

"What? Why?"

Bunny's phone rang. "Yes, officer?" She listened. "Please send them up."

She stood. "The reporters came early. Shall we go to the sofa? Paul, can you and Max move that loveseat closer?"

"Let's see." I put my arms out and wiggled my fingers like I summoned The Force in a *Star Wars* movie. The loveseat floated up an inch and moved over a couple of feet. "Good?"

She stared at me with both eyebrows raised. "Um, yes, yes, that's fine."

After two quick knocks, the door opened, and an NYPD officer let a young woman and an older man into the apartment.

"Miss Sophia!" said the woman.

"Emily, such a pleasure to see you again. How are you?"

"Great. My parents send their love." She turned to the couch, where the four of us sat in a row.

"This is Junie, Max, Gemma, and Paul," said Bunny.

"You're the grandson, right?" Emily asked. I nodded, then we smiled as she took several photos.

"Say I'm her favorite grandson. That'll tweak my cousin Lance."

"As you heard, I'm Emily, and Michael is the section editor. He's the one who has to approve you as her number one in the article."

She put a recorder on the coffee table. "Our goal here is to be sure we get everything."

First, she had the four of us say and spell our full names. "I make everybody do that, even if your name is Joe Smith," she said. With her hand by her mouth, she pretended to whisper, "Michael goes all red in the face when reporters misspell names."

He pantomimed his head exploding.

"Remember, a recorder is running," said Emily. "Paul, I talked to Lance, who seems very nice, so don't mess with your cousin. He

231

described the Grigori abilities as insight and convincing persuasion techniques. Some outlets call it mind-reading. Is it?"

"Mind-reading? That's silly. My grandmother knows when people feel sad and she cheers them up. Is that a mental power or emotional awareness?"

"Either or both," she answered.

"You seem to know my grandmother–"

"Everybody knows Sophia," added Gemma.

"True, she has a ton of friends." I agreed. "But has she comforted you, or been extra nice when you had a bad day?"

"Sure. She even told me not to cry when a guy broke up with me in college. Said there's a lot of swordfish in the sea, and some swords are better than others. Make certain I compare a few to find the one I want."

Cal Ray laughed. Gemma and Junie grinned at each other.

"Were you thinking of swordfish so she could read your thoughts and come up with that?"

"Not at all. Never heard that expression before."

"Aren't swordfish like, really long," giggled Gemma as she elbowed me.

My lips curled up for a second, but I got control. "It didn't take a mind-reader to figure out someone hurt you, did it?"

"You're right," agreed Emily. "The black clothes and the tears no doubt gave it away."

"If Max could read minds, his grades would improve," said Junie.

"Hey!"

"Believe me," I said. "If I could read minds, I'd live large in Las Vegas playing poker and stacking cash."

Max laughed and shook his head. "White boys and poker. Crazy."

"In most states you can't gamble until you're twenty-one," said Emily. "But I understand your point."

Our discussion continued for another fifteen minutes. As she was winding down, I asked, "Did you research the James Randi Prize?"

"I don't know that one."

"Randi was a magician who later created the James Randi Educational Foundation to emphasize critical thinking and debunk paranormal claims. His goal was to stop fakers from cheating people. He offered a cash prize in 1964 that reached up to one million dollars from 1996 through 2015. Nobody won a penny."

"Maybe the tests were too hard?"

"Not so much. Identify playing cards in a sealed envelope. Name three out of twenty objects in the next room if you claimed to be a remote viewer. Use telepathy to read what Randi was thinking, things like that. No winners. Over two dozen groups around the world still offer prizes for any display of ESP, telepathy, or telekinesis, including the Center for Inquiry Investigations Group with a $250,000 prize. No prize money won yet."

"We'll check into those, thanks." She put the recorder back in her purse, then stopped. "Sorry to learn about your father's injuries. Is he better now?"

I looked at the carpet. "Don't know. My parents are pissed at me for talking about the crimes at their company. Bad for business and so on. They threw me out."

Emily wrote in a small notebook. "Sounds like a real emotional burden. How are you holding up?"

I shrugged. "Families fight. I've got my friends, my grandmother, and even some new friends. I'm OK. Not singing 'Tango of Sorrow,' yet."

"Excuse me, what?"

"Sorry. Old song by a retro swing band named Blue Plate Special."

"If you say so."

Gemma's phone rang. She gasped when she saw who called. "My mom. Wow. Better get this."

She took a couple steps but turned back. "My parents haven't spoken to me since the fight at school. We did the right thing, and everybody's mad at us." She left for the bathroom.

Emily asked Max and Junie about their situations.

"My parents haven't thrown me out," said Junie, "but no calls to come home, either." Max seconded his situation was the same.

Emily said, "Our sources say the insider trading cases will disappear. Faster if they testify against their employers."

"That's good news," I said.

She asked her boss, "Can I tell them about the articles scheduled for tomorrow?"

He turned to the group. "I ask you to keep these details to yourselves until we release the official story, OK?" We agreed.

"A handful of coworkers of Grigori members came forward and disclosed how the billionaires rely on them," she said. "Stories are all, 'They say they read minds and persuade people, but it's just cold readings,' using the same techniques as fortune tellers. They watch for clues like a carnival psychic and keep going when they get an emotional response. But the wealthy idiots eat that crap up and convince themselves it's magic. In all the interviews we did, colleagues believe they swindled their billionaire bosses, not gave them secret information learned by mental powers."

"They uncovered some Grigori tricks," I said.

"A word of advice to you guys," said Michael. "There are over 700 billionaires in the U.S., and it seems like every one of them hates you. Or they fear you. Or both."

"On that cheery note," Emily stood. "Thanks for your time."

She shook our hands, and added, "Tell Gemma goodbye for me. It's been fun."

After they left, I looked for her. The hall bathroom the door was open, and she waved me in and put the phone on speaker.

"You pissed off the wrong people, but I can help," said her mother.

"Probably not."

"Dammit, Gemma! Your prom is coming, and I spent a fortune on your dress and ticket! Stop this craziness and come home right now!"

She looked at herself in the mirror and touched the crease left from her split lip. Then stood up straight and pushed her shoulders back. "I'm tired of being yelled at. Is Daddy home?"

"He's at work."

"Tell him a cookbook will include dishes named for me soon. I'll send him a copy."

"What are you babbling about?"

"Bye, Mom." She tapped her phone and her mother's strident voice disappeared.

She dried her eyes and fluffed her hair. Chin up, but she had a sad, meager smile.

"You OK, gorgeous?"

She wrapped her arms around me and gave me a kiss. "Mom says you're not good enough for me."

"I'm not taking that personally since she hasn't met me, and because parents always tell their kids their crush isn't worthy, right?"

"Mine does. Usually she's right, based on my history."

"Do you agree?"

She kissed me again. "Not this time."

Chapter 45: The Ghost of Yasmin

That night, back in the hotel, Gemma hit me with an eager look. I waggled my eyebrows.

"You're going to explain this song stuff right now."

Not what I hoped for tonight. "It's a long story and we've got a tough day tomorrow. I don't know if I can get through it."

We sat in two upholstered chairs on either side of a tiny table.

"C'mon, how long will it take to explain these weird songs?"

I looked out the window at the lights in buildings between us and Central Park. "They connect to why I asked you to the Spring Dance."

She bounced in her chair. "Now I have to know what caused you to do anything as bizarro as ask me out in ninth grade. I thought about spitting on you every time we got close."

I winced at the memory and her hand covered mine. "OK, I'm treating this like a silly story and it's deeper, right?" I nodded.

"C'mon." She plumped the pillows up on the bed against the headboard and motioned for me to sit beside her. I kicked my shoes off and climbed up.

"This way I can hug you for support and kiss you when you need it."

"We have this honesty thing, but I've never told anyone every detail, even Bunny."

"If it's important to you, it's important to me."

I realized I wasn't getting out of this, so I took a deep breath and started the tale of my first love, Yasmin Kelly.

"We met when I was four years old. We'd just gotten into our penthouse after they redid the building. Not long after, the Kelly family moved in five floors below us. Their daughter, Yasmin, was ten years older."

"She wasn't a girlfriend?"

"Way more important. She watched me when my parents went out or worked late or whatever. I'd go to her place, or she'd come up, and we were basically together all the time. She even put an air mattress in her bedroom and I'd nap while she did homework. Called me her little shadow."

I had to stop a minute and look out the window. I imagined I heard Yasmin warn me not to pull the scab off this wound.

Gemma hugged me and I continued.

"My parents focused on Goldstone, so there wasn't much time left for me. Bunny helped give me a family life, but Yasmin became my big sister. If I'm a decent guy today, it's because Yasmin loved me when my folks were too busy."

I stopped and wiped my eyes. Gemma handed me a tissue. "She must have been special because you're pretty decent."

"Thanks. When I was ten and she was at City University, she dove headfirst into music she said was 'unknown but deserved recognition.' Taught me everything she discovered. At eleven she smuggled me into my first concert."

"Must've been fun. You're smiling."

"Yeah. She started a blog and it became popular. We hit the clubs to see ska punk bands with horns when I was older and could kinda pass. She even got me backstage to meet her favorite group, the Cherry Poppin' Daddies."

"Kinda rude name."

"Kinda rude music on some cuts. But amazingly fun and inventive."

"Play me a few soon?"

"No problem."

"You keep using past tense, so I'm guessing she moved away. Where'd she go?"

"An Irish Catholic cemetery."

"Oh, shit, oh, oh, oh, I'm so sorry, oh, damn."

I gave her back the tissue she'd given me.

"The week after Thanksgiving, she went on a grad school field trip. In one of those car service vans that hold fifteen or sixteen people."

"Oh, no."

"Yeah. Driver slid sideways. The pole hit right where she was sitting, crushing her left arm and leg. Both needed amputation, at the elbow and knee."

"She lived?"

"And came home ten days later. I spent every minute possible helping her the same way she helped me when I was little, so I dropped everything that December. Slept by her bed during Christmas break to be there and get her pain pills and stuff during the night. She needed them because things weren't right and she knew it. Distracted herself by teaching me her outlook on music. Told me where she looked for bands and why she did it. Taught me to listen over and over until I could hear the joy through the noise. School restarted, and I had to leave her during the day."

"So that's when she, ah–"

"Passed, met her maker, whatever. She didn't give up or stop fighting. A blood clot killed her the Thursday after we returned to class in January. She died while I was at school. All I saw ahead of me, without her, was darkness. Everything was black."

"Gone. Just like that. Forever. The pain chewed an enormous hole in me, right beside the one from Sparky. Nothing had ever hurt that deep. Not even Sparky getting killed, but I was younger and didn't understand as much."

"Sparky?"

"Grandfather. Bunny and Sparky."

"Of course. Can't have Bunny and Grandpa." She blew her nose and wiped her eyes.

"I didn't leave my room or stop crying for three days." I took a few deep breaths. Gemma kissed me on the cheek and hugged me again.

"Dad came in, screamed that Barylan men don't mope and cry, we do things. Slapped me for moping so long."

"You were fourteen! Disgusting!"

"So, I did something. I ran to Bunny, and she healed me. Now I see it's partly because of her empath powers, but mostly just being my grandmother. She got me back into the world."

"What was Yasmin like as a person?"

I smiled at all the memories. Which ones should I tell her? "When she concentrated, the tip of her tongue stuck out, just a little. When I saw it, I knew to stay quiet, because something exciting was going to happen.

"Always tucked her hair behind her left ear, but never her right. I told her not to get a hook for a left hand because she'd put her eye out. She laughed until tears came and called me the funniest person she knew. I told her it was Max. No, Max is great, but I crafted my jokes personal for her, so that meant I was special.

"She reminded me over and over she raised me to become the best guy possible for a lucky girl. I said you're the one I want. Oh no, I'm your sister from another mother, Paulo."

I stopped for a minute. "Nobody else called me Paulo, and nobody ever will. Not the way she did, with her little half grin."

"One day in middle school I came home pissed. Who knows, might've been something you threw at me. She held me and told me the world may have moments of ugliness and cruelty, but our job was to overwhelm it with beauty and kindness. That became our goal."

"Wait, I saw an entry when I going through my diary about the dance. In the spring of eighth grade, you stopped fighting back so much when I insulted you. I wrote you took half the fun out of it."

"Now you're connected to Yasmin. Amazing how one small girl who didn't have much time touched so many people.

"With every goodbye, she told me to go forth and do great things. Started when I was eight. I can't do great things, I'm only a kid, I told her. You can do small good things today to learn how to do big great things tomorrow.

"Bunny took me to her funeral, filled with hundreds of her college friends. Hundreds. One asked me if I was Paul. When I said yes, she told me Yasmin bragged on me constantly.

"Dozens more came and fussed over me and repeated things she told them. Twenty girls had a story I'd forgotten from when I was five. Yasmin was leaving to a party, and I wanted to go. I'm going to chase hunky guys until I catch one, she said, and you can't run fast enough. I told her to chase'em my way, and I'd trip one and she could grab him before he got away. Something five-year-old me made up that I don't remember, but she carried it with her forever. Her friends said it became code. If you felt sexy, you didn't need Paul's help. If your confidence was low, you'd say I need Paul's help tonight. Or an insult, like hey, with your hair, you'll need Paul's help for sure. And Yasmin just laughed and laughed.

"She was a history major and told me over and over the past is full of stupid until one smart, special person stands up and leads people toward the light. That tyrants fall because someone has the courage to stop them. Many people want things to stay the same or go back to the old ways, but there's always a beacon shining toward a future that's better for everyone, not just the rich. Told me I was such a man. I said no, Max is the leader, not me. She laughed and told me to get bit by a radioactive spider and become a superhero like Spider-Man.

"She must have known, a week before she died, things were worse. Prepared me to go on without her, but subtly so I didn't catch until later. Built me up for the future."

Gemma got the box of tissues from the nightstand and handed me two.

"I checked on her that last day before school. She told me she loved me like she always did. I was her special guy above all other guys forever. It was going to be OK, because she was right-handed, and I was there to do the stuff that needed two hands. I promised I'd be her left hand and foot.

"She got serious, held my hand, and pulled me close. Told me she couldn't have children after the accident. But it was OK, because she had me for the past ten years, and seeing me grow up was the greatest joy she'd ever had. Watching me develop from the cutest little boy in the world to the smartest and sweetest young man in the world was more than she ever expected.

"Her last words to me were to go forth and do great things."

I had to stop for a while. We used several tissues.

"I got the laptop, CDs, albums, music, and notes she left for me and took over Yasmin's Obscure But Deserving Music Report. Been doing it for the last four years. Now I call it the Ghost of Yasmin's Obscure But Deserving Music Report. Nobody knows who's writing it because I keep her photo on it. That's why I don't do sports or Chess Club or debate or anything else."

"For her."

I exhaled. "As long as it's still going, I know she's still around in some way. She'd have a song title or lyric for every occasion. When I quote one, I sense her with me."

We sat without talking for a few minutes.

"You said she's in an Irish Catholic cemetery?"

I tried to say yes, but the word stuck.

"Did she have red hair?"

It took another two minutes before I was able to speak. "Yeah, but straight and not so red or long. Creamy Irish skin with a sprinkle of freckles across her nose. Way shorter than you. I was taller than her by twelve."

"But I reminded you of Yasmin?"

"I had a stupid kid idea her spirit or something might magically make it to the only other red-haired girl I knew. I pretended to ask her what I should do. She always told me to act brave and go for it. So, I asked you to the dance."

"And I treated you like dog shit! Damn, I was so dumb."

"I was the dumb one. It took me a couple of years to realize none of it was your fault because you had no idea. It turned out seeing someone with red hair and green eyes was oddly comforting in a weird way. Underneath the aggravation."

"From me being an asshole for so long."

"Sorry this honesty curse we have dropped something so heavy on you. But that's not the final bit."

"More? What?"

"The driver limped away from the van and they never found him, but his tequila bottle was under the seat. The car service company hid at the bottom of a ton of shell companies. Certainly part of a management firm, no doubt set up to cut every corner to let greedy managers siphon the money that should go to certified drivers and vehicle maintenance."

"That explains a few things."

"For all I know, the top man over those companies is Holden."

Chapter 46: Enemies in High Places

We met at Bunny's the next morning for breakfast. She stacked newspapers and magazines on the table. The *Wall Street Journal*, *New York Times*, and the *Washington Post* had front-page stories on the Grigori and billionaire scandal. Tabloids, print and online, won the headline contest. "Crooked Bastard Billionaires," said one. "We Lose at Poker Because Billionaires have X-ray Glasses," said another. "Mind-readers + BillionBullies = Screw the Public."

"I think we broke the Internet," said Junie.

I took Gemma's hand. "We should check on Holden to make sure he's in the office today."

We watched him in his office take one phone call after another. "Don't worry about your investments. We're fine." Next call. "This is just politics." Next call. "There's no reason to call our loans early."

"Time to pay him a visit," I said.

Cal Ray brought the car out front, and the four of us jumped inside. Bunny climbed in, too. "You want to come?" I asked.

"After all this, you think you can leave me home?"

In the Goldstone lobby, Bunny looked around and stopped. "You go on ahead. I'll stay here as a lookout."

* * * * *

In the elevator, I opened my senses to everyone around me.

"You ready, bro?" asked Max.

"I can sense every emotion and hear every thought. Holden's confidence is wavering." That was the simple answer. He alternated between being pissed at the problems I'd caused him, and proud I'd learned how to fight by listening to him all these years.

The elevator opened, and right in front of us loomed the giant granite reception desk with Goldstone Equity Management carved into the front. They painted the letters in gold leaf to make the point money was the goal above everything.

As we walked into the lobby. Gemma gasped. "Reggie?" A man and a woman sat at the welcome desk. The guy, in his mid-twenties, stood.

"Gemma? I haven't seen you in a couple of years. How they hanging? Or they still pointy?"

I sensed her emotions rotate from surprise to anger. Underneath the rage was a dark pit of shame. "You know him?"

Her fury exploded. "Meet Reginald von DickFace."

The depth of her outrage increased, then changed back to humiliation in a flash. The regret and disgust radiating from her almost made me gag.

"I remember when my—"

"Enough!" I interrupted. "We're not here to look up dumped guys from her past. I'm here for Holden."

Reggie moved from around the desk and stepped in front of me. He had a linebacker build, and beside him I felt thin and young, which I was. But I was far angrier and more determined.

"Holden's busy."

"I'm—"

"I know who you are. The golden boy who turned on his family!"

As he talked, I could sense him Push me, as wispy, translucent words floated from his head to mine. *"Go away, go away."*

I laughed in his face. "This is hilarious, you're the new baby Pusher my mother's trying to train!"

Gemma gasped. I sensed a wave of confusion from her.

Surprised, Reggie tried to Push harder, but I grabbed his fear and slammed it back at him so hard he staggered backwards.

Max stepped in between the two of us. "I'll bounce this asshole while you talk to Holden."

"Relax and let me handle this pathetic little failure."

The woman behind the desk picked up the phone and whispered into it. Junie stepped beside her and took the phone from her hand. She touched the console and said, "Phones stop."

I turned to Gemma, who had moved behind me. "I can tell this guy hurt you. What should I do with him?"

"Fry his ass!"

I smiled at him with the warmth of a snake ready to strike. *"Go over to the corner on my right, sit in that corner, and piss yourself,"* I ordered him mentally. *"And shit yourself, too."*

Reggie walked stiffly away from us. I Pushed more. *"Stay there in your own filth until the police come to get your statement."* He sank lower and his gray slacks darkened in the front as he settled on the floor.

"If you ever see Gemma again, leave the room. If you can't, go to the nearest corner and piss yourself."

She touched my shoulder. "Two security guards coming from the hallway on your left."

We walked forward toward them. "Max–"

"Got it."

Cal Ray watched them cry out and crash to the carpet. "Man, that's better than shooting them. Quiet 'til they yell and holler." He pulled his Smith & Wesson out of its holster but kept it under his jacket.

Gemma picked up a glass paperweight the size of a tennis ball from a desk. A manager in his forties came out of his office almost twenty yards away, his fist in the air at the disruption. The paperweight smashed him smack in the chest. He gasped and slunk back into his office.

"Nice throw," said Cal Ray.

"Tennis coach made us throw baseballs to help our serves."

"Bet yours is dynamite."

"Damn straight."

Cal Ray gathered the guns from the security guards. Gemma picked up another paperweight.

In the foyer of Holden's suite, his personal assistant banged on her dead phone. She saw me and my friends and dropped it.

"Paul, stop right there. Don't make this worse."

"Sorry, Vicki. Don't get in our way."

I grabbed the knob of the heavy oaken double doors that opened into Holden's vast office. He'd locked them. "Coward!" I yelled and kicked both open so hard they banged into the wall and rebounded.

"Guarding your six out here," said Cal Ray.

I marched in, followed by Max, Junie, and Gemma. Holden sat at his desk, leaning back, feet up, with a Hollywood smile on his face.

"Do you have an appointment, young man?"

"Go ahead, try it."

Holden pulled his right hand out from under the desk. He aimed a large silver revolver straight at my head.

I Moved the gun back towards him. He couldn't point the barrel away from his right temple, even using both hands.

"Not smart, Holden, not a bit. I wanted a nice friendly chat, and you got all hostile."

I called Cal Ray, and he stepped into the room. "You want a new gun? It's shiny."

Cal Ray pulled Holden's weapon from his grasp. "Oh, what a beaut. 357 Magnum long bore with a custom ivory handle. Excellent balance. The Senator may take this for his own collection when he sees it."

"Keep it close. I might need to hit him with it. Or shoot his kneecap."

"This'll blow his leg clean off. Big mess. Let Max do his thing." He went back out to guard the door.

"Let's talk, Holden. First, I've got a bunch of new friends hurt by Akme Johnson. You'll make that right."

"Go to hell."

"Is that any way to speak to your godson? Man, that hurts."

"Your parents'll pay for this."

"No, because from now on you'll act as nice as you are rich. You'll set an example for every other billionaire with Grigori help to cheat and lie and cover up murders."

"Didn't your parents teach you how the world works? It's a rough place, not like your cushy private high school."

I focused on Pushing Holden. "*Make reparations to the people in East Texas for Akme Johnson's damage.*"

"Not doing that," he said through clenched teeth. Blood vessels throbbed on his forehead.

I pulled a chair out for Gemma. "Sit, guys, this may take longer than I thought."

I tried another Push and spoke out loud at the same time. "Make reparations to the folks in East Texas for Akme Johnson's behavior."

Through tight lips, Holden grunted, "No." His left eye bulged.

I sat back in my chair. No one had ever resisted a direct Push. "Impressive. How are you doing this?"

Struggling, he answered, "Extraordinary men get wealthy because they possess the strength of mind and character normal guys don't."

"What a load of rationalized bullshit."

"Many CEOs succeed because they're psychologically tough," said Gemma. "But it's toughness from raging narcissism and being non-violent sociopaths. They're bullies upfront and cowards behind the facade."

I Moved Holden's right hand onto the top of his desk. Another nudge and his fingers splayed out.

"I can control your body, but not your mind yet. So, I'll need to break your concentration with a considerable amount of pain."

I grabbed a large crystal award on a thick marble base from one of Holden's bookshelves. "Which finger do you want me to smash first?"

"You can't hurt the man you've looked up to all these years. The one who paid your parents so much money and gave you that Rolex. You're not strong-minded enough."

I lifted the trophy. "Pinky it is." I brought it up, wavered a bit, up a little higher, and put it down on the desk.

"You're right, we've got too much history. All on my side has been admiration and even, well, love, like family."

"Let's stop this nonsense. You go home now, and I won't press charges."

I waited to let him consider what I might do to him, but he didn't worry a bit. Gemma figured him out, and his mental state remained defiant. He was a sociopath and battle-tough after years of manipulating other people, even without powers. I'd have to hurt him a lot, and that would scar me as well.

She touched my arm and whispered, "Yasmin."

"Max, luckily, doesn't know you from a street beggar. Right shoulder."

"Gladly." With a twirl and a flick, Holden screamed.

The door opened and Cal Ray pointed his gun inside. "Ah, Max at work," he said as he backed out and closed the door.

The intense pain caused Holden's arm to hang limp.

"Ready to negotiate the new operating philosophy for Goldstone Equity Management?"

"No," grunted Holden.

"Other shoulder."

Holden screamed again, but not as loud. "I can't breathe," he croaked.

"Where've I heard THAT before," said Max. He pushed the needles deeper.

Holden stiffened in agony. "OK," he whispered. "Make it stop. I'm begging you. Stop."

One wave of Max's hand and Goldstone collapsed face first on his desk. His huge heaving gulps of air were the only sounds in his enormous office.

"Junie, take your backup drive and suck everything you can out of Holden's computer and the network."

"My pleasure." She pulled his Lenovo ThinkPad X1 Carbon executive laptop closer to her and plugged in a 16-Terabyte external drive.

"You can't get in without my password," croaked Holden, still recovering.

"Hide and watch." She put her palm flat on the keyboard. His login screen appeared with his name and password displayed. She dragged his files to her drive and the file icons flew across in a blur.

"Here comes some genuine pain," I said. "I know better than to trust you. Unless I have serious leverage, you'll double-cross me before we get to the parking garage." I waved the folder from Isabella.

"Let's talk about human trafficking."

Chapter 47: No Mercy for Swine

I tapped the folder Isabella sent me on the desk twice. "Guess what's in here?"

Holden's face fell. "Shit."

"Pretty much."

I opened my folder and flipped through the contents. Gemma leaned over for a better view and backed away. "That's disgusting."

I put a photo of young women crammed into a shipping container in front of him.

"I've never seen that picture before," he said.

"Of course not," I said. I laid out bills of lading and transit instructions. "Are these familiar?" Each had a logo of one of his companies at the top.

He sank back in his chair.

"You want to lie and tell me you didn't know, and how dare these lower-level managers pull this crap, don't you?" I asked. "I'm a good lie detector. Go ahead, tell me how this got started."

He didn't say a thing, so I eavesdropped on his thoughts.

"How the hell did he get this? Who sold me out? What can I say that will fool him and explain this?"

"You can't fool me and explain it away."

His mouth dropped open. "I thought you were a persuader."

"I am."

"But you just heard my thoughts like a telepath."

"Yep. Here's the answer to your next question." I levitated the crystal award from on Holden's desk. It floated up two feet, hovered, and smashed down hard, gouging out a chunk of the mahogany surface where his pinky finger had been.

"You can't do that."

"And yet."

"So the reports are accurate? You have multiple powers?"

"Another talk for another time." I used my Inside Voice to Junie. *"Start your video."*

"Holden, turn to me and tell me how all this began."

He swiveled his chair to stare out the window from his office up on the top floor. New York City glittered in the sunlight. Sunbeams sparkled as diamonds on steel and glass.

"At first, it was what you said," he admitted, still looking out the window. "This happens in logistics companies, large ones, because so much comes and goes and so little gets checked."

"How did you find out?"

"Complete accident. A drug sweep at a warehouse discovered a bag full of cash. They weren't looking for it, but they found it. The money was to pay off border guards and customs officials. That supervisor rolled on the two above him."

He turned around and glanced at me before he focused on the chunk gouged out of his desk. "It came up the ladder. One of the accounting supervisors running it from inside this building brought the case to me. He had project details and a PowerPoint presentation explaining the enormous returns available for moving people from A to B. We could do it more humanely, safer, and better than the cartels and crooked coyotes at the border. Make it appear to be a rogue operation if the wrong customs person found the container."

"When did it start from Europe?" I asked.

"After a year of success from Mexico, we tried it with two people hidden in one of our planes. Then four. An entire plane supposedly flying back for equipment upgrades, full of nothing but illegals, made it once. They come over anyway, so we at least make it safer and more comfortable."

I pulled out more photos. "See this girl in the container flying out of Romania? Here she is in an ad for underage girls. Here's her police booking mugshot. You're not bringing in farm workers or manicurists, you're importing sex slaves."

"We're giving these women a better life, getting them out of their shithole countries."

Gamma slammed her fist hard on the desk. "No! You asshole! You're kidnapping innocent children and ruining their lives! Paul, ask Cal Ray to bring me one of his guns and I'll shoot this son-of-a-bitch myself!"

"Don't get high and mighty with me!" he yelled. "I have rights. I'm a leader in the business community!"

"And a video star now," I said. "Got what you need, Junie?"

He burst out laughing. "You little bastard! You are your father's son."

"Not sure that's a compliment."

He leaned forward and stared at me. "You cost the company ten billion dollars this week, do you know that?"

"Just on paper, right?"

"You idiot, it's ALL on paper! Didn't your parents teach you anything?"

"Yeah, stories of Grigori honor and service and making the world a better place. They left out the trafficking and murdering."

He looked at Junie. "Your camera stopped?" She nodded. "Have you uploaded it somewhere?" She smiled. "Public?" She shook her head.

He relaxed and leaned back in his custom leather chair. "Paul, Paul, Paul. I'm fucked. What weird song do you have for me?"

"My first choice was, "No Mercy for Swine," by the Cherry Poppin' Daddies. But I decided another song of theirs was the best choice. So, the song is, "When I Change Your Mind.""

"Those titles make sense. You're in control now. What will happen to me?"

"I could give Gemma your gun."

He chuckled and raised an eyebrow.

"You're not getting off that easy. First, who keeps trying to kill us?"

"Me, well, forced by other billionaires reliant on the Grigori who are afraid of you exposing them just as you're doing to me. The recent headlines you generated rattled them. And the Grigori Council wants you dead, but they make me pay for it."

"Why did you attack my father?"

"THAT was the Grigori Senior Council, the actual power behind the scenes. You're in deep shit with them as well." He waved to get me to look at him. "I didn't want any of this, but I had no choice."

I couldn't help but laugh. "How many times have you given me those 'captain of your own ship' and 'make your own destiny' speeches? You had a choice to stop it before it started. A choice when you were first approached, a choice every day it continued, and a choice when they said to murder me. You had choice after choice, and you chose wrong each time."

Gemma's phone rang. "Bunny? What? OK."

"Dragavei sent more commandos to save Holden, but they got here when the police did. The cops grabbed most of them, but a few made it to the stairs. We don't have long."

I turned to Gemma. "Hold my hand."

"Now? Oh." She grabbed my right hand and squeezed.

I ordered Holden to, "*Stand up, turn in a circle, sit back in your chair.*"

Without a word, he did what I Pushed him to do.

"What the hell?"

"Here's the deal. First, pay off every victim of Akme Johnson."

"But—"

I Pushed more. "No excuses! Fix the damage, personal and environmental. Second, No more murders, cover-ups, trafficking, and so forth. No more criming."

"OK, OK. You're not turning me over to the police?"

"You're now a shining example of a new breed of billionaire as decent human being. Invest only in companies that follow Corporate Social Responsibility guidelines, and only those firms. You'll still be wealthy, but one enormous yacht is enough."

"But my returns—"

"Will be stable and avoid self-inflicted losses from fines and litigation," said Gemma. "And tons of great social media! Your face will be everywhere, getting you more investors."

"Third, Gemma and Junie will go over your business decisions when necessary."

"I will NOT report to children!"

"Suit yourself. Work with us or stand trial for human trafficking." His face fell, and he nodded.

"Fourth, protect us and our families from your billionaire friends trying to kill us."

"Sorry, kid, they don't ask my permission."

I turned to Gemma. "Want to watch Holden fly like an eagle out the window?"

"He can do that? Amazing."

"Why are you still here? Just break the window and fly away. You'll be free."

He jumped up, grabbed his chair, and slammed it against the glass wall behind his desk. It bounced. He grabbed it again and threw it even harder. A star appeared in the glass. He smashed it a third time, and a small hole opened.

"Holden, you can't fly, but you will jump out of this window if you don't help protect my friends. Now stop that and sit."

"Damn you."

We heard a gunshot outside the office. I stood and pulled Gemma to my side. Her hand still in mine, I said, "Finally, if any of us or my cousins Lance and Quinn die before you do, the guilt and pain will drive you to commit suicide the next day."

"That's crazy! What happens if one of you has an accident?"

"Lousy luck for you, just as it was for Jenkins last month. Keep your estate paperwork up to date."

I turned to Junie. "You got the video for that second part, right?"

"You know it."

There was another gunshot, followed by a three-shot burst.

Cal Ray burst through the door. "About finished? We have incoming and I could use Max's help."

"On it," said Max. He ran out with Cal Ray. Five seconds later, three people screamed with pain.

I walked to the door and motioned for Holden to walk through first. "You're going to clean this up now."

"I can call off my dogs, but I can't protect you against at least three hundred pissed billionaires. Good luck, son."

"Sure you can. Pass this warning to the billionaire club members at your monthly meeting. Get on board or you're next. Simple enough?"

He nodded, but I held the door closed. I could sense roughly two dozen people outside, but no one radiated fear. "What's going on out there?" I asked Gemma.

"Ah, lots of people standing around making videos of Max and Cal Ray marching guys over to the police."

I opened the doors, but Holden didn't step out at once. "I'm fine, and I'm coming out," he yelled. "Stand down."

He strutted out and smiled like the billionaire he was. He motioned for me to stand beside him.

"Many of you remember Paul Barylan from his internship last summer. He and his friends have convinced me there's a better, more socially responsible way to run Goldstone Equity Management."

He put his arm around my shoulders. "It's a beautiful day, ladies and gentlemen."

I smiled into at least a dozen phones taking videos, then we walked to the reception desk. Four New York police officers handcuffed three Dragavei Associates commandos as Cal Ray and Max watched. Wes and Elena came out of an elevator, waving their FBI badges in front of them.

"Are you guys behind this?" Wes asked me.

"No, Agents, I am," said Holden. "Security exercise gone wrong. We'll sort it out." He sniffed and looked around until he spotted Reggie sitting in the corner. "What the hell happened to him?"

"He got a quarter of what he deserved," said Gemma.

Chapter 48: An Uprising Is Born

Two days later, we lounged in Bunny's living room watching Senator "Big Dave" Kingston give a speech from the Capitol steps, live on cable news.

"That's why the Grigori Research Association members are working with the largest companies in America to help them become exemplary corporate citizens."

"They haven't agreed to any changes, so he's putting the GRA in a public bind. Clever," said Bunny.

The Senator waved at Holden on his right. "No person better exemplifies this outstanding new approach than Holden Goldstone, owner of Goldstone Equity Management. For example, he acquired a company in Texas that hid a terrible record of workplace safety lapses and environmental damage. To make things right, he's pledged to revive damaged waterways and habitats and pay full reparations to workers and family members hurt by the company."

Kingston stepped over and shook Holden's hand.

"The human trafficking evidence in our pocket sure makes Holden play nice," said Max.

I added, "Wes said they couldn't find any leads to follow about the murder for those other two I heard my parents discuss."

"He is also the founding member, along with my companies, of the First Four Initiative, named for Paul Barylan, Gemma Hargraves, Max Orlov, and Junie Johnson," continued Kingston. "Other members include Quinn Barylan, Lance Zolotov, and Sophia Popova. FBI Special Agents Wes Turner and Elena Martinez represent law enforcement."

Kingston stopped for a round of applause. "The First Four principles are Honor, Integrity, Community, and Service. These are the guiding—"

My phone rang, so I excused myself and went down the hall. When I saw who called, I froze.

"Hey, Mom," I squeezed out.

"Just so you know, your father's fine. He starts his new job next week."

"What?"

"You ruined Goldstone, you idiot! We can't make any money being sweet and nice and growing love petunias instead of profits!"

"That's not how it works, I promise."

"If you want any belongings from the house, come get them tonight between seven and nine while we're at dinner. We'll replace the locks in the morning."

"Mom, I–"

"Goodbye, Paul. You're eighteen now. You're on your own."

"Wait–"

"Find a new phone. This line goes dead tomorrow." She disconnected without another word.

I stumbled to the guest room, then slumped to the floor in the corner. The roaring in my ears was so loud I couldn't think.

Bunny came in and sat on the bed near me. "Your mother?"

I nodded.

"You radiate abandonment. Are they moving away?"

"Just from me."

"Ah."

"I worried it might happen, but I didn't believe they'd do this."

"So sorry."

I moved over, leaned against the bed, and put my head in her lap. "It's so ... stupid."

"Let's sit here for a moment."

"OK."

* * * * *

Junie turned off the TV and told Max, "I want a latte. Gemma? Latte?"

"After lunch? You don't drink coffee this late," said Max.

She glared at him and raised an eyebrow. "*Dumbass, get lost so I can talk to Gemma about girl stuff.*"

Max launched off the sofa. "Lattes on the way, babe," he announced on his way out.

"At the throwdown, Paul seemed to know how bad that guy hurt you. No details, but serious. Have you two talked yet?"

She covered her face with her hands. "I will."

"What's the deal, G?"

She shifted and stared at the floor. "Remember that year my parents fought all the time, and I turned sixteen and partied like an idiot?"

"Course. Your 'Red is Ready' stage."

She winced at her former nickname. "Reggie started me on that idiot downhill slide. I did stupid things with him. No, wait, he Pushed me to do those awful things."

"Mr. Poopy Pants? But he's way old!"

"Things I never told anyone, even you. Sometimes I'm not sure if they're memories or nightmares, but they're terrible either way."

"Photos and videos?"

She closed her eyes. "And more."

Junie's right leg bounced until she stopped it with her hand. "Paul looked mad enough to kill that guy, but he shamed him instead. Matching your shame?"

"Maybe."

"Way more than topless mirror pics to make guys hit you back?"

"Way worse."

"Sucks, girlfriend. I'm sorry, but you better come clean soon or you'll worry yourself to death." She stood. "I need air. Gonna catch up to Max."

Gemma slumped on the couch, staring into space for a few minutes. Bunny came and sat across from her. "Where are Junie and Max?"

"Starbucks." Gemma looked around the room. "Where's Paul? He got a call and disappeared."

Bunny used a tissue to wipe her eyes. "The call was from his mother. They, well, told him to stay away."

"Daaaamn, that's intense. How is he?"

"Asleep. He needs time alone to process this."

She took the tissue Bunny handed her. "What's this?"

"Your support will help him the most. How long are you going to hide your past and lie to him?"

"Oh, shit. You know?"

"I can sense you're an emotional mess over this. You should rejoice at what you've accomplished, but this is tearing you up, and I'm afraid it will soon hurt Paul."

Gemma leaned her head back on the couch and talked to the ceiling. "My boobs aren't big, but they came in early, like my height. I could pass for older and did every weekend. My parents fought constantly, and I avoided it by partying, usually with college guys." She shook her head. "Did stupid things. I can't let him find out."

"He'll stand by you."

"I'm afraid to take that chance."

"The guy he, well, punished, at Goldstone's is an ex?"

Gemma dried a tear, then looked at the tissue Bunny gave her. "You knew how hard this would be, didn't you? Yeah, he was in college and I just turned sixteen. I didn't know he was Grigori." She wiped a tear from her other eye. "I'm disgusted he was my first."

"Our bodies haven't been our own since man walked upright."

"He took pictures, videos, and more. If Paul sees those, he'll hate me."

"I don't think he could ever feel that way about you. It's sad, but don't lots of teens get private photos circulated today?"

"These are way more than nude selfies. Since he just lost his parents, he might want to cut off his past and start over and sweep out the old junk, like me. He told me the story of Yasmin, and that made me realize I'm not good enough for him. I want to stay together, but I'm scared if he discovers my past, he'll pull the plug."

"Gemma, that guy was Grigori, so none of it was your fault. It was illegal, statutory rape, even if you consented. Even if it was your idea, it was illegal. I doubt he ever wants to see you again after the episode yesterday. He certainly doesn't want to face Paul. He has to realize if he released any private images, he'd be in far more trouble than you."

"I'm scared to tell him, so please don't say anything."

"I'll try to keep what you've told me in confidence. But don't underestimate his connection to you, mentally and emotionally."

"You can tell it's strong?"

"I feel your emotions intertwine when you're close. Few couples I know fit together as you two. You need to give him some space today, but give him some credit tomorrow. He's an empath too, remember. I know he respects your privacy, but sometimes we can't help but sense things. You want to tell him before he stumbles across it by accident."

"Like when he got that call. You knew it was bad."

"His pain was a slap in the face it was so intense."

"How am I going to compete with his memories of Yasmin? She was amazing and magnificent and loving and the perfect woman he's looking for. I'm not her."

Bunny wiped her eyes. "Yasmin was wonderful to him, and he adored her. But that's his past, and he knows it."

The door opened and Max and Junie burst into the apartment. "Latte's for everybody!" said Max.

He gave one each to Gemma and Bunny and looked around for Paul.

"I'll hold it for him," Gemma said.

* * * * *

An hour later, I came out, waved to Max and Junie in the dining room, and collapsed beside Gemma. She saw how wasted I was and warmed my latte in the microwave and brought it to me. Then she got a brush from her purse, said, "Serious bed head, babe," and worked on my hair while standing behind me.

Bunny asked silently, "*Are you OK?*"

Before I could answer, I smiled and ran to the door.

"Surprise!" she said.

I opened the door and Quinn and Lance walked up, luggage in hand. Our group hug exploded into the room, and Bunny came over for hugs as well.

Quinn pulled me away, grabbed my head, and kissed both cheeks. Then she squeezed my butt and yelled, "Honk honk!"

Gemma's eyes narrowed, and she crossed her arms. I escaped from Quinn's clutches and dragged her closer. "Meet my cousins."

She half-smiled and put out her hand out, but Quinn threw her arms around her. She let go, stepped back, and studied her.

"You are NOT what I expected, based on the girls Paul was hitting on in LA."

"What?"

"Emma has her Ms. America smile and blonde hair and boobs and all. Morgan, too. Even Daphne, who kept trying to kidnap him, was blonde."

"Don't forget her expensive new naughty pillows," added Lance.

Gemma peeked down at her own breasts. Before she could speak, Lance hugged her.

"Not so harsh, Quinn. She has a natural look that pops big with those killer freckles. And her hair is amazing!"

I put my arms around her from behind and kissed her cheek. "There weren't any girls in LA as special as Gemma."

"Max, Junie, come meet the West Coast rebel leaders," I said.

After the introductions, I grabbed Lance with one arm and Quinn with another. "So, you guys orphans now, too?"

"Mom supports us, because of Bunny, but she couldn't stop Dad from throwing me out," said Lance. "The order came from the Grigori Council."

"One parent held each arm and tossed me out like the garbage." said Quinn.

Before they could get depressed, I sensed Kingston and Cal Ray had parked in the garage. "Bunny! Set two more places for dinner."

Quinn said, "What?"

"He's got this long range Spidey-sense for people," Max told them.

"These guys are on our side." I tapped my Rolex. "If I want anything from my house, I have two hours to get it. Locks change tomorrow."

"Need help?" asked Lance.

Shaking my head, I said, "I have my laptop, phone, tablet, music, and grabbed some clothes." I looked across the room. "Got her."

"Odd way to look at your new girlfriend," said Quinn.

"She's scared to tell me about past boyfriends."

"Interesting. You worried?"

"Not as much as she is."

Quinn gave me a big smile. "Want me to search her memories?"

"Absolutely not. Serious," I said. "We may need a Grigori code of ethics one of these days."

* * * * *

259

After dinner, Kingston suggested we all fly back to Texas first thing in the morning. "Too many death threats against you guys. Even with the police in the building, you need to move somewhere safer."

I put my phone down. "Thanks for giving us some glory in your speech, but we need new numbers now. People texted, phoned, tweeted, and called me a Socialist, a Communist, a Marxist, well, all the ists. Names so disgusting I've never heard them before. And worse, including my senior picture with cross hairs over my face."

"Some think I'm a guy, so they want to cut off my penis. Then come vagina insults, followed by rape threats," said Quinn. "And some dick pix to make up for the one they snipped."

"So many synonyms for whore and vagina," said Gemma.

"Do they call you the N-word before saying they want to rape you?" Junie showed her a text.

"Me too," said Max. "But less rapey and more lynching."

"We'll get y'all more secure phones," said Kingston.

"He's right, Cousins. You'll love Jefferson, Texas, and the haunted bed-and-breakfast we stay in."

"Haunted?" Quinn waved her arms in the air and went, "WoooOOOooo."

"Our new friends Carli and Ugly Junie will show you around."

"Big Junie now. After we left, Carli changed his name," said Junie.

"I'll call Chief Fred first thing in the morning," said Cal Ray. "We'll need some extra eyeballs."

"I'll come with you this time," Bunny told me.

Junie counted noses. "We have the rooms, but bathrooms don't work."

"I'll stay in Marshall. You six need to unwind for a bit without me in your way," said Bunny.

Junie thought to Gemma, "*You owe me ten bucks.*"

"*Junie the matchmaker wins again.*"

Later, Quinn sat by me on the sofa, so close she might as well be in my lap. She put her arm around my shoulders and talked to me, lips almost kissing my neck. Typical Quinn.

From across the room, Gemma leaned toward Bunny and said, "She can't keep her hands off him. She knows Paul's her cousin, right?"

She placed her hand on Gemma's. "The Grigori encourage cousins to marry."

"No way!"

"I did. It magnifies the Rasputin connection and makes the bloodline stronger. Maybe more difficult to legalize today, but not impossible."

Gemma frowned and exhaled slowly. "You warned me the other day, didn't you?"

"Why I said you need to clear the air sooner rather than later."

Chapter 49: Shut Up and Dance

The morning sun blazed in the butterfly garden outside our window a week after we returned to Jefferson and the Haunted Grove. This became our new home, since three of us were officially thrown out of families, and the other three weren't sure if their parents wanted them back or not. I was up on my elbow, smiling at Gemma.

She yawned, stretched, and finally opened her eyes. "You watching me sleep?"

"No, well, yes. I was thinking."

"About?"

"How much I love you."

She turned to face the other way. I heard her choke back a sob.

"Wow. Not the response I wanted."

She turned to look at me and wiped away a tear. "You wanted–"

Badly mimicking her voice, I said, "Oh, Paul, you thrill me in ways no man ever has. You complete me. Your manliness makes me swoon. I love you bunches."

She laughed. "This is not one of those mushy Hallmark Channel Christmas romances, thank you very much. And every girl knows not to believe a guy the first time he says he loves her when they're in bed."

"What's the real problem?"

Her smile faded. She looked at the ceiling and bit her lip. "Lying to other guys was so easy. But it's just impossible to lie to you."

She faced me again, opened her mouth to speak, but chickened out and faced the other way.

"I don't think I know what love really means. Thought I did. Told every guy I dated I loved him. No, you still can't ask. Hoped it might make them say it back. But the closer they got to me, the sooner they'd leave me. Or I'd push them away."

"The more I'm with you, the more time I want to spend with you."

She turned back over and kissed me, then pushed me off my elbow so I was flat, and put her head on my chest. "That's what they said, too. At first."

"On the plus side, and you didn't dump me after two weeks."

"You picked up an extra week, remember, with the foot massage special exemption."

We were quiet for a moment.

Softly, I sang, "You may say I'm crazy, but I'm crazy about you."

"I get a song lyric? Sweet. Who?"

"The song is 'About You' by Distorted Penguins on their album *Magic* released in 2001. The pride of West Virginia, maybe. At least they're from there."

"Thanks."

"The Reggie problem still has you twisted up, doesn't it?" I stroked her hair. "Tell me or don't, but give yourself a break. Remember what you said in this very room? Don't worry about the past, just be happy we're together now. I am. Happy, I mean."

"I wish it was that simple. Let's have a great time tonight and talk later, OK? After I figure some things out?"

* * * * *

At 7 PM Bunny knocked on my bedroom door and walked in smiling. I had on my tux pants and shirt, and she held up my bow tie and cummerbund.

"Again? Those ties are stupid," I said.

"This one is smarter than the last one," she replied. "Pre-tied, so you just hook it. I'll adjust the fit for you."

She threaded the ribbon through the loop on the back of my tux shirt collar and I hooked it in front. "A little loose." She pulled it through the tensioner clasp until the tie tightened.

I put on my coat. She stepped aside for a good overview.

"You look great."

"My last tux was a new Armani," I said. "This is from Mack's Rental Clothes of Marshall, Texas."

"Does that bother you?"

263

"That one was a gift. This one I earned." I could sense how happy she was for me. "You're looking pretty good yourself."

"Dave asked me to bring a couple of evening dresses, but I never thought I would chaperon a high school prom."

The doorbell rang. "You're ready to go," she announced.

Carli and Big Junie handed out corsages in the entryway.

"Yo, Paul," yelled Big Junie when he saw me at the top of the stairs. "Hurry, or I'll put this corsage on Gemma myself."

"The hell you will," barked Quinn. "You're MY date tonight."

"Wait, what?" I asked. "Junie and Carli aren't together?"

Carli said, "We tried that last year. Been friends since preschool, so it felt like dating my brother."

"Or my sister," said Big Junie. He leaned close to Lance's face. "Which means if you hurt her, I'll hunt you like it's deer season."

Lance looked at Max. "*He's kidding, right?*" he thought.

"*Probably.*"

I held out my arm, Gemma took it, and we walked to the door.

"Whoa," said Kingston. "Pictures first."

After a thousand photos and videos, Gemma pulled me onto the porch. We stopped and stared at our ride for the night.

"Carli! You said we had a limo!" she yelled.

"I said we had a country limo."

"It's two horses pulling a trailer with hay bales for seats!"

"That's a country limo," laughed Carli. "C'mon, girl. It's fun."

Sexy Junie turned to Big Junie. "Is that thing safe?"

"Oh, it's hella dangerous. I'll help you up the step."

"You be careful," said Bunny. "We'll take the horseless carriage and meet you there."

A Jefferson Police car arrived. A small, wiry man with longish hair combed in a swoop, chewing gum like it was a contest, walked up to Big Dave. "Hey, guys," he said. "This is Chief Fred. You're not exactly street legal, so he'll escort you."

Cal Ray shook hands and tilted his head toward Max. "If something happens, Max has some kind of magic bullets."

"Magic bullets? That a thing now? What'd y'all drop in my lap?"

"The best young people you'll ever meet," said Bunny, "who will change the world."

"Yes, ma'am, I heard." He turned to Cal Ray. "So, buncha pissed people?"

Cal Ray chuckled. "Big time, and too many to count."

"They can work themselves up as mad as all gitout and that means nothin' to me. But if they try'n touch one of my citizens or visitors, they best be ready to fight."

He walked toward his car but stopped at the trailer. "Howdy, folks. Y'all ever need anything, just ask for me. Want me to flip on the lights for a disco?"

We laughed. "What's the party word, Max?" I asked.

"Boogie down, Chief!"

Carli pointed to the hay bales at the front of the "limo" with plastic crowns and tiaras on them. "Non-Texans sit there and put on your headgear."

"Crowns and tiaras? Why?" Gemma asked.

"We voted y'all the royal court for the Prom. People want to say thanks for making Akme Johnson pay what they owe. Hundreds of families'll live better because of you guys."

During the ride, Carli asked Gemma, "Where were you going to prom back home?"

"Mandarin New York. Five star hotel, and tickets cost two grand."

"Daaaaamn," said Big Junie.

"Sounds at least a hundred times better than the Jefferson High School gym," said Carli. "Guess the tickets oughta cost forty times more."

Gemma patted my knee. "That's OK. I have things here I didn't have in New York. I'm in no hurry to go back."

* * * * *

Holden Goldstone stood before his conference table. He scanned ten local billionaires, each focused on stopping the growing support for the First Four Initiative.

"Gentlemen," said Holden, "thank you for your time. I can't do much publicly to stop Paul's misguided crusade after that damn Senator's speech. But I can help you crush him before this gets worse."

"Investors complained all week, and I cajoled and threatened and promised we followed socially responsible investment guidelines," said the man to his left.

"That true?" a man asked.

The first man laughed.

"I just hope we're not too late," said the owner of 4,256 apartments in the city. Over three hundred lawsuits were in the court system for illegal evictions and discrimination complaints.

"We can handle this," Holden told them. "But you can't kill Paul or his friends, for two reasons. First, they'll become martyrs, even if it's an accident. Second, and more important, he implanted mental booby traps in my head that will kill me if he or another member of the group dies."

"How do we end this?"

"Bring me one of his friends or cousins. Best choice is that red-headed girl. With my hands around her neck I can force that ungrateful little shit to end this nonsense."

The conference room doors banged open. A tall man, bald head gleaming in the bright lights, looked with intense dark eyes over a crooked nose.

"Anton?" said Holden. "Why are you here?" He stepped forward to challenge him, hesitated, and moved back.

"You failed multiple times to solve this problem. We must extinguish this financial attack now or lose untold billions of dollars."

He dismissed Holden with a wave. "You didn't have the balls to handle that kid or the Senator. Sit." He walked to the head of the table and stared at each of the billionaires. "I know who you are, but four of you haven't met me. I'm Anton Kruschkov, leader of the Grigori Senior Council. If you men do what I tell you, we can stop Paul Barylan and his friends dead in their tracks."

The slumlord leaned forward. "When you say dead, do you mean—"

"No matter what it takes, we WILL stop them."

Music Mentioned

The Ghost of Yasmin's Obscure But Deserving Music Report

Links to all the music mentioned are here:
TeenTelepaths.com/music

Cherry Poppin' Daddies
Bigger Life
Hammerblow
Hi and Lo
Impossible Dream
No Mercy for Swine
Saddest Think I Know
Steamrolled
Teenage Brain Surgeon
The End of the Night
The Enemy Within
The Search
Up From the Gutter
When I Change Your Mind

Beatles
Yesterday

Blue Plate Special
Tango of Sorrow

Brian Setzer
Rumble in Brighton

Bowling for Soup
Shut up and Smile

Distorted Penguins
About You

Faders
Girls Can Make You Cry
No Sleep Tonight

Save Ferris
Sorry My Friend
The World Is New

Secret Agent 8
When Push Comes to Shove

Skasmopolitan
Slut Named Rachel

Walk the Moon
Shut Up and Dance

Lyrics from "The Saddest Think I Know," "No Mercy for Swine," and "Teenage Brain Surgeon," by the Cherry Poppin' Daddies, and "About You" by Distorted Penguins, are used with permission from rights holders.

The Teen Telepaths Series

Awakening, Book 1
Uprising, Book 2
Final Battle, Book 3

www.TeenTelepaths.com

Facebook: Teen Telepaths

About James Gaskin

James writes books, articles, and jokes about technology and real life, including super-powered teenagers.

Join the mailing list (your name is never sold or used by anyone else) and get the free short story, "Double at the Dairy Queen," that takes place the day after *Awakening* ends, and the day before *Uprising* begins.